The assassination of Olof Palme

The Contract (The Mission) ....

.... To Assassinate Olof Palme ....

Christer F Hedberg

Copyright © 2021

Christer Hedberg

All rights reserved.

ISBN: 9798460031481

DEDICATION

Harold Carnsew, Sydney, Australia for having had the patience (and knowledge) to go through the book, correcting misspellings and illogical sentences despite his age.

Harold, You are a Unicum!

The assassination of Olof Palme

The Ultimate Reasons leading to the Assassination of Olof Palme - The Prime Minister of Sweden

- Based On a True Story -

Want to dig deeper ? Buy the book - you will be surprised

What did really happen?

Has the perpetrator really been found or .. ?

Is the solution really as straight-forward as they say or ...?

Is there more to the official version than what they say ..?

(which must not or cannot be divulged)

Do you really believe the official version reflexed what happened?

A crime fiction/true story

(factual fiction) book,

based on a true story,

recorded witness testimonies,

logical reasonings leading to

a probable cause scenario

over the assassination of

Olof Palme

The Contract (The Mission)

Table of Contents

PREAMBLE..12

Background..18

    The gigantic mistakes during Olof Palme's time as Prime Minister..................21

    Löntagarfonderna (The Employee Funds)...................26

    Palme's Legacy..29

    CCB - Civil Cooperation Bureau..................................33

    Covert structures and activities...........................34

Stockholm – November 1985.....................................35

Lisbon – November 1985..47

London – November 1985...55

Durban – November 1985..60

Stockholm, End of November 1985............................66

Stockholm, December 4th, 1985..................................77

Stockholm, December 5th, 1985..................................83

Stockholm, December 8th, 1985..................................91

The Contract (The Mission)

Stockholm, December 10th, 1985 104

Stockholm, December 14th, 1985 106

Stockholm, December 16th, 1985 109

Durban, December 19th, 1985 112

Durban, December 22nd, 1985 114

Durban, December 25th, 1985 115

Durban, December 28th, 1985 117

Durban, December 30th, 1985 118

London - January, the 2nd 1986 119

London - January, the 5th 1986 120

London - January, the 10th 1986 122

January, the 14th 1986 123

January, the 15th 1986 127

January, the 16th 1986 128

January, the 20th 1986 129

January, the 21st 1986 130

January, the 22nd 1986 132

January, the 23rd 1986 137

January, the 24th 1986 140

January, the 25th 1986 142

The Contract (The Mission)

January, the 26th 1986 144

January, the 27th 1986 147

Durban - January, the 28th 1986 148

Lisbon - January, the 28th 1986 150

London - January, the 28th 1986 152

January, the 29th 1986 156

January, the 31st 1986 157

February, the 1st 1986 159

February, the 2nd 1986 161

February, the 3rd 1986 165

February, the 4th 1986 169

February, the 5th 1986 173

February, the 6thth 1986 178

February, the 7th 1986 181

Stockholm - February, the 8th 1986 184

February, the 9th 1986 188

February, the 10th 1986 192

February, the 11th 1986 194

February, the 12th 1986 197

February, the 14th 1986 199

The Contract (The Mission)

February, the 15th 1986 201

February, the 18th 1986 207

February, the 19th 1986 209

February, the 21st 1986 220

February, the 22nd 1986 227

February, the 26th 1986 229

February, the 28th 1986 231

March, the 1st 1986 237

March, the 3rd 1986 241

March, the 8th 1986 243

March, the 14th 1986 244

March, the 16th 1986 245

March, the 17th 1986 250

March, the 18th 1986 252

March, the 24th 1986 - Stockholm 254

March, the 25th 1986 256

March, the 26th 1986 258

Stockholm, March, the 28th 1986 259

March, the 31st 1986 260

April, the 1st 1986 263

The Contract (The Mission)

April, the 2nd 1986...265

April, the 3rd 1986...266

April, the 4th 1986...267

April, the 6th 1986...269

April, the 7th 1986...270

April, the 8th 1986...273

April, the 16th 1986...278

April, the 17th 1986...279

April, the 21st 1986 - Stockholm...281

April, the 21st 1986 - Pretoria..286

April, the 24th 1986 - Stockholm...291

April, the 25th 1986 - Stockholm...293

April, the 26th 1986 - Stockholm...294

April, the 28th 1986 – Stockholm..300

April, the 29th 1986 - Stockholm...302

May, the 6th 1986 - Stockholm..304

May, the 8th 1986 - Stockholm..306

May, the 9th 1986 - Stockholm..307

May, the 12th 1986 - Pretoria..310

May, the 12th 1986 - Stockholm..313

The Contract (The Mission)

May, the 14th 1986 – Stockholm 319

May, the 17th 1986 – Frankfurt 321

May, the 18th 1986 – Frankfurt 327

May, the 19th 1986 – Frankfurt 329

May, the 19th 1986 – Pretoria 330

May, the 20th 1986 – Frankfurt 331

May, the 22th 1986 – Stockholm 334

May, the 26th 1986 – Stockholm 335

June 2nd 1986 – Durban, South Africa 337

1987 – Pretoria, South Africa 339

1988 – Durban, South Africa 341

September 1990 – Stockholm 347

October 1990 – Durban, South-Africa 348

Granskningskommissionen (GK) 353

"The Investigation Commission" 353

E P I L O G U E 355

GAMLA STAN 358

THE END 358

The Contract (The Mission)

PREAMBLE

Numerous attempts have been started to find the cause and those responsible for the assassination of Olof Palme, one explanation (excuse) dumber than the other, full in line with the Swedish "Tomtebolyckan" - A happiness to be compared to that the Trolls live in. (A Troll is a being in Scandinavian folklore, dwelling in isolated rocks, mountains, or caves, living together in small family units, and are rarely helpful to human beings).

And there we have the Swedish naivety when it comes to describing a particular course of events - what is not likely cannot not have occurred, what is probable must have occurred. Theories not really anchoring in reality, based on evidence lacking a practical reality basis like the Kurd problem, South Africa, Iran/Contra, Chile, CIA, EAP, a lonely drunkard, etc. - one theory more absurd and illogical than the other, only missing the Martians with their UFOs. With so much brain diarrhoea at once is hard to take things seriously.

It is hard to have confidence in the Swedish Police and their investigation methods and ability to solve problems when you hear and read the results of all investigations having been undertaken regarding the assassination of Olof Palme and then coming to the conclusion that the investigations can only be regarded as amateurish and naive attempts to sweep the real events under the rug. This leads me to the conclusion that this must be about a – for Sweden - a much larger and more serious conspiracy than all the – sometimes naïve - conspiracy theories so far having been published. That such a conspiracy would have its roots within Sweden's borders is something nobody really and honestly has regarded as a possible option or really worthwhile discussing in Sweden as such a phenomenon cannot and therefore will not have its

The Contract (The Mission)

roots within the borders of Sweden, a typical Swedish attitude, the reason being that the Swede is honest and socially engaged and responsible - oops. Bad Swedes must not and therefore cannot exist. The Swedes seem to live with the assumption that if only the laws are just, then society will also be perfect.

Consequently they start to search for guilty ones abroad where there are enough potential and credible clients found to perform a similar deed. Instead of concentrating on qualified causal research, based on Swedish history and culture they shoot in all directions, the main thing is to find someone who could have been "mean" to the Swedes - preferably someone from the right wing scene and ideally from abroad - the Swedish virginity must not be questioned - knowledge is power, not having a clue of anything is also ok.

Lately, however, a few, for the Author. more imaginable and also credible scenarios have been publicised having lifted the investigations to a level resembling an international level from Swedes who have managed to "liberate" themselves from the obsession that all evil must come from abroad and therefore must be run by capitalist '"demons" (the Swedish journalism is unarguably unparalleled in the world when it comes to rectification and unilateralism – compare with pre-Russian Pravda) - unfortunately these scenarios have (deliberately?) not been adapted by any official investigation or audit committee as creditable - might then of course lead to something, which in the end might turn out to be embarrassing.

I have – as a result of all the information that has been publicised, in an attempt to find the reason for the assassination of Palme - come to a different conclusion and have based my book on this new information, conclusions not necessarily having to be true, but on the other hand cannot be branded as untrustworthy either, namely: How and why did Palme get assassinated if the perpetrators did not belong to any foreign conspiracy and the principals are not to be found

The Contract (The Mission)

abroad? The book is of type speculative fiction, i.e. the scenario cannot be proven but might be real.

That John F. Kennedy was assassinated by a conspiracy is imaginable for almost every Swede. However, that Palme was killed as a result of a similar plot is for almost every Swede regarded as inconceivable.

This may sound somewhat strange, but unfortunately something very typical for the Swedish mentality and character nowadays. Has in fact the Swede – when it comes to the crunch – lost the ability to think autonomously, instead always hiding herself/himself behind the collective "Tomtebolycka" – an almost incomprehensible and unbelievable naive "looking away" attitude (like burying your head in the sand) - not daring (or simply refusing) to examine claims that differ from the Swedish model.

Why then does the average Swede find it impossible to imagine that local intelligence or security services might have been involved in the assassination of Olof Palme? Are the Swedes so naive or is it all about our deep-rooted (desperate) way of nationalism and the peaceful - not to be questioned - Swedish "folkhemmet" – the mantra - the castle of freedom, security and justice?

Until Sweden stops putting the blame on foreign powers, there will never be a satisfactorily solution to the Palme syndrome, instead the question : **Why did it happen?** must be answered.

and this question is the path I have tried to follow and understand: How and why could someone have done this to the Honorable Swedes? It could very well be that for some people murder may be legitimate - others not. It may also not be the right solution to a particular problem, but it may help us understand in general why things have gone astray.

"Clean up your own backyard before you barge into someone else's" as the Swedes' firmly believe that they're special, thereby producing the most charitable explanation for the ludicrous incompetence of the immediate official response that most probably ever has been given for a murder of Palme's calibre. If Palme had been struck down by a meteorite, it would probably have seemed more credible than the official version given by the Swedish police stating that Palme had been killed by a lone Swedish alcoholic, but he also appeared far too Swedish to assassinate a prime minister on impulse, even one as widely loathed as Palme. However, had he appeared in a novel about foreigners, he might have made a credible suspect.

The Contract (The Mission)

N.B.

It should be noted, that South Africa i.e. the government in Pretoria and in particular Minestry of Defence, most probably, and to a certain degree was having their role in the assassination of Olof Palme, something, which I have not pursued in great detail in this book, as this is something which effectively is beyond the scope of this book.

Further to the assassination: The go-ahead with the assassination and primary support is likely to have come from Washington. It was certainly not out of fear of exposing the wrongdoings of the South-African regime that made USA stay in the background, limiting their support to be more financial than being a part of the physical "action" itself.

(Very often there is a confusing misuse of the word "Apartheid" - Apartheid is a political ideology, defined by South-Africa in the 1940s - not to be compared with a regime running a country, which could adapt any ideology and still be in power, hence the South-African regime got support from US – not the ideology itself)

USA under Reagan enjoyed close ties with the South-African regime's security apparatus, seeing it both as a bulwark against "communism" and a useful ally in the disruption and suppression of left nationalist movements, which most certainly also included similar movements in Europe as well – including the Olof Palme movement. In 1981, Reagan declared that the Apartheid regime had "stood beside us in every war we've ever fought" and was "strategically essential to the free world in its production of minerals". Together with the Thatcher government in Britain, the Reagan administration sought to block sanctions on South Africa and provided crucial support to keep the regime intact towards the end of its "Apartheid" days.

The Contract (The Mission)

A conclusive proof of why and by whom the assassination of Palme took place (apart from circumstantial evidence), will probably never be found, however you have to understand that President Reagan, not exactly being the cleverest guy around, felt being sort of blessed, having a privilege, which enabled him to exercise the power of being the "President" of the United States wholeheartedly during the same period as Olof Palme was Prime Minister of Sweden, a power which he regularly used for making things go "his way".

In-fact, by criticising South-Africa Olof Palme indirectly was also criticising Ronald Reagan and USA.

Clarification:

Throughout the book I often use "Russia" instead of "Soviet Union" although the latter – from a historical point of view - may be the correct way for specifying the name of the historical entity where the book takes place. However nowadays most people see "Russia" as the more appropriate way of describing "Soviet Union", even during an epoch in time where using the denotation "Russia" more or less was abolished even for correctly describing "Russia" as an historical entity within the "Soviet Union".

Christer Hedberg

Inzell, Germany

10/06/2021

The Contract (The Mission)

Background

When Palme was shot dead around 20 people witnessed the killing, including Palme's wife, nobody has ever been prosecuted for the crime. Suspects over the years have ranged from members of the Kurdistan Workers' Party to a number of different far-right extremists, but the cops' blunders and poor leadership led them nowhere.

Many people have speculated that this meant the hit was an inside job. In fact Palme was deeply unpopular with many sectors of the Swedish society, so there was no lack of motivation, quite the contrary, either from inside or outside the government. Conspiracies of all kinds swirled around the killing.

Palme had publicly opposed the US Vietnam War and the apartheid system in South Africa. He also spoke up for an active peace policy and rapprochement with the Soviet Union.

For the Swedish military and intelligence officers, he was a traitor to the fatherland. In the evening of February 28, 1986 - four weeks before a planned visit to Moscow - Olof Palme was shot dead in a street in Stockholm

The assassination has morphed into a vast national obsession, a kind of a keystone in Swedish identity, generating countless number of books. It has become a great playground for enthusiasts of political conspiracy theories, many of whom are dissatisfied with the official verdict. Many people believe that Sweden has good reason to suppress the truth—and that the United States might be involved.

At the site of Palme's death, grieving Swedes left thousands of red roses, the symbol of the Swedish Social Democratic Party he led. On the other hand, Palme was loathed by the hard-right nationalist underground movement, clinging like lichen

The Contract (The Mission)

to parts of Scandinavian society. It's considerably more prominent nowadays.

There are good reasons to indulge in the idea that there's more to this story than the enigmatic figure of a single man. One or more gunmen hired from the Swedish fascist underground or possibly even the Swedish police having cooperated with the South African government together with Britain and the U.S. in eliminating Palme is another theory.

The theory goes like this. During the so-called "high" apartheid era, from 1948 to the early 1990s, the South African government was a death machine, executing 134 of its own political prisoners, killing a number of anti-apartheid activists, and commissioning several extrajudicial assassinations abroad of politicians who either opposed apartheid or meddled in the country's shady trade affairs.

This is not an outlandish theory. The former police hit squad commander Eugene de Kock once testified in court that the Palme killing was part of "Operation Long Reach," the secret campaign to counter the apartheid administration's foes abroad. Bold new evidence supporting this theory from former apartheid torturers, have been compiled, many of whom have been long protected by the amnesty they received as part of the Truth and Reconciliation Commission's agreements.

The other reason we have known so little about the international crimes South Africa committed during apartheid is that the U.S. might prefer it that way. In the mid-1980s, the South African government was having trouble navigating a global market bent on excluding it through boycotts. It got around the problem by partaking in secret trade deals with Iran and Israel, brokered by then-CIA Director William Casey. When Olof Palme won the reelection in 1985, he recommitted to his long-standing anti-apartheid foreign policy, which took the form of interfering in those shadow trade networks in arms and oil. In 1985, Sweden intercepted a delivery of arms en route to Iran, revealing to the world that Israel was selling explosives to Iran.

This broader scandal is known, of course, as the Iran-Contra Affair. If Palme was intending to expose details from Iran-Contra in the latter half of 1985, then suspicion for colluding in his assassination would logically fall on the CIA, as well as South Africa. It was, according to this theory, in the interests of Iran, the U.S., Israel, and South Africa to have him disappear. South Africa, conspiracy theorists point out, was the party with the death squad contacts handy.

(Minor excerpts from the document "Who killed Olof Palme?" by Joseph Livingstone is included)

The Contract (The Mission)

The gigantic mistakes during Olof Palme's time as Prime Minister

Olof Palme's political legacy has been discussed extensively as a result of the assassination at Sveavägen in 1986. However, his work regarding the Swedish economic policy, by contrast has received little attention. This is regrettable as Palme's two terms as prime minister - the years 1969 to 1976 and the years 1982 to 1986 - was in fact filled with unique and far-reaching (disastrous) economic policy measures {misfortunes}.

Four episodes deserve to be dragged into the light to illustrate the apocalyptic legacy of Palme:

- The price regulations   1970-71
- The bridging policy   1974-76
- The super devaluation in   1982
- "Löntagarfonderna" - the employee funds – in   1983

These experiments are exceptional both in Swedish as well as in international economic and structural policies.

Of course Palme did not design the details of economic policy himself. He was not even particularly interested in economics. However, as Prime Minister, he carried the ultimate responsibility for his government's policy. He also drove the financial issues vividly and skilfully in any debate. Therefore, we can speak of an economic legacy from his time as head of government.

In the early 1970s, the Palme government introduced a general price freeze. The purpose was to be in the position to face the wrath of housewives who were demonstrating against rising food prices. Price outage marked the beginning of a

The Contract (The Mission)

period of 20 years of the price control as an element (attempt) of stabilisation policy - longer than in any other industrialised country.

Sweden was dragged down in a regulatory morass with extensive control bureaucracy, negotiations, price spies, appeals, trickery, cheating and police reports. All this was from the ever start a very harmful activity as the research clearly shows that price controls are not capable of stopping inflation - they do not attack its causes. Instead, they create large costs to the society by impairing a market functioning economy.

Price controls are imposed by politicians, who lack the knowledge or courage to tackle inflation by tightening the economy and thereby having to impose unpopular policies. This short-term behaviour stood out as a running landmark for the Palme government, which was a low-water mark in Swedish stabilisation policy (one of many).

When the first oil crisis in 1973 came about, there was the fear that Sweden would suffer from weak domestic demand and unemployment. As a consequence, the Palme government then decided to try to overcome the expected economic downturn by stimulating demand with a highly expansionary fiscal policy.

During the years 1974-1976 the so-called bridging policy lead to Swedish prices and wages raised far above the level in the countries to which Sweden had a fixed exchange rate. The result was a loss of competitiveness and a deepening cost crisis. It then hit Sweden with full force after the Social Democratic government lost power in the elections in 1976. When they handed over the ticking bomb crisis to the incoming conservative government, Palme argued that the new government came to an already "readymade table".

The Contract (The Mission)

However, the truth was another. The table was in fact already empty. The crisis could only be rectified by two devaluations, which eventually restored Sweden's costing position.

The bridging policy virtually meant that Sweden missed the international economic recovery that followed the first oil crisis. Thus Sweden ended up lagging behind the rest of the world.

The bridging policy (experiment) was a very expensive experiment for Sweden.

After six years in opposition Palme returned as prime minister in 1982 in the aftermath of the second oil crisis in 1979-80. The first action was to write down the value of the Swedish Krona by 16 percent. The purpose of the super devaluation was to acquire a competitive advantage for Swedish exports by undervaluing the Swedish Krona - a new recipe in a never-ending unsuccessful Swedish economic policy.

Short term the super devaluation seemed to be a success. But it did not get the necessary aftercare to be successful. Instead prices and wages were being pushed up, thus contributing to the fact that Sweden's growth became lower than in most other countries.

Palme was attracted by the super devaluation because it made it possible for him to live up to his catchy election promise of "more room for the elbows and less austerity" and the lively description on how Ludvig Svensson's curtain factory would face brighter times ahead. Like price controls and bridging policy the offensive devaluation was a method to avoid having to take politically unpopular measures short-term.

Regarding structural policies, the introduction of employee funds is the key action taken during Palme's time as Prime Minister. The aim was that through the state, the ownership of Swedish industry was to be transferred to LO – the Labour Union. The funds rested on a Marxist view of the capital.

The Contract (The Mission)

There was no understanding of the role of the entrepreneur, the market dynamics of the economy and capitalism as the driving force behind Sweden's prosperity.

Löntagarfonderna (The employee funds) created a deep confidence gap between industry and Palme's government. It lead to that Swedish entrepreneurs like Kamprad (IKEA), Rausing (Tetra Pak) and Persson (H&M) moved out. (The latter moved back home to Sweden in the 1990s, after the - at that time - Prime Minister Ingvar Carlsson guaranteed that there would never again be any introduction of any employee funds). The centre-right government that came to power in 1991 then fortunately abolished said funds. Since then, the fund idea has been politically dead.

It is an irony of fate that Palme himself came to give the green light for the decisions that made his economic "prescriptions" impossible and obsolete, namely the deregulation of the financial markets in November 1985. The lack of aftercare of deregulation then led to the 90's crisis and the end of the fixed exchange rate, creating totally new opportunities for the economic politics.

With today's floating exchange rate, an independent central bank with primary objectives such as low inflation and international capital mobility, there is no room for price regulation, bridging policy, super devaluation and employee funds. These measures now belong in the museum of economic policy.

Unfortunately, Sweden still has to live with the aftermath of Palme's experiments. The gigantic mistakes in the 1970s - and the 1980s, lead to the Swedish economy was lagging behind the rest of the world. The challenge for today's economic policy still is to recover what was lost during the Olof Palme's time as Prime Minister.

(Source: Lars Jonung "The gigantic mistakes .." - Dagens Nyheter 16th of March 2006 – free translation from Swedish)

The Contract (The Mission)

If the employee funds were political-strategic blunders of large dimensions that can be blamed on the unions (Metall and LO) then there is no doubt that it was Olof Palme, who himself made sure to drive down the social democracy in an ultimately extremely destructive struggle for public monopolies.

The Contract (The Mission)

Löntagarfonderna (The Employee Funds)

A first model was launched by the LO economist Rudolf Meidner, the Socialist politician Anna Hedborg and Gunnar Fond in August 1975 on behalf of the trade union congress in 1971, which the same year approved a motion from the Swedish Metal Workers' Union authored by the then chief investigator Allan Larsson. The motion proposed that the issue of collective capital formation should be investigated.

The reason for the inquiry was that the solidarity wage policy would lead to that workers in high-productivity firms would restrain their wage demands, whilst workers in the low-productivity firms could increase their wage demands. A side effect being that the most highly productive firms, then could make bigger profits than what otherwise might have been the case. By the unions, this was called "excess profits" and they wanted this "excess" to go to the employees – for example through so-called employee funds. But the actual "salary increases" in the low-productivity firms meant in practice a labour movement to the more high-productivity firms and sectors, thus ensuring a high and equal wage progression for employees and to ensure full employment.

The creator of the "Löntagarfonderna" - Rudolf Meidner - argued that the solidarity wage policy road was fully paved with corporate failures. But with active labour market policies, the establishment of "Arbetsmarknadsstyrelsen" - the Labour Market Board, and a full employment, these structural changes in the labour market has not been a major socio-economic threat in the 1950s - and the 1960s , the so-called golden age. The Left-wing movement of 1968 had also brought with it new demands on wages, working conditions, influence and participation.

The main idea of the first proposal for the employee funds was that 20 percent of the affected corporate profits would be converted into so-called targeted stock dividends that should

The Contract (The Mission)

be received by the employee funds whose boards should have a majority of the representatives of the employees. In the long term the funds would then be in the position to own more than half of all shares in the major Swedish companies.

In LO's (trade union) newspaper "Fackföreningsrörelsen" - The Union Movement", Meidner declares that the proposal was intended as a direct attack on the capital owners might;

"We want to deprive the capitalists of their power, which they exercise just by virtue of their ownership. All experience shows that it is not enough with influence and control. Ownership plays a crucial role. I refer to Marx and Wigforss, stating that "we cannot fundamentally change society without also changing the ownership. ".

(Source: Excerpt from Wikipedia - free translation from Swedish)

Note:

After the Social Democratic election victory in 1982 a modified form of the employee funds, where companies during the years 1984-90 paid "profit tax" as well as "profit sharing tax" was introduced.

On the 4 October 1983 the first 4 October demonstration comprising more than 75,000 participants took place in Stockholm. The rally was on initiative from Småland entrepreneurs and was organised in cooperation between different business organisations. Also a petition with 533,702 names were collected as a protest against the employee funds.

After the bourgeois election victory in 1991 a bill stating that the funds would be dismantled in a way so that they would not be able to be rebuilt was introduced and also executed.

A full scale Meidner model would have needed to be augmented with other policies. For example, if enacted, Sweden would surely have experienced devastating capital

The Contract (The Mission)

flight. And it's not hard to see how workers with access to wage earner funds could become as abusive to the rest of the society as wealthy shareholders.

The Contract (The Mission)

Palme's Legacy

Olof Palme, Sweden's then Prime Minister, was assassinated on February 28th 1986. His death shocked millions everywhere. The murderer has still not been found, at least he has not been convicted. The crime was an attack not only on Palme, but on democracy itself.

Palme is now part of history but history is something that must be freely analysed, not just silenced out of deference. So, as we recall Palme's assassination we should also remember how he behaved and what he represented.

Olof Palme's legacy in foreign policy

Palme was a powerful, eloquent critic of the US and the war in Vietnam. He cursed Soviet oppression in Czechoslovakia and General Pinochet's murders in Chile. Because of these stands, Palme has often been portrayed as a consistent adversary of tyrannies. But this is not quite true. In fact, Palme systematically refrained from criticising many oppressive regimes and, indeed, embraced some of the cruelest dictators, or at least tried not to offend them.

Do not "vilify" the Soviet Union, said Palme, Chairman of Sweden's Social Democratic Party for 17 years and Prime Minister from 1969-1976 and, again, from 1982-86. Do not engage in "anti-Soviet agitation" or "the business of anti-Sovietism," he declared in 1984, a typical neutralist stand in Palme's Sweden.

No doubt, Palme reflected the spirit of his times. The West's Marxist revival after 1968 deeply impressed journalists and socialists, not least in Sweden. The Vietnam War changed the

The Contract (The Mission)

world view of many young people. Palme, however, carried this spirit forward so long after many others had seen the liberal light. "Neither communism nor capitalism represents a dream of liberty for the peoples of Europe," he said only a few years before the peoples of East and Central Europe freed themselves from Communism to embrace democracy and capitalism.

Palme also exploited ideological differences over diplomacy to wound other democratic parties in Sweden. The conservatives were lapsing into "the crusading spirit, aimed at the liberation of Eastern Europe, which prevailed in conservative quarters in the West during the Cold War," he said in 1983 - a moment of heightened tension between the West and the USSR. Eventually, Sweden's Liberals and Conservatives, after 44 years of Socialist rule, came to power in 1976. None of the threats to Sweden's foreign policy, which Palme confidently predicted, materialised in their nine years in office during the last quarter century.

His views were often nettlesome to those he criticised. But his early opposition to United States escalation of the Vietnam war, his condemnation of white minority rule in South Africa, and his disapproval of the Franco government in Spain and the Soviet invasion of Czechoslovakia were expressions of a distinctly independent conscience. In 1982 he even asked NATO and the Warsaw Pact to establish a nuclear-free zone in Europe.

Divisive at home, Palme tried hard to divide the West at a critical moment. In the 1980s Social Democrats in Sweden and Germany developed a close ideological collaboration in foreign affairs. The so-called "Palme Commission" (including the influential Egon Bahr) suggested a policy of "common security" between East and West, and nuclear weapon-free zones instead of NATO's policy of deploying cruise and Pershing II missiles to counter the Soviet advantage in theatre nuclear weapons.

The Contract (The Mission)

This alliance between the two parties led to serious distortions of fundamental Western values. Palme and Oskar Lafontaine, then one of the leaders of the opposition in Germany, did not see the Cold War as primarily a conflict between freedom and tyranny. When Palme visited East Germany in 1984 he never criticised repression there, nor the Berlin Wall. Instead, Palme praised East Germany's leader, Erich Honecker, underlining shared goals and the mutual struggle for peace and development. Palme's main speech mentioned "détente," "trust," and "friendship," but never "freedom".

Much the same pattern came about when Palme visited Cuba. He shared a podium with Fidel Castro at a mass rally in Santiago de Cuba. Palme spoke appreciatively of "socialist revolution," never mentioning his own party's conviction that "revolution" should take place only after free and honest elections. Indeed, Palme used Marxist slogans, but said nothing about human rights and political freedom, giving the impression that Sweden and Cuba embraced similar ideologies.

In a joint statement with Fidel Castro, Palme claimed that the two men were united in all the areas they had discussed. They even confirmed their happiness that the struggles for freedom of "the Vietnamese and Cambodian peoples have been crowned with victory." *This was said in the summer of 1975, two months after Cambodia's Khmer Rouge embarked on a genocide that killed two million of the country's seven million people.*

Was Olof Palme really unaware of Pol Pot's massacres? Newspapers in almost all democracies, including Sweden, were informing us of the Cambodian horrors. Palme, however, thought it more important to present a united front with Cuba's tyrant than to worry about atrocities committed by Communists in Indochina. *Palme, indeed, seldom condemned oppression in Third World countries. He constantly condemned apartheid in South Africa, on the other hand he*

The Contract (The Mission)

never criticised Mao's China, the most murderous regime to arise after World War II – estimated number of victims: 70 millions.

This double standard was particularly pernicious in the Middle East, where Palme never censured an Arab country, regardless of its corruption or cruelty. The only nation in that region he repeatedly attacked was its only democracy, Israel. He even equated the Israelis with the Nazis.

Still, more than thirty years after the murder of Olof Palme, Sweden and the West must still come to grips with what Palme left behind, his anti-Western agitation and his willingness to see fundamental ideals of freedom as merely relative values (see Africa). For people seeking or defending democracy and human rights, Palme was an unreliable partner. It is that aspect of his moral "example" that should be recalled.

(Source: Per Ahlmark - "Palmes Legacy 15 Years on", Project Syndicate - February 21, 2001 – minor adaptions undertaken to better reflect today's situation)

The Contract (The Mission)

CCB - Civil Cooperation Bureau

The South African **Civil Cooperation Bureau** (CCB) was a government-sponsored hit "squad" during the apartheid era that operated under the authority of Defence Minister General Magnus Malan. The Truth and Reconciliation Committee pronounced the CCB guilty of numerous killings, and suspected even more.

When South African newspapers first revealed its existence in the late 1980s, the CCB appeared to be a unique and unorthodox security operation: its members wore civilian clothing; it operated within the borders of the country; it used private companies as fronts; and it mostly targeted civilians. However, as the South African Truth and Reconciliation Commission (TRC) discovered a decade later, it became evident that the CCB's methods were neither new nor unique. Instead, they had evolved from precedents set in the 1960s and 70s by Eschel Rhoodie's Department of Information, the Bureau of State Security (B.O.S.S) and Project Barnacle - a top-secret project to eliminate SWAPO detainees and other "dangerous" operators.

From information given to the TRC by former agents seeking amnesty for crimes committed during the apartheid era, it became clear that there were many other covert operations similar to the CCB, which Nelson Mandela would label the *Third Force.*

The role envisaged for the CCB was the infiltration and penetration of the enemy, the gathering of information and the disruption of the enemy. The CCB was approved as an organisation consisting of ten divisions, or as expressed in military jargon, regions. Eight of these divisions or regions were intended to refer to geographical areas. The CCB provided the South African Defence Force (SADF) with good

The Contract (The Mission)

covert capabilities and clear instructions: destroy the terrorists, their bases and their capabilities. This was also the South-African government policy.(Source: Excerpts from **Civil Cooperation Bureau** - Wikipedia)

Covert structures and activities

The 1980s saw an extensive proliferation of covert structures and front companies specifically designed to obscure links to the state. Thus, for example, *the entire CCB operation was run via front companies*, employing operatives who formally resigned from the SADF and SAP (South African Police). A significant number of operatives remained in the 'security business' by establishing security companies, a cover that legitimately allowed them to have arms and to employ people with military or police training.

This process of 'privatisation of the security forces' relied to a large degree on a decentralisation of lines of command and control. Thus, on the one hand, the state increasingly emphasised the importance of centralisation and co-ordination – indeed, the notion of a 'Total Strategy' increasingly drew non-security departments and personnel into the ambit of tightly co-ordinated security policy.

The Contract (The Mission)

Stockholm – November 1985

The autumn had almost left to make way for the long Stockholm winter with rain, darkness, sleet - you name it. It was the worst season of the year where the people could only wait for Lucia to come with "the light" (longer days) again on December 13th.

They also must have got it wrong back then, when they tried to figure out from when the days would be longer again, as in reality the days starting to get longer did not start until a week later. But never mind, people did not give a damn about that week anyway as long as Lucia came, always with an excuse to get pissed at 5am in the morning,

But being November it was still more or less a question of surviving the gloomy days which you had at this time of the year until the days started to get longer, not being able to do much more than just eat, sleep and work. And the government was no exception. Everyone was waiting for the "light", although they were most probably waiting for another "light" than the average citizen.

At "Riksdagshuset" - the Parliament House - where the government was residing were four members of the government core team comprised of three men and one woman plus the chief Economist of the SE Bank and consequently a very influential person within the Government when it came to discuss economical matters and its implications - Klas Eklund - coming together, trying to find a solution to the so called "Palme problem" as they called it. The

The Contract (The Mission)

"Palme problem" was in essence how to find a way to make Palme change his somewhat revolutionary approach towards almost everything – towards the industry, the military, SÄPO – the Swedish Security Police, towards western foreign countries and their policies and political systems, towards the establishment, the rich people, you name it, and to more conform and commit to earlier decisions having been taken and agreements having been signed. Palme's view of the world more and more had become his personal view – the view of an Emperor, not the view of an official representative of a democratic country, and this fact had slowly begun to become an embarrassing and even a serious problem for Sweden – not only for the government, the military and Swedish secret police, but also for the Swedish export industry meaning it had increasingly becoming more difficult to close contracts with foreign companies even with companies where there has been a very long relationship.

One of government core member stressed that the main problem with Palme was that he was chronically suspicious and tended to listen and believe in every gossip he came to hear. Also, everyone not sharing his views automatically became a suspicious right-wing person in his eyes and therefore a political opponent just the way people like Hitler acted and Fidel Castro was acting, he said. He also mentioned that you automatically were a political opponent of Palme if you did not play his game. Anyone not being in favour of Palme's views more or less became his enemy.

His comments resulted in vehement protests from the other core members, however, the person originally having raised the issue did not comment on the protests from the others.

Instead he continued –

- I know Olof Frånstedt – the former head of SÄPO – that he mistrusts Palme because of his listening and belief in any gossip he becomes to hear and this is by any mean not the way a representative of a country should act. This behaviour now has resulted in that Palme now wants us, I

The Contract (The Mission)

mean Sweden, to stop any cooperation with CIA in favour of the Soviet KGB, something, which I personally find is very difficult to come to grips with and cannot understand. Although Sweden is a country officially being neutral, we bloody well belong to the western hemisphere and not the eastern, something which has been guiding our decisions all along. Is there anything driving his desires, which we are not aware of? I don't know but I have my own thoughts on that subject.

- When a prime minister of a sovereign country vehemently tries to impose such a change regarding our foreign policy it can only mean the Soviets have some sort of hook on him, which he cannot run away from. Or to bluntly put it – should that be the case, we are here talking about pure blackmailing from the Soviets. To me this is the only plausible reason for his actions and behaviour, as a prime minister should not try to impose his own foreign policy, something, which he to my opinion unfortunately is trying to do.

- I do not know if you are aware of the fact that Palme is having or has had regular meetings with the KGB-agent Nikolaj Nejland, which is a matter of great concern, something which to my opinion more or less only confirms my theory I just outlined. Is he working for the Soviets or what lies behind his recent actions? As we most probably cannot make him divulge the reason for his behaviour – we must then find and take other necessary actions.

The other members of the meeting had now become completely silent and were probably also somewhat chocked over the uncompromising view of Palme that they just had come to hear.

He then continued by saying -

- Please bear in mind that Olof Palme also made his conscription as intelligence officer at the same place where

The Contract (The Mission)

our notorious "friend" Wennerström was working. I am not trying to suggest anything here, just letting my own thoughts play with some possibilities and what their consequences might have been. You are all free to draw your own conclusions..

- One of the other core members – the woman - then said somewhat annoyed
- How did you get hold of all this information?
- Let us say that I have very good connections to some vital source within the security community, but let us leave it at that
- Do you then really insinuate that Palme is a spy?
- I am not stressing or implying anything. I am only presenting the facts here and now. It is for you to draw your own conclusions.
- I still cannot believe that what you are saying is true.
- Let's look at it from another angle then. Let me give you a couple of examples.
- Why the overwhelming applause for Eric Honecker in East Germany? In Palme's main speech when he visited Honecker in Stralsund in 1984 he mentioned "détente," "trust," and "friendship," but never used the word "freedom". Why was there no mentioning of the Berlin Wall? Instead, he comes up with total crap, underlining shared goals and the mutual struggle for peace and development.
- And what about Fidel Castro? Much the same happened when Palme visited Cuba. He shared a podium with Fidel Castro at a mass rally in Santiago de Cuba. Palme spoke appreciatively of "socialist revolution," never mentioning our conviction that "revolution" should take place only after free and honest elections. Indeed, Palme used Marxist slogans, but said nothing about human rights and political freedom, giving the world the impression that Sweden and

The Contract (The Mission)

Cuba are embracing similar ideologies, which I find somewhat embarrassing.

- Why is there no criticism of the Soviet Union? Quite the contrary; He is even saying - Do not "vilify" the Soviet Union and - Do not engage in "anti-Soviet agitation" or "the business of anti-Sovietism". Why this never-ending criticism of USA and their politics – domestically as well as foreign. Has this become a typical neutralist stand in Palme's Sweden?

- And why the embarrassing silence regarding Pol Pot and Cambodia and what is now taking place in Vietnam. To my opinion the whole scenario does not add up at all. I can smell a rat here.

- So you mean he is a spy?

- I did not say that, but I personally think that he hides something, which might long-term have a devastating impact on Sweden as a sovereign country if we do not curb it in time.

- What do you mean with curb it?

- To put it bluntly - find a way in getting rid of Palme. And it is not just about what we now have discussed. We also have "Löntagarfonderna" - the employee funds – and his overall attitude and general view towards "The Capital" and private ownership, something, which to my opinion threatens to bring Sweden to a grinding halt if we cannot find a different way in achieving what we originally were stating as our goal.

- The purpose behind "Löntagarfonderna", he continued, is to transfer the ownership of the Swedish industry to LO – the labour unions, and the "Löntagarfonderna" base their overall view on the Marxist way of how the capital shall be handled and used. There will be no room for the role of the entrepreneur and private ownership in Sweden anymore. Is this what we want? Is this not fraud against our voters and

The Contract (The Mission)

what we stating as our official program?

- Instead of having a system, he continued, where you are letting the dynamic of the market economy and the capitalism be used as a vehicle for maintaining and improving what we already have obtained.
- But isn't our goal to better spread the wealth in Sweden?
- Yes, I agree, but we cannot sell an idea, which in reality is aiming at obtaining a different result than what we publicly are stating. That is not fair politics. And it has nothing to do with social democracy anymore either. It is nothing but pure socialism. The industry is not stupid. By now they know in essence what we, or at least Palme, are aiming at and there is also no way in hell that we can force the companies to pay for something and invest in something which eventually will lead to a takeover of said companies by the unions. They are fully capable of realising that for them a state monopoly of the industry governed by the unions is the preferred solution.
- And the exodus of companies and skilled people has already started. Just look at what has happened to IKEA, H&M and Tetra Pak – three family-owned companies who used their own money to create companies and new jobs in Sweden – they have moved out from Sweden, thereby putting ten thousand new job opportunities elsewhere as well as making people lose their jobs as a result of their move to another country – sorry but the way the government momentarily is acting they see no future for their companies in Sweden anymore. Not to mention the tax evasion – Sweden is loosing billions of Kronas every year in that the companies are now paying their tax elsewhere. Is this really something we want? Also Rudolf Meidner, with his dogmatic views on what will happen to family-owned companies does not make it easier to get any sympathy for our ideas.

The Contract (The Mission)

- For example, his words to the Tetra Pak owner Hans Rausing will discourage anyone from even being prepared to set up and invest in a company in Sweden -
- "The nature of the business, the family owned, we will not have in the future of Sweden."
- When Hans Rausing then asked him if he could imagine to introduce some kind of tax or fee in order to avoid the forced sale of the family business,
- Meidner then bluntly replied -
- "It will not be possible, no one should be able to buy his freedom"

- Have we totally lost our minds? Is this not close to using the same approach that was used in the Nazi-Germany in the 30s for getting at the family companies the Jews possessed? Just take over the industry with a minimal compensation or eventually without any compensation at all – at least to me it is nothing but pure stealing.

He then continued -

- If we cannot find a different approach in how to better spread the wealth in Sweden, I believe in the end Sweden will only consist of idiots in the future as Hans Werthén is saying. And there will be nothing to spread either. We must differentiate between theoretical ideas and dogmas and what effectively is possible to implement. We are here to govern Sweden and not to experiment with nice-to-have ideas and see what happens. If the industry and the skilled people have lost confidence in what we are standing for, then the shit will hit the fan and the consequences will be disastrous. In fact I am inclined to believe we have almost already reached the point of no return now and I do not think it will help us trying to build up a Swedish version of the "Berlin Wall" in order to force skilled people and companies to stay in the country, as the "highly- priced" East-Germany has done, he said and smiled.

- To my opinion we are about to cut off the branch we are sitting on, not a very clever way of doing politics, I believe. Believe me, once the skilled people have left the country they will never come back. It is like a relationship, once you have found out your partner has betrayed you and you have found another one to live with, you'll never return.

- Without a healthy industry, private sector and skilled people we are, sorry to say, fucked, he continued. No one is going to vote for us anymore and then it does not help us that we additionally have implemented impractical ideas and dogmas in essence preventing us from taking the necessary actions needed to revert it all. We have to be pragmatic in what we are undertaking and proposing, having the prosperity of Sweden as our first goal – nothing else counts. No personal goals here. If we don't have that before our eyes when governing Sweden, there will not be anything to spread in the end, regardless of how we may want it.

- Having said that, we also have to come to grips with our devastating tax system, something, which Palme vehemently defends, but in essence threatens to kill us. Please, bear in mind, that during Sweden's "golden age" – the 50s and the 60s, the tax burden in Sweden was lower than the OECD average. It is not until Palme came to power, that we have reached a tax burden level being considerably higher than comparable countries. In fact we have the highest tax rates in the Western world! It is only due to the immense expansion of the Public Sector, which actually started with Palme, that we have got this immense tax problem.

- Even more progressive taxes do by far not serve its purpose. Instead of bringing about a just and equal society it instead creates a society of wranglers, cheaters, peculiar manipulations, false ambitions and new injustices arise,

The Contract (The Mission)

something which does not have much to do with what we social democrats stand for. The black market is progressing at record speed and Sweden's official growth is virtually zero and now is the worst in Europe. We cannot bury our heads in the sand anymore pretending that the problem does not exist. People need incentives to work legally otherwise they turn to other means for securing their survival – it is the nature of the law for survival.

- I cannot understand his belief in expanding the Public Sector at the same time criticising and vehemently blocking any attempts trying to curb private ownership at the same time denouncing any form of private ownership as the root of all evil, something which after all has enabled us to create the welfare state we all now are enjoying. Why Palme is trying to destroy it, I cannot grasp. And attempts to explain and excuse his views by referring to the poverty he saw in USA in the 50s is total bullshit. You do not make the situation better in USA by destroying the foundation of the Swedish welfare state.

- At the age of twenty, he was a reserve officer and an employee of the intelligence service and did work for the infamous T-Kontoret ("T office"): a Swedish intelligence agency, active between 1946 and 1965, I believe. As you probably also might know, the T-office later got transformed into the even more infamous IB - InformationsByrån. However IB didn't actually exist as a working unit. Not even the Parliament knew about its existence. When Palme left for USA 1947, there was no belief in socialism at all – quite the contrary. He more or less had a good time, during his time in USA, drinking beer and socialising and singing Russian Marches with another "conservative upper-class" guy, whom Palme there got to know, namely Birger Elmér later the one becoming the task to rebuild T-Kontoret and thereby creating IB! Quite a coincidence don't you think, I can smell a rat here! Someone saw the opportunity to convert Palme with substantial help from – well you might guess who - for the

The Contract (The Mission)

socialistic crap free of charge.

- Anyway, during Palme's stay in USA in the end 40s he is said to have experienced something, which suddenly triggered his "social pathos" but that what triggered him most certainly has not anything to do with what the socialists in this country now are using in their propaganda when trying to sell off their dream-come-true society.

No one at the table said anything, baffled by the outspoken and outright honesty, something, which totally contradicted the way politicians normally were communicating with each other in Sweden.

He then finished by saying

- Of course we could always have a chat with Palme about his views and about what I here have laid out, however I personally believe it is a waste of time as someone or something seems to have a hold on him. I also believe that all his actions and his disbelief regarding private ownership in favour of "Löntagarfonderna" is a result of this. Let us bluntly call it blackmail as there is no country as far as I am aware of, apart from the countries behind the Iron Curtain and Cuba, which is pushing for a socialist society more than Palme is doing and we all know what sort of welfare and freedom pure socialism has brought to these countries. Palme may view it differently, but to me nothing more horrendous could happen to Sweden than such a political system being brought upon us.

- What do you mean we should do then? , one of the others cautiously asked.

- I honestly don't know, the only option I see is somehow to force him to resign for health reasons, but for that we have to have a majority of the government with us or we have to denounce him in public but to be successful we need hard evidence for what I have said and that will be very difficult if not impossible.

The Contract (The Mission)

Hot and ferocious discussion followed without reaching any consensus what was to be undertaken. Finance Minister Feldt commented that he doubted a change regarding how Palme viewed things was possible as anything which contradicted his views drove him nuts, something which Feldt had experienced himself when he dared to question whether it was right to solely allow for a state governed child care or if it should not be possible to allow for private initiatives as well. Feldt also having dared to criticise "Löntagarfonderna" had led to a verbal outburst from Palme.

Mr Eklund – the Chief Economist - said that a full-fledged implementation of "Löntagarfonderna" would, based on similar approaches in other countries, most probably would lead to a stagnating economy and eventually ending in a political system like Yugoslavia's, a country not being exactly one of the more prosperous countries in Europe. He fully agreed with the previous speaker that future investments and initiatives by private individuals would virtually come to a grinding halt and that any investments to be made would consequently have to be done by the state, a system which has been proved being far too inflexible and bureaucratic to work in a market oriented economy. In essence Sweden would begin to even more lag behind other countries than what was the case already, momentarily facing a buying power equal to that of Portugal, one of the poorest nations in Europe.

He finally said that, regardless what political system one might prefer, he could not understand why the government having taken the decision for a political system, which ultimately would lead to more and more government control over the economy and simultaneously proved to lead to less and less economic growth for Sweden, cannot be revised.

The Government is striving at obtaining even more control over the economy, instead of giving Sweden the resources of going in the opposite direction. This was something, which he, as economist could not comprehend. He had the feeling that governing a country sometimes was a try-out-game for many politicians, where they could try out just about everything they felt like doing, without having to be afraid of facing any consequences.

Ironically, he thought for himself that, whilst someone having taken the same measures during a dictatorship with a corresponding result, which most certainly would have led to a liability for the consequences with a corresponding and "rightful" punishment, a democratically elected government would quite the contrary most certainly not only walk free but also be in the position to put the blame for any disaster on the new government. Also a lifetime pension would also most certainly be waiting for the "democratically elected" government as a righteous reward for their "experiment".

In essence, the result of their discussions was that they disappointingly had to admit that they could not agree on anything and that they would have to wait for the next Social Democratic party convention in order to raise their concerns. Raising the issue with Palme in private would only give him time to collect ammunition to defend himself at the next party convention - a typical Swedish approach where consensus and negotiations was the preferred name of the game instead of having to take any real decisions. Any deviation from of this behaviour was to be regarded as having "abused" said rules of etiquette and was therefore regarded as unethical and improper behaviour. To put it bluntly, Sweden was in fact, by always desperately aiming at finding a consensus in and thereby senselessly discussing everything without having achieved anything, which was intended to be undertaken, regardless of its consequences, at the brink of negotiating and discussing the subject to death.

Lisbon – November 1985

The winter had reached Lisbon. Although the temperature was not too bad, it felt bitterly cold due to a biting and blustery wind from the Atlantic together with rain, which made the temperature feel colder than it actually was.

Nipping on his almost empty glass of beer **José Eduardo Tavares Silva - José Silva** – thought about his present situation and gloomy future. He hated the weather in Europe, could not stand the fucking winter they had, the more north you travelled the worse it got. He could not understand how people could live in such a climate where you were freezing all the time.

He also had come to hate the communists with their fucking world revolution theory how to save the world from the "capitalist venom", which was not anything but a greedy philosophy how to make the communists take over the power of the world instead.

He also had come to hate the western powers for having allowed his country to be raped by the communist vultures and he hated having been forced to leave the only country he knew and loved - Mozambique. He has become bitter towards the world.

He had grown up in Maputo, the capital of Mozambique. As Mozambique had been an integral part of Portugal for more than 400 years, he automatically had become the Portuguese Citizenship by birth.

The Contract (The Mission)

The voyage of Vasco da Gama in 1498 marked the arrival of the Portuguese, who began a gradual process of colonisation and settlement in 1505. After over four centuries of Portuguese rule, Mozambique gained independence in 1975, becoming the People's Republic of Mozambique a socialist state - shortly thereafter. After only two years of independence, the country descended into an intense and protracted civil war lasting from 1977 to 1992.

He was born Portuguese, therefore, as he could not see any reason why he all of a sudden should be forced to accept another citizenship, it left him with the only option – to leave Mozambique – his country – when the "liberation army" FRELIMO came to take over the country – still another opportunity for the socialist movement to once again prove its incompetence.

The growing fear of retaliation amongst the whites to be carried out by the blacks and a ninety day ultimatum to either choose Mozambican citizenship or leave the country, eventually drove the majority of the Portuguese – predominantly the white - population out of the country, including his parents, who then had to leave the country for Lisbon, Portugal.

Before the communists came, no one had hated the other. Then came the fucking Russians, Chinese and Cubans with their socialist crap and so called "help" philosophy aiming at "helping" FRELIMO to liberate the country, which was not anything else but another way of colonialism. FRELIMO was nothing else but a bunch of uneducated locals, greedy for power, calling themselves liberators, aiming at liberating the country from the "imperialists" (the white - i.e. Portuguese - population), despite the fact that it already had been proclaimed "liberated" (i.e. independent) in 1975 as a result of a leftist military coup takeover in Portugal. Unfortunately a democratic takeover was not in the interest of the communists and FRELIMO which, as a consequence took

The Contract (The Mission)

power of Mozambique and intensified their own "liberation" war.

Had not Portugal tried to improve the conditions for the black population as they had build new railroads, irrigation systems, hospitals, schools, etc. ? They might have been somewhat late in realising what had to be undertaken, but - a fault confessed is half redressed - as they say, he thought for himself.

A new law to force the white (the white - i.e. Portuguese - population) had been passed by the FRELIMO party, now effectively running the country, ordering all Portuguese citizens to leave the country within 24 hours with only 20 kilograms of luggage. Unable to salvage any of their assets, most of them returned to Portugal penniless.

What FRELIMO hadn't realised with their decree was that almost all knowledge and know-how left Mozambique in one go leaving the country with a local industry, which now neither could be run nor maintained or serviced anymore. Almost all necessary spare parts and equipment needed to keep the industry rolling had so far been taken from Portugal, a country not particularly interested in helping FRELIMO out in securing their takeover of the country. Also the knowhow necessary to keep the production rolling was gone. This led to an almost total breakdown of the infrastructure and the production of necessary goods came to a grinding halt.

Stupid and naive as the blacks always were, he thought bitterly, they never thought about what the implications, resulting from their actions, would or could be. No planning ahead – just immediate action was the name of the game.

But it did not matter. All attempts Portugal had taken to improve the conditions for the population people did not matter anymore. FRELIMO'S hunger for power and one-sided socialist propaganda just rolled on. Even the western powers stopped their support for resistance movements like RENAMO aiming at preventing a takeover by the communists.

The Contract (The Mission)

He therefore joined RENAMO in an attempt to prevent Mozambique to be "liberated" and taken over by the communist pack.

RENAMO was originally sponsored by the Rhodesian Central Intelligence Organisation (CIO), it was founded in 1975 as part of an anti-communist backlash against the country's ruling FRELIMO party.

When the support from South Africa eventually faded out, as a result of outside political pressure and their peace treaty with FRELIMO, the options for a successful victory were close to nothing and he decided to join the Civil Cooperation Bureau (CCB) – the South African "Green Berets" - a unique, integral and supportive unorthodox security operations unit of the South African Defence Force, where its members wore civilian clothing and used private companies as fronts for their covert operations.

Officially CCB was working within the borders of South-Africa. Unofficially CCB was used for covert operation outside the South-African borders as well and he worked there as a mercenary to help South Africa in their attempts to stop the communists from penetrating southern Africa from their Angolan setups.

Had not Mozambique been an integral part of Portugal for almost 500 years? How fucking long does something have to belong to a country before it is recognised as an integral part of that country, he wondered.

He also had build up a hatred towards Sweden and their never- ending claims from their Prime Minister Olof Palme to free the African "colonies" from the white "aggressors". it felt like they have to play the role as the moral conscience for just about everything and everyone in the world. You name it and they were there to tell the world what was right and what was wrong. Why the fuck does a small and far away country like Sweden have to tell the world what was good for Mozambique and how and by whom the country has to be run.

The Contract (The Mission)

Also, what gave Sweden the right to publicly condemn the way Portugal ran Mozambique and as a result consequently trying to influence the masses to become hostile towards the Portuguese government? Why the fuck? Who cared for the 250 thousand whites who did not take the same standpoint and who had lived in Mozambique all their lives and as a result of Sweden's "intervention" had to leave the country? Why the fuck? Fuck Sweden and their Prime Minister, he thought.

Jose finished the beer he had in front of him, but did not feel like leaving the restaurant for the rain outside and ordered another beer. The only thing you can do in this fucking weather was to get drunk, he thought bitterly.

However, there is one good thing with Europe, he thought, and that was that they allowed you to stay until you decided to leave the bar or restaurant yourself, regardless if you ordered something or not and not, as was the case in the US, the moment you had finished your meal they handed you the bill, something, which he found being utmost disturbing.

He thought about his years as "missionary" (mercenary) in Angola after having been forced to leave Mozambique and then joined the South-African Special Forces to fight the communists in their attempts to take over Angola as well as trying to hinder them in their attempts to cross the border to Namibia ultimately aiming at penetrating southern Africa.

How he missed Africa, he thought. He had no feelings for Europe and their people although he still possessed a Portuguese passport, as Mozambique had been an integral part of Portugal – not a colony – when he was born.

Europe was a continent where everyone knew what was good for everyone else, knew what was good for Mozambique, knew what was good for Angola, knew what was good for South-Africa, knew what was good for South-Rhodesia without even having spent one fucking second on the African continent. And those who were to blame for what was taking place in

The Contract (The Mission)

Africa were always the white Africans, no-one even being remotely interested in paying one single thought what was to happen with the "normal" whites, people who had lived all their lives in Africa without having paid any thoughts about political conquests or racial advantages. People not having second thoughts, people who were only aiming at doing a decent every-day job, like any European with only one difference; they were not born in Europe because their parents had decided to emigrate to Africa and not to America or Australia.

He was so fucking tired listening to all these never-ending discussions about the bad and privileged white people in Africa so he could vomit. Why the fuck were all whites in Africa regarded as crooks and outcasts only because they happened to be born there? He felt he must find a way to start "breathing" again and had been through a lot of scenarios aiming at making it possible and finding a way for him to settle in Africa again. The only viable option he saw was South Africa and for that he needed money – and a lot.

He also paid some thoughts regarding what might have happened to his "mates", the South-African Piet van Cleef and the South-Rhodesian Martin Carlisle. Together they have had a good time, despite the raids they regularly had to make into Angola, raids that often officially had not taken place – that's why we - the "missionaries" (mercenaries) were there, he thought and smiled for himself. The three of them were fighting as a separate unit within CCB, being independent from any restrictions, which CCB may have to impose on their own folks. It always was a good feeling when you stumbled on one of those fucking commies and had the opportunity to send him to the "happy hunting grounds" as some sort of retribution for what they had done to him, his family and his country – ruined and castrated it, he thought.

He never had had any regrets regarding what he was undertaking, instead he found that the fucking commies should see to that they were going home. Clean up in your own

The Contract (The Mission)

fucking backyard before coming to Africa, he thought. Then they as well as we would have fewer problems, he thought.

He also paid some thoughts about whether Piet or Martin had managed to dig up any new connections or had got any message regarding new assignments, other than having to fight for a lost cause in Angola. Slowly he was beginning to get unsettled. They had agreed to keep in touch by putting two small classified ads in Financial Times. If any of them had received an offer they had agreed to put in an ad on a Tuesday in Financial Times – "Not interested in CCB? - Answer under Chiffre .....", where the others were to answer with contact information in case someone was interested in their skills. Should there be a phone number available where someone could be reached it was preferred to have the number – backwards - as a written reply to the chiffre. The chiffre also said from whom the ad actually originated.

Another ad, in case one of them were looking for assignments saying "missionary assignments welcomed - Answer under Chiffre....", also in Financial Times, was agreed to be put in on Wednesdays to Fridays, – one day per person, in case there was only one position available. As it was not that suitable to directly search assignments as "mercenary", they had chosen the word "missionary" instead, when looking for new assignments as those, familiar with the "mercenary" subject, most probably knew what really was meant with the word "missionary". As they wanted to avoid unnecessary publicity, they also avoided advertising in well-known "Law & Order" magazines, which could lead to that you got too well known in the market, something that often might be disadvantageous for the "business". The name of the game as a "mercenary" was to keep a low profile with what you were doing.

It was now more than a month ago since they had split up in Cape Town after having finished a couple of minor "cleansing" tasks at the Namibian/Angolan border and it was about time to do something more substantial, he thought, instead of just "hoboing" around, doing nothing. As it was Tuesday he

The Contract (The Mission)

reminded himself not to forget to go to the Lisbon main train station and buy a copy of Financial Times. Shouldn't there be anything the following week, he might be forced to contact CCB stating his availability for a new assignments, although he was hoping, due to Britain's increased involvement in the African colonial wars, Piet and Martin would have managed to build up some good connections with British special forces like Ulster Defence Regiment (UDR) and SAS – unofficially they occasionally needed people for "impossible missions" - and he could envisage having to "take care" of something, should anything else pop up, other than just chasing Cubans in Angola.

The Contract (The Mission)

London – November 1985

Martin Carlisle took a sip from his pint of beer, having put both his elbows on the bar and his hands on his cheeks with empty eyes, which did not really register anything and thought somewhat depressed and absent-minded about his present life and his present situation.

It was cold with a never-ending drizzling rain, i.e typical London weather for December. He has come to hate London and its eight million inhabitants. Everything was so fucking cramped, you were stumbling over people everywhere and everything was full – busses, the tube, restaurants, streets, roads – everything, you name it. It was as if you were living in a nightmare. He was longing back to Africa and his South-Rhodesia, where he was born, with enough space, sun and warmth the whole year around.

Unfortunately everything had been taken away from him only because the fucking communists with help from China and the Soviet Union had meddled about with something which they neither would understand nor was it any of their business. They should have minded their own business, he thought

Perhaps Ian Smith could or should have taken a different approach towards the black population when he had the opportunity, but on the other hand, had he not tried to find a way for the blacks to gain majority and to "gradually" be brought up to "standards of Western civilisation." and didn't he negotiate with moderate black politicians aiming at reaching the best solution for South-Rhodesia?

The Contract (The Mission)

Ian Douglas Smith was a Rhodesian politician, farmer, and fighter pilot who served as Prime Minister of Rhodesia from 1964 to 1979. He was born to British immigrants in Selukwe, a small mining and farming town about 310 km (190 mi) southwest of the then Southern Rhodesian capital Salisbury. He has been described as personifying white Rhodesia and remains a highly controversial figure. He was the country's first premier not born abroad, and led the predominantly white government that unilaterally declared independence from the United Kingdom in November 1965, following prolonged dispute over the terms.

Firmly believing that blacks are not ready to be handed power over South-Rhodesia, he - pointing to the chaotic situation in South-Rhodesia after 1980, vehemently tried to prove that he was trying to prevent South-Rhodesia from suffering the same fate as other black majority-ruled African states – unfortunately he failed after having fought against communist encroachment for almost fifteen years.

In the end having been forced to sell off the country to Mugabe and his fucking communist mob mainly due to international pressure was unnecessary and totally wrong. The black people had never had a better life and will never get a better life than the life they had had under white mastery, he thought bitterly for himself.

In an attempt to save what the whites had accomplished Martin joined the Selous Scouts, a special forces regiment within the South-Rhodesian Army, Martin thought, where he got trained as a sniper aiming at ending the terror on the population carried out by uneducated and unorganised Mugabe-terrorists with only one goal; to plunge the country in an abyss without caring about the implications for the population – even for the black majority.

Most of the blacks, which he had met and talked to during their "cleanup" operations, did not want any changes to take place at all. They had work and enough food on the table and

The Contract (The Mission)

were treated decently by the white farmers, they said. Unfortunately, they were ultimately forced and threatened by the terrorists – Mugabe's communist mob - to join them for their "cause".

To destroy once one of the most beautiful countries, something that Mugabe now was about to do, was something that Ian Smith would never had done. Instead of chasing away the knowledge from the country, thereby destroying the base for a well-functioning society, he should have strived at reaching a cooperation between the whites and the blacks in order to continue the build-up of South-Rhodesia, based on what the whites had accomplished.

Instead Mugabe decided to behave like a child – you more or less have to treat all blacks as children, he thought. Since 1980 and the institution of a majority Black government, South-Rhodesia was re-named and all traces of a previous British Rhodesia, was removed including white rules, laws, property, and nomenclature. As a result of Robert Mugabe's policy everything reminding people of a previous white mastery disappeared – apart from the language english - the language the whites were speaking.

The blacks will never have it as good as when the whites ran the country as they are completely lacking the prerequisites for administrating and running a country, Martin thought bitterly.

He had never regarded himself being a racist. He had only grown up and lived in a society run by the whites without ever having paid any thoughts regarding being privileged at the expense of the black population or having had any hostile feelings towards them. Fuck, the blacks were the racists, not the white population, he thought for himself.

It does not help seeking help from collective run countries like China or Soviet Union, countries being utterly incompetent in coming to grips with the problems they had in their own countries themselves, he thought. A better solution for the

The Contract (The Mission)

blacks would have been, despite the differences, to seek a joint solution together with the white population as they were the ones ultimately knowing what was needed to save the country from a complete chaos and anarchy, something the whites finally have come to realise – although probably not understand - that the only plausible solution, which would have to have been executed for saving the country would have been a joint approach by the whites and the blacks.

Unfortunately such a solution did not interest Mugabe and his mob and the international "conspiracy" against the ruling South-Rhodesian white population.

As a result of Mugabe's seizure of power, he and his parents were forced to leave the country – the only country he was familiar with – as he still was British citizen as a result of his parents having come from England and never seriously had thought of the possibility to apply for a South-Rhodesian citizenship whilst he was living there.

However, he did not come to grips with life and the environment in England and therefore took the decision to go South Africa and there joined the South-African Bureau of State Security – BOSS - South Africa's "Green Berets", as a "missionary" to help South Africa prevent the Communists from infiltrating southern Africa, the last free frontier left in Africa. His education at the Selous Scouts more or less had given him "free entry" to join BOSS - they did not allow anyone just to go "on board" – the requirements were high. Also his experience with guerilla warfare was another useful merit he possessed being very useful to them.

He also thought with rage of some countries in Europe – countries not having a clue about how Africa and South-Rhodesia was functioning – eventually leading to that Mugabe and his murderous pack received international help and support in order to continue their "freedom struggle" in South-Rhodesia, especially Sweden with their fucking upper class prime minister – Olof Palme, a "yeller" who never ceased to appeal for a takeover by the blacks, however when it came to

The Contract (The Mission)

the crunch not really interested in the consequences of his fucking screaming - for the white as well as for the black population – career-obsessed as he was. Was there really any international conflict that he could stay away from and not put his fucking nose in? Martin doubted there was.

He stopped his self inflicting thoughts instead wondering for himself what his "buddies" from his last assignment at the Angolan border were doing. They had had a stressful time together with little sleep and food and the Cuban Communists lurking behind every bush. However, they were lucky to have known the terrain much better than the Cubans. Sometimes, he felt really sorry for them poor sods - he thought, most of them not having any experience in guerilla warfare, something that he was trained for and had been practising for several years. You just sat there and snapped one after the other - was like shooting off clay pigeons.

The Contract (The Mission)

Durban – November 1985

Piet Van Cleef sipped on his wine and took a bite of his steak his girlfriend had prepared to celebrate his return from Namibia.

He had just recently returned from a longer mission ("cleansing assignment") along the border between Angola and Namibia, a mission which he had received from the Civil Cooperation Bureau (CCB), South Africa's "Green Berets", an area where hordes of Cubans were to be found and which slowly was about to become a real problem, not only for Angola but also for South Africa, a problem that had to be solved at all costs. South Africa could not under any circumstances allow any communist infiltration attempts by the communist "liberators" (from China, the Soviet Union and Cuba), who momentarily all were to be found in Angola, to become successful.

He preferred to work as a mercenary - or "missionary" as they preferred to call themselves - for CCB as there were enough "missions" which you could choose from and you were in the position to decide where and when you wanted to carry out your task. The payment was also much better as a "missionary" than being employed directly by the CCB.

He was born and raised in Durban, South Africa without really having paid any real thoughts when it came to apartheid and racism.

Every now and then he had some thoughts how South-Africa came to be a country and he could not fully comprehend why being white on a black continent was regarded as something

The Contract (The Mission)

abnormal, and almost unethical by the rest of the world. After all, our roots in Africa are close to 500 years, he thought, and why doesn't it legitimate us – the whites - to be an integral part of the African continent as no one was actually living in the southern part of South-Africa at a time when the gradual process of white settlements begun. No settlers, no settlements, no tribes, no indigenous people, nothing was there, which could be claimed by someone.

Compared to how America and Australia came about with their colonisation. Their way of gradual process of colonisation was never really criticised, Piet thought for himself. There was not even any colonisation having taken place, he thought for himself also thinking that it was not fair, the way South-Africa was condemned by the world community.

The Portuguese mariner Bartolomeu Dias was the first European to explore the coastline of South Africa in 1488, attempting to discover a trade route to the Far East via the southernmost cape of South Africa, which he named *Cabo das Tormentas*, meaning Cape of Storms. In November 1497, a fleet of Portuguese ships under the command of the Portuguese mariner Vasco da Gama rounded the Cape of Good Hope and the first whites arrived.

By 16 December 1497, the fleet had passed the Great Fish River on the east coast of South Africa, where Dias had earlier turned back. Da Gama gave the name Natal to the coast he was passing, which in Portuguese means Christmas. Da Gama's fleet opening the Cape Route between Europe and Asia.

His forefathers, arriving and settled down in South-Africa almost 150 years ago were emigrant Boers from the Cape Colony, who came by land over the passes of the Drakensberg. These so called "voortrekkers" were led by a certain Piet

The Contract (The Mission)

Retief then passing through almost empty and deserted upper regions.

Consequently his parents were also born and raised in South Africa, even his grandparents. Also he had had and had black friends – also black females with whom he, when he was younger in the 60s, and the racial issue was not seen as something, which you thought might lead to conflicts of any kind and therefore would prevent or restrict you from keeping them as friends., you every once in a while, although it was forbidden by law to have intercourse between the races - you hate ared one-night stands with them. He also often took his black friends with him and went swimming and surfing on "white" beaches, something that was silently tolerated as long as they were together with whites. Apartheid was more or less something that you and even the blacks has come to accept and come to live with without really thinking about its origin, intent, pros and cons. The main thing that mattered was that everyone had a job and there was food on the table. The only thing, that the authorities were pretty strict about, was that the blacks had to be back in their townships during the night and then to return to the "white" areas to work the following morning. If they missed out on having returned to the townships on time, they had a problem. This often led to the situation, where they had to be "hidden" by the "whites" in areas where the "whites" were predominant until the next morning (provided someone was prepared to hide them). Should someone be caught not having followed what the law prescribed, you had a problem (including Coercive Interrogation) unless you didn't know a white South-African, who was prepared to "stand up" for you.

He did not directly regard himself as a racist and had worked and lived with black "colleagues" without any problems whatsoever when CCB conducted raids into Angola. He had even swung a "beaker" together with them, but he found it hard to imagine that the blacks should and could govern South Africa some day.

The Contract (The Mission)

Every single country where black people had come to power in Africa either after having gotten their "freedom" from their colonialists or "liberated" themselves, those countries had gone down the drain in record time. As there had never been any real countries in Africa before the whites started to populate the continent anyway. The tribe-thinking mentality of the black people immediately had led to that the blacks had begun to fight each other, being more interested in coming to power in the country and getting the power over other tribes eventually had as result that your own tribe with its members was put in all strategic positions in the government without really being interested in the country as such and that he would not under any circumstances allow for similar experiments to take place in his South Africa.

Apartheid was most certainly not something that solved South Africa's current problems. More rights and responsibilities for the blacks - yes, but the blacks running the country as a result from events similar to those in South-Rhodesia and Mozambique – unthinkable.

He had met many hateful white "missionaries" from Mozambique and South-Rhodesia who had lost everything they had owned and had had, in countries where they were born and had grown up without racist ulterior motives and where the communism now had helped the black "liberation armies" to shatter everything the "whites" had built up over the centuries and it was the main contribution from him to South-Africa to help prevent any communist influence – by all available means - from entering his own South-Africa. Also European "loudmouths" from countries that did not have a clue how things worked in Africa and how it was to live in Africa had significantly contributed to the current misery on the African continent.

A prime example of this interference was Sweden and their government, with their crazy "loudmouth" Olof Palme in the lead - his behaviour could be compared with that of other

The Contract (The Mission)

famous "loudmouths" like Hitler and Fidel Castro, somethingwhich also irritated him like hell as he was of the opinion that South Africa has to walk a path that was possible for South Africa and not any path a fucking "loudmouth" in Europe had proclaimed to be the real one, just to be able to use the political core of other countries' problems for his own ego, You cannot just abolish apartheid without also being able to foresee the consequences by doing it. They should not expect that by abolishing apartheid it would solve all problems at once, problems that had taken themselves – the white population - decades trying to come to grips with.

Was it not social as well as mental injustices in the European countries that once had forced large parts of their population to emigrate, particularly to Africa, to seek new opportunities to survive. Had anyone at the time, interferred in how those countries would go about in solving their social problems? Fuck them, he mumbled for himself.

Sometimes when he thought of what many countries thought and said about South Africa, he became very angry, as it was often done without reviewing and taking historical facts into account.

The Europeans they all sit there in their fucking rocking chairs and thinking "clever" things about how we are to solve our problems, without having any idea what they're talking about. They are not the slightest interested in the historical fact that the white and black race came to South-Africa virtually at the same time; the black race coming in from South-Rhodesia, while the first European colonists came over the sea route to Cape Town. At that time – 500 hundred years ago - South Africa had been uninhabited except for a few Bushmen - he thought for himself.

But with these facts, it is not possible to make politics as it does not fit into the schema for the "innocent" (and corrupt) European politicians and as a consequence of their wrongdoings they virtually send whole nations into chaos and anarchy, something which had happened with nations like

The Contract (The Mission)

Mozambique, South-Rhodesia and Angola, he thought for himself. You cannot for god's sake using a European solution on an African problem without taking the consequences of what you are proposing into consideration as well - and he got even angrier the more he thought about it.

The Contract (The Mission)

Stockholm, End of November 1985

It was a typical late November in Stockholm, the sun was not to be seen, just added a little extra light to an already dull day at the horizon, the weather was extremely unfriendly and the depressing darkness was present almost all day - a biting wind mixed with never-ending slushy snow or cold rain, which made you feel only wanting to stay in bed all day. It was pre-Christmas time, which left people with their only viable choice outside their home – to go Christmas shopping.

However, not all people went shopping. instead many used their time to catch up with things having been postponed and put aside due to the long days of the Swedish summer where Sweden almost came to a grinding halt, where people were occupied with celebrating midsummer and getting pissed as a result from eating all the crayfish and drinking an almost obscene amount of "schnapps" having to be consumed with the crayfish every August. The "schnapps" drinking was obligatory

On such an unfriendly Wednesday sat such a person, living in Djursholm, one of the noblest areas of the Stockholm area, trying to catch up with what he had been postponing during the summer months. He was sitting together with a long-time friend who was just visiting him, discussing the present rundown situation of Sweden

- Isn't it depressing, to see Sweden almost going down the drain after having experienced and lived in a strong and wealthy country for so many years, yes even decades, the host said thoughtfully!

The Contract (The Mission)

- Indeed it is, his long-time friend agreed. Although we had the Social Democrats running Sweden for decades, we were all primarily striving at improving the Swedish welfare model and not working for your own personal ego and beliefs as now seems to be the case. As you know we often had our verbal disagreements with Tage Erlander, our former Prime Minister, but even he realised that you cannot and must not touch, I mean challenge, the basic foundation of the Swedish welfare state.

- Something, which unfortunately now seems to have been put aside by today's politicians, especially by those who have been elected and trusted to run the country. Nowadays it seems they are about to slaughter the cow that is giving us the milk, just for some short time goal of being able to sell the meat, in order to be in the position to give the masses the tranquillisers that you accidentally might have promised them by the last election, just to be able to stay in power. We are here talking about the famous Swedish enviousness – a very questionable and self-destructing trait.

- I agree. Nowadays, the politicians are aiming at turning our political system into a mechanism for legalising oppression, repression and stealing, the other one said, almost spitting out the words.

- More and more people as well as companies are giving up fighting and instead taking the decision to leave the country. The socialist – not social democrat - movement is slowly penetrating every part of our society and our lives. People are slowly getting brainwashed.

- They don't seem to realise that by buying Palme's "socialist" crap, sorry – so called promises, they are destroying the fundamental principle of Sweden – how to work together for a better Sweden – long term. By just simply grabbing what is possible to get – short term, you are destroying the basic foundation for being in the position to even keep those

The Contract (The Mission)

short-term goals.

- I have the feeling it has gone thus far in that those of us disagreeing with what Palme – our Enfant Terrible - and the socialists are proclaiming. are beginning to get afraid and do not have the courage to speak out anymore – instead they prefer to stay silent. Do they fear some sort of retaliation? Anyway, this behaviour gives people in general and the socialists in particular the impression that the non-socialists are in minority, something, which is totally wrong. The tragedy is that they even seem to believe that they are in the minority themselves. Nowadays it seems as if the socialists are the only ones really stressing their political views in public. This situation is very precarious for a democracy, as it sort of tends to legitimise the socialists being in power without even having to be elected.

- I agree with you. Many prestigious companies like H&M, IKEA and Tetra Pack now have left Sweden. Imagine what incredible sums of company tax Sweden is losing as a result of all short-sighted decisions and actions taken by the present government.

- And then we have the "Löntagarfonderna" - the employee funds - a purely Marxist approach, with the aim to transfer the ownership of the Swedish industry - with help from the state - to the unions, and LO in particular, effectively - by state decree – enabling them long term to purchase and run all businesses in Sweden – with money stolen from the companies in the first place, calling it "övervinster" – excess profits. This is the first step towards the creation of a Mussolini-style corporative state. The result of such an approach we all can see in the countries behind the Iron Curtain and Cuba.

- Also MBL - "Medbestämmandelagen", another bureaucratic morass, requesting by law that a company has to inform and consult the union representatives in said company in everything you intend to do, something which does not exactly make life easier when it comes to run a business and having to take fast business decisions in order to secure a particular deal. We are not alone in the world - there is a fierce competition out there – something which some people seem to have forgotten.

- I think something must be done or we will end up being one of the poorest countries, if not the poorest, in Europe. In the end we probably will have to face the same destiny as the countries behind the Iron Curtain. By the way we have, according to recent statistics, in the meantime reached a buying power equal to that of Portugal, utterly embarrassing and depressing bearing in mind that Sweden was number one on the country prosperity list only 25 years ago. It can never end well, when the state now is counting for 40 percent of the work force, or should I say 40% of a mostly unproductive work force eventually producing even more useless bureaucratic obstacles for the industry. As the bureaucrats are not generating any money to finance the crap they are producing, it can only be financed through our "eminent" taxation system - at least we are number one when talking about crappy tax systems, he mumbled for himself.

- In the meantime it has become a tax system that is circumvented by more and more people and even companies with the sole goal just to survive as a production unit thereby only postponing having to file for bankruptcy. With tax brackets well over 90% you cannot exist on what is left after tax anymore. I read an article not a long time ago stating that in the meantime over 50% of everything produced and traded with in this country is done with black money. For God's sake, people are beginning to get scared, that they cannot live on what they legally earn anymore as the option changing what is causing the resentment - i.e our tax system - does not seem to be a valid option.

- Let us also not forget the "Angivarlagen", the guest interrrupted, the law that has made it compulsory for all citizens to report any knowledge of people, which may have

The Contract (The Mission)

the intention to evade tax. What is bad for Palme and the state then becomes illegal by imposing a new law instead of modifying the existing ones. However it is quite unacceptable under any rule or law that is worthy it's name that anyone should be forced by the law to become an informer.

- ... and the Swedish courts now effectively are about to be transformed into a political power instrument not having been experienced since the days of Adolf Hitler. This is what is called democracy in Sweden, the host commented ironically.

- ... and then all of a sudden we now have a problem with our foreign policy as well, something which we have never experienced before. As long as Tage Erlander was our State Minister, the world could rely on Sweden being a neutral country although, to be fair, we were always more leaning towards the west than towards the east, but at least we were the incarnation of a stable country, the world knew what we stood for, implying a stable relationship when it came to do business with our partners. Now our present State Minister – Palme - has decided to change the rules in that he seems to have found new "comrades" telling him to tell the old "comrades" more or less to go to hell, solely based on his personal flavour. All of a sudden Sweden now has been put under the same umbrella as countries like East Germany and Cuba, by the way a country which Palme admired and during his visit there publicly supported and praised, something which – incidentally - also goes for countries like Vietnam and Mozambique.

In his eyes USA all of a sudden has become the country of oppression and fascism. Has he completely lost his mind? He is virtually destroying all our business relations in USA in one go, something that has taken us years to build up. How is Sweden going to survive when there are no partners left to trade with, a country dependant to 90% on exports? The autonomy of the Kingdom of Sweden is at stake.

The Contract (The Mission)

I can recall in an interview Dagens Nyheter had with the former rightwing leader Gösta Bohman some time ago, Bohman there accusing Palme for being mentally instable and calling his infamous handling of the truth a "real national security risk".

- Agree, and even the fascists in the Soviet Union are now looked at very favourably by our government, no sign of criticism anymore and East Germany is only seen in a very positive and favourable context from reading the outcome of the meeting Palme and Honecker had in Stralsund when he was visiting Honecker. I get the creeps from having to register the way the government is handling our foreign policy.

- And even a liberal newspaper like Dagens Nyheter has begun shifting their political views. You only have to read the incredible crap Olof Lagerkranz wrote down after having returned from his travels where he had studied China, Vietnam and the Soviet Union. Dagens Nyheter being a liberal newspaper – my ass! It is embarrassing having to read about the way he compares China and the Soviet Union with USA, putting the future of the world in the hands of those fascists, condemning those who effectively had built it up to be what we now are enjoying.

- Perhaps it is true what always has been rumoured, and that is that Palme is an informer for the Soviet Union, having been hired by the Soviets in the 50s, during the Wennerström era, the guest commented. Please bear in mind that Palme also did his conscription at the same place as the place Wennerström worked. Supposedly there is or was a second person working together with Wennerström, someone who did not get caught when Wennerström was caught and whose name never was revealed. I don't know, but I find Palme's behaviour utmost confusing and one sided in direction of the Soviets.

- And look what has happened with Vietnam and what they are doing with people either having sympathised with the

The Contract (The Mission)

previous regime or having a view different from that of the present regime – the so called "boat people" – a very democratic behaviour of the present Vietnam regime indeed. Is this what Palme and his "comrades" are aiming at for Sweden? I don't think so, but if they don't agree with the outcome of the Vietnam "liberation war" why don't they say anything? All of a sudden Palme has become very silent and non-committal when it comes to comment on what presently is taking place in Vietnam and the South East Asia – either because his views has shown to be embarrassing or because he agrees with what is happening over there, I don't know. Why isn't he making the world aware of what is happening to the people over there now as he so vehemently was doing during the Vietnam war? Another very strange behaviour indeed, don't you agree, now when Vietnam hasn't turned out to be what the world had envisaged. However I personally never believed in any democratic movement to take place in Vietnam after the end of the war anyway. And why wasn't he condemning Pol Pot's massacres in Cambodia that killed more than two millions people - some reports estimate it being up to 4 millions - of the country's seven million people?

- I personally can smell a rat here; we here are registering something, which is not quite kosher. They, I mean Palme and his "comrades" are up to something and if no decisive action is taken soon, you and me and the whole Swedish establishment will cease to exist in the long run. Remember the way the establishment were wiped out in Soviet Union or better said Russia and Eastern Europe, with the takeover of the communists? Not to talk about what will happen to everything that the establishment possesses. It is bad as it now is with the tax burden being imposed on us. Also look at what has taken place with the assessed value of properties, which is the basis for the property tax – increased manifold. In the meantime one skilled person and profitable company after another is leaving Sweden due to what we now are experiencing. To a certain extent you can

The Contract (The Mission)

register the same pattern or let's call it exodus as was the case with East Germany until the wall was built between East and West Germany, then prohibiting more people from leaving East Germany; even the socialism needs skilled people.

- I must agree with you when you are mentioning East Germany or DDR – Deutsche Demokratische Republik - as it officially is called. Sweden has already become a DDR in mini format, where one branch after the other of our society is put under state supervision, either being socialised or being state controlled. In essence the freedom for companies to decide what to produce and what to undertake with their assets has more or less become extinct.

- It cannot go on like this much longer, something has to be done and done fast, before Sweden totally goes down the drain, with incalculable implications for all of us and I am here speaking for the so-called "working class" as well. If there is nothing left to share, even they will suffer heavily, most likely heavier than the "upper class". Pity they do not realise what implications they will be facing from the way Palme momentarily is running Sweden. The "working class" is about to cut off the branch they are sitting on. It cannot be that we have to write off the Krona by 16 %, having an inflation of over 10 percent and at the same time the people must accept salary increases of only 2 percent. Effectively he is even betraying those people he is stating he stands up for. Compare that with West-Germany and it makes you wonder what he really is up to.

- I fully agree with you. Let us see if we can arrange some sort of meeting with other concerned an vital parties and discuss possible undertakings. In the meantime I will, through our "ears" within the government and the social-democratic party, see if there is any concerns there, and, if that is the case, see if any preparedness is due to have the present situation be changed for the best of Sweden – not

The Contract (The Mission)

for the party – short-term. I will also - very discrete of course - try to raise the subject with other people of importance in the political arena that I know. I also intend to ask some of my business partners who have expressed their concerns regarding the situation we are facing to attend the meeting as well. Of course this is a very delicate problem, and therefore has to be handled with corresponding seriousness and of course any inquiries must not under any circumstances be possible to have them be traced back to us.

- I will try to get in touch with people I trust within the military Defence Forces, the police and SÄPO to see how they assess our problem and ask them if they are interested in a joint meeting. However there should not be more than 10 people in all attending such a meeting, just to minimise any possible leaks. Let's finish the talk and start acting upon what we now have discussed and see if there is any room and necessities for further actions having to be taken before such a meeting.

They then parted with the intension to individually pursue the actions agreed and to meet again in a week's time. The one initially having organised the meeting felt a slight excitement over what they just had been discussing. He knew he was on dangerous ground here, in trying to interfere with the future direction of Sweden. On the other hand, he thought, I am old and have had my fun and there is not much they can do to me anyway. I might not be at the peak of my cunnings, but I still have far too much influence and power in most areas of the Swedish society than just to be ignored in case something was to happen to him personally. However then at least Palme would then have to explicitly explain what is going on and what he is standing for, the direction of his political ambitions and intentions and, at long last, what they were aiming at resulting in. I don't trust him more than a rattlesnake, ready for the final bite, regardless what he claims, he thought for himself. He is only after fulfilling and expediting his personal goals, not

The Contract (The Mission)

the slightest interested in what becomes of Sweden after his mandate has finished.

He then sat down in his library, trying to walk though what had been discussed and called the butler (who also acted as his chauffeur) for a late cup of tea, something which he always had every evening, before he went to bed. Today however, he found it difficult to stop thinking on possible implications of what they had discussed and almost started to play through different scenarios how the situation could be managed and mastered. He took the phone and dialled one of his most trustworthy friends within the social-democrat party at his home. He knew many within the party, which more or less shared the same basic views with him, but for political as well as private reasons, could not openly make their views public. Many of them had served during the Tage Erlander era and felt very uncomfortable with the present path the party now was taking.

- Hello Sten, it is me. Can you spare me a couple of minutes? I know I should not phone you at home but I would like to have a chat with you about a fairly urgent and crucial problem. I would prefer not to discuss it over the phone so would it be possible for us to meet sometime next week at my place? Of course we have to be cautious as our friendship would most certainly not be favourably viewed by certain members of our government. I suggest I let someone pick you up with a car - a rented car – and let him drive you here, just to avoid any personal consequences, should the subject be known. After our meeting this someone will then drive you back to a place of your choice.
- Let me see, I don't have any appointments or meetings on Friday, would Friday be all right with you?
- Suits me fine. I will then arrange to have you be picked up at your home at eight o'clock, if it suits you.
- Should be fine.
- Ok, then. See you on Friday, he said and hung up.

After he had hung up, he wondered if he was doing the right

The Contract (The Mission)

thing, but eventually came to the decision that he had to do it for the future of Sweden, not for personal gains. If the present situation were to persist, he thought, the foundation for a prosperous Sweden would disappear and it would need decades to have it be rebuilt and he felt he had to do something. As he preferred to wake up early, he finished his tea and headed for the bed.

The next day he also made some additional phone calls to crucial business partners. They also expressed their concerns regarding the present political situation in Sweden – which seemed to have gone haywire - as well as the ever increasing strained business climate in which they had to work within and adhere to and he agreed with them to have a meeting be arranged in a not too far away future in order to have a more in-depth discussion regarding the situation they were facing.

The Contract (The Mission)

Stockholm, December 4th, 1985

Three days later he became a phone call from his friend.

- Hi, it's me. I had an informal chat with some trustworthy people within the military forces, SÄPO - The Swedish Security Police - as well as people within the police and they told me that they were anything but pleased with the present political situation and probable implications. They stressed that something should be or even must be done to solve the imminent problem soon as possible as it slowly was becoming not just a high but also a first priority task. Can I come over to discuss the matter in the next couple of days with you?

- Of course, let's go for tomorrow – Thursday - at 08:00 pm. If you fancy, you can then have some supper with us. Would that suit your schedule?

- Sounds all right with me. I will then tell you somewhat more in depth what I have heard from the people I met with..

- The next day his friend came over and they had their supper, some home made bread, salad Nicoise, matured Västerbotten cheese and "Gravad Lax" together with a refreshing German beer from the north – Jever Pils – a beer that he imported, due to lack of decent beers at the "Systembolaget" - the Swedish state run liquor store company. After supper, they withdrew to the library for some coffee and to have a more in-depth discussion regarding their common problem.

The Contract (The Mission)

- As I said over the phone - his friend said - I have had some informal talks with trustworthy people within the Military Defence Forces, the police and SÄPO and it turned out that they all are aware of the problem and find it very alarming the way Sweden is run at the moment. They say - if we don't act fast, the moment where we can stop the madness will have passed as Sweden wtll then effectively already have been turned into a satellite of Soviet Union. Any attempts to do anything would be too late and might result in an immediate intervention by the Soviets as it happened in Hungary and Czechoslovakia.

- They also said that they had come to hear about a planned journey in spring, better said in April, where Palme is to meet with the new president and General Secretary of the Communist Party of the Soviet Union, Michael Gorbachev, in Moskva, which have made them wonder why a meeting all of a sudden has to take place so soon after Gorbachev has been elected.

- Many, especially within the military complex and SÄPO, feel that there has been too many visits to and praise for countries, predominantly speaking the "communist" language something, which they find not just somewhat curious but also suspicious. His never-ending anti-Western agitation worries them as well. For example, they say he is constantly condemning apartheid in South Africa, yet he never has criticised Mao's China, the most murderous regime having aroused worldwide after World War II. He is even equating the Israelis with the Nazis! I get the impression that the military complex completely seems to have lost confidence in Palme and his unpredictable actions. SÄPO even has come to regard him and also has registered him as a security risk, unofficially of course.

- From their perspective, his behaviour seems to point at two possible things; he either is a convinced communist or was - probably sometime in the 50s as many people have been suggesting - been hired by the Soviets as an informer and that they now, Palme being the prime minister of Sweden, are calling in the debt, now tightening the screws to force him to act as an "errand boy" for the communist movement as they otherwise would expose him and reveal his undertakings for the Soviets.

- They firmly believe that Palme got hired by the Soviets as he studied in the USA at the same time as Wennerström worked as military attaché at the Swedish embassy in Washington, which in retrospect I think was not just a coincidence. They supposedly met at a festive event at the Soviet embassy in Washington where Palme most certainly then got hired as a Russian spy. And what the hell did he do at the Soviet embassy if this wasn't the case? You cannot possibly attend any formal events at the Soviet Embassy without a formal invitation or having been recommended by someone and I don't think that you will get an invitation to come to the Soviet embassy for just being a nice guy and most definitely not from the Soviets, no way.

- They also say, with his behaviour and corresponding actions taken into account, his intention can only be to make Sweden a socialist state as well, his actions probably being dictated and demanded by the Soviets. SÄPO – the Swedish Security Police - also says that they have found out that the Soviets have very detailed and concrete plans indicating a possible invasion of Sweden, something that SÄPO finds more than alarming.

- The question is: how did the Soviets come to know all this vital information? From Palme? Palme supposedly also has issued a message to SÄPO, telling them to cancel any cooperation with CIA and instead start cooperating with KGB; They ask themselves if Palme completely has lost his mind, the way he acts. Therefore, they say, something has to be undertaken and undertaken fast, ideally before he meets with Gorbachev probably to reveal and hand over even more classified information with the sole purpose to integrate Sweden in the communist sphere.

The Contract (The Mission)

- Sounds like we all seem to share the same view when it comes to judge Mr Palme. BTW, I have also made some informal phone calls to some influential and very competent business partners, which I think highly of and they also stress that the problem has to be solved and solved fast, one way or the other as there otherwise will not be much left of what can be regarded as a profitable business in Sweden anymore.

- In the meantime many companies are seriously thinking of moving their headquarters and production facilities abroad as they are expecting devastating political decisions or shall I say decrees – in the near future, which will cripple their possibilities to do business in a normal and orderly manner even more than what is the case today. Things are bad as they already are, they say, and further escalations in terms of new laws imposing further business restrictions, higher taxation or new mandatory employee contribution crap can and will not be tolerated. This will inevitably lead to an avalanche of companies closing down their operation in Sweden or at least moving their headquarters to another country. Or to put it bluntly: if we have to face what we just have discussed, Sweden is fucked. This would erode the Swedish economy even further in that any corporate taxation claims are suddenly void as there is nothing to tax anymore.

- It is depressing having to register that it had to go this far. It really surprises and scares me that the government is not capable of realising the implications of what they are imposing before it is too late – you only need common sense to see the consequences of your actions. However, we are here dealing with politicians and they quite often don't seem to function like ordinary human beings. And once you have lost the confidence in the government, there is no turning back. People as well as companies then will take decisions to "save themselves" so to say. And once they have left Sweden, they are gone for good. It is like a marriage, where your partner has been unfaithful too many

The Contract (The Mission)

times – in the end you give up and file for a divorce, because you do not trust your partner's promises anymore. And we are here not trying to find ways how to avoid having to pay our part in supporting the Swedish welfare state. No, it is more a question of avoiding being robbed.

- My contacts within the military complex, the police as well as SÄPO they all have agreed to attend such a meeting to discuss and try to find a solution to this problem. However it can only be done with utmost secrecy, as no one would like to face a situation where you are being accused for treason.

- Of course we have to be careful and discrete, the host continued. We only have to find a suitable place where we can have this meeting. If we agree to have one person from the military, one from the police, two from SÄPO, two from the industry, one from the government and us two, it will make nine people all in all and this number I believe should be sufficient in order for us to be in the position to come up with something useful to work with.

- I would suggest that we meet at my summerhouse at Älgö in the Stockholm archipelago. It is very easy to reach the property by car. Let us also try to have the meeting as early as possible, so that people can return home on the same day. Of course there are provisions for a sleepover if those not coming from Stockholm would prefer not to return home the very same day.

- Let us also agree, he continued, to meet up at the Saltsjöbaden train station, and I will make arrangements to have the parties be picked up from there, just to avoid someone becoming curious why there are so many cars lined up at the property.

- Let me first have the meeting with our Social Democrat friend coming Friday, he finally said, and the meeting scheduled either for the Sunday that follows or for the following Sunday. Ask your connections what is feasible for

The Contract (The Mission)

them.

They then had some small-talk in general about other things and the friend left around 11 pm, waiting for the outcome of the meeting with the government representative, to be held the following day.

The Contract (The Mission)

Stockholm, December 5th, 1985

The following day his social democratic friend was picked up by a rented Volvo from his home at Tyresö in the South of Stockholm at 08 pm. Unfortunately they had to drive through Stockholm in order to come to Djursholm in the north, a more than 50 km long journey taking over an hour to finish. He finally arrived at the destination around 9 pm. Upon the guest entering the house, the host said ..

- Hello Sten, nice of you to have been able to come with such a short notice. I would very much like to discuss a couple of things with you and hear your opinion on what I have to say. Lets go to the library and I will explain to you what I have on my mind.

- In the library the guest was offered a good whisky, which he thankfully accepted before the host started to explain what he had on his mind. After having sat down in a comfortable Chesterfield armchair, he then started by saying ..

- As you might realise the Swedish industry is very concerned with the direction Sweden is heading at the moment, both in terms of what is happening domestically as well as regarding our foreign policy.

- Fortunately you are not the only one having second thoughts in the areas you did mention, the guest interrupted. And that goes for many Social Democrats as well, especially those having served under Tage Erlander, the former Prime Minister. With Erlander we had a domestic and foreign policy, which was predictable and in

The Contract (The Mission)

sync with other vital areas of the Swedish society. Also our foreign policy was in sync with what happened in the rest of the world. With Palme something else is taking place. He tries to impose his views of what he believes is important on Sweden without bothering to synchronise with other vital areas in Sweden. And this goes for our foreign policy as well. His beliefs are seen as the beliefs of Sweden although they often aren't, as he is not consulting anyone regarding what he might be up to and what politically is feasible. And this approach worries a lot of older members within the social democratic party. Momentarily he is relying on the younger 68-generation having pure socialism as their primary goal regardless what it may cost. The democratic way of resolving a conflict is not something, which actually appeals to them. Or even Palme for that matter, I must say. They all live in a black and white world. If you are not with them you are against them. Bear in mind that throughout the history many takeovers have taken place with only a minority of people having agreed with the views of the "takeovers". This, for example was the case with the Russian October Revolution and the takeover in Russia by the Bolsheviks. The Mensheviks had some months earlier won a "democratic" election led by Alexander Kerensky - a Russian lawyer and revolutionist. However it did not suit the communists and they started an all-out civil war aiming at overthrowing the Czar – therefore the October Revolution came about.

- Coming to talk about Palme, he still seems, the guest continued, to have the support of his ministers, although there are signs of rising tensions as he is interfering in and tries to decide almost everything by himself, I mean without consulting anyone - especially when it comes to laying out and deciding our foreign policy and domestic labour matters, for example pushing for "Löntagarfonderna".

- So far no conflict has erupted, but it will happen unless viable ways can be found in either getting rid of Palme or make him take another approach.

- However I see a problem there, he continued, in making him take another approach as no-one through the years, being so fanatic as he is, has come to change his mind. In essence he is power-obsessed, in that he is not approachable for anything not reflecting his own narrow way of thinking. He is arguing for the sake of arguing, not to reach a consensus regarding a certain subject. No, that has never been and will never be his approach when it comes to finding ways of reaching his goals. He cannot distinguish between agitating and discussing, neither could and can people like Lenin, Hitler, Mussolini, Fidel and Mao. As very skilled and consequent agitators being superior in their way of agitating they inevitably see the agitation as the only way to reach their goals. The masses get exhausted by just listening to all their agitation, effectively not understanding much of the "propaganda" being broadcasted anyway and eventually they give in for the agitator's arguments. This way of acting and thinking must not under any circumstances be adapted to a democratic society. Such people are a danger to the society itself in that those people do not bother adapting to any democratic rules having been agreed and laid out over decades anymore.

- However, you might argue that the very thing that gives a democracy its greatest strength, might also become its biggest weakness: the people. An often cited fear is that if the people are ignorant of certain issues, or just generally not well educated (and informed), they may make errors when casting votes. If they do not fully understand the implications of their votes, it could allow for a person being ruthless or having no conscience from our standards to gain power, and thus, begin to reverse some of the inherent freedoms in a democracy. Democracy is also remarkably inefficient and slow and taking that in a broader perspective actually a danger to itself as a working vehicle for establishing a keeping the democracy democratic. And this is what I momentarily feel is happening with Sweden and its democratic system.

- This is most certainly also the main reason for the severe discrepancies between Olof Palme and SÄPO, he finished. From what I have heard he presumably demands SÄPO having to know everything about the work they are undertaking. He is interfering in their daily work they say, an attitude more based on his political pathos than on rational thinking and this severely cripples SÄPO in their work. The question inevitably pops up: Why does he want to know everything? Sorry to say, but to me there seems to be an urgency for having to collect information expected or requested to be delivered, needless to say to whom. You might not share my view, but you must at least admit it sounds strange.

- I know what you think, but although it sounds strange at first sight, I cannot possibly believe that a prime minister will use his power to get at and consequently deliver secret and vital information to another country. However, regardless of what you might think, the situation is serious enough for the necessity to take some decisive actions aiming at resolving the matter. I am a convinced social democrat, but most definitely not a revolutionary person. and not someone believing in the socialism by force and its dogma, and I am most definitely not prepared to let Palme, just for personal reasons and gains, destroy what we have managed to achieve in Sweden over the decades.

- I am not a social democrat, the host said and smiled, but at least the path our former Prime Minister Tage Erlander was heading was predictable, honest and in the name of Sweden and not steered by any selfish private goals and unpredictable decisions. It was something, which even I could live with. And the "fights" we had were at least always fair.

- In confidence I also have to say that one of the primary

The Contract (The Mission)

reasons for wanting to have this meeting with you is that I have also received an internal and very alarming paper from Klas Eklund, the Chief Economist at the SE Bank and, as you probably know, also working for and with the Social Democratic government. He is stating that nervous discussions are momentarily being held behind "locked" doors by the core team within the government how to go about with these clusterfucks of problems in general and consequently the government is facing an ever increasing problem with Olof Palme and what to undertake with Olof Palme. Should they try to convince him simply to resign or to resign for health reasons? And if what Klas Eklund is writing is true it is bloody well about time that something is being done asap.

- It is unfortunately true, Sten answered reluctantly. The government is facing an ever increasing problem with Olof Palme. He is more and more acting on his own, however I expect this information stays between us and also that the information you have come in possession of does not become publicly known as you you probably know it would have disastrous consequences.

They discussed further for an hour, but in essence agreed that something had to be undertaken in order to secure the democracy and social welfare and prosperity of Sweden for future generations.

As the Social Democrat was about to leave, he said:

- I will try to find out, very discreet of course, to what extent the dissatisfaction or more precisely the disagreement with Palme's policy has emerged within the government. However, we must at any price avoid that any alarm bells start to chime.

- I fully agree with you, and believe me here we are not talking about personal gains. No, this is only a question of saving Sweden as we all know and love it. The democracy cannot and must not be used as an excuse to rape a

The Contract (The Mission)

country. Even Adolf Hitler was elected in a democratically held election, then misusing the democracy politically or better said, using the weaknesses of the democracy to achieve his own personal and fanatic goals. And I sincerely hope we are not about to fall in the same trap or should I say – fall for the same trick as The Weimar Republic did in 1933 in Germany.

- Don't worry, I understand. Let me hear from you.

- By the way, I have proposed the other participants to have our meeting next Sunday at my summerhouse at Älgö in the Stockholm archipelago. I hope it will suit you as well.

- Hang on for a sec, Sten said, and took out his calendar. It should be fine. I don't have anything going on that weekend which cannot be postponed.

About 11 pm, the guest was driven home, both having reached the consense that a meeting was to take place in the very near future, together with representatives of other areas crucial to the culture of the Sweden's society.

The following day he phoned up two of his most trustworthy business partners and told them briefly about the outcome of the chats he and his friend had had with the other people involved and agreed that Sunday in a week's time would more suit both of them.

He then phoned his friend up and told him about the outcome of the chat with his Social Democrat friend as well as what his business colleagues have said. His friend said that he had had chats with his connections within the Military Complex, the Police and SÄPO – the last two units being represented by one man - Hans Holmér – the former head of SÄPO and at present having a position as District Police Commissioner being the primary representative of the police forces in Stockholm county and that they have agreed to have a meeting the following Sunday.

The Contract (The Mission)

Some 200 km from Stockholm, one of his business partners had a somewhat frustrating chat with his wife over that he was forced to attend the meeting the following Sunday.

As they already had agreed to go for Christmas shopping on that weekend, she was - as every woman - far from being amused having to change plans. As he could not tell his wife the real purpose of the meeting, he had to come up with an excuse.

- I have to go, he said. The meeting is of utmost importance in order to find a common solution and approach regarding "Löntagarfonderna". We cannot and must not let the government introduce them as it would be the end of Sweden. Can you imagine the Swedish industry having to adhere to what LO - the Swedish labour union - dictates, having to be run by a bunch of useless people not having done a decent piece of work in all their lives. They have spent and devoted their whole life just trying to avoid having to work and instead let the legislation see to that they get the money they need. They are only running from one intrigue meeting to the next, just looking for ways in pulling the legs of the Swedish industry. And I am one of those "victims". If "Löntagarfonderna". gets introduced, there will be an avalanche of businesses going abroad, only worsening an already serious economic situation in Sweden, in that there will not be anything to tax anymore. This would most certainly lead to a catastrophy for all people of Sweden.

- I know it is important what you are saying, but what about all the shopping we had planned. When are we going to do all our Christmas shopping?

- Tell you what, he said. Let us take the car to Stockholm early on Saturday and spend the weekend in Stockholm. Then we can go shopping together on Saturday and you can then go shopping on your own on Sunday. In the evening, we then can have a nice dinner together in a posh restaurant. I will arrange for a room for 2 days at Radison. From there it is a piece of cake to reach the Stockholm

The Contract (The Mission)

Shopping Centre. Either – if the weather permits - take a nice walk through "GAMLA STAN" or take the tube from SLUSSEN to T-CENTRALEN – only two stops.

* That would be lovely, his wife said, raised from the couch and gave him a swift kiss and a hug. There are much more opportunities to go shopping in Stockholm than here.

He smiled for himself, thinking that all women are so easy to read. Just give them the opportunity to spend some money and the rest is of no importance to them at all. They are then not even interested if you are telling the truth or not or where you are heading. He just had to be careful what he was saying in case she would start to ask what persons were to attend the meeting.

The Contract (The Mission)

Stockholm, December 8th, 1985

The days went by and the preparations for the meeting were in full force. Come Sunday and they met at Saltsjöbaden train station at around 11:00am, as had been agreed. Food and assorted drinks for a brunch when they all arrived had been prepared and brought to the summerhouse; Gravad Lax, Shrimps, Janson's Frestelse (Jansons Temptation) – a Swedish speciality, Salad Nicoise, Caesar's Salad, rare roast beef and home made bread. Everything prepared and delivered by a local deli shop not far away.

After the brunch they went for a coffee in the dining room, where they also started to discuss the purpose for showing up at the meeting.

The host for the meeting stood up from his coffee and started introducing the meeting to the participants.

- Hello, I very much appreciate that you have been able to make time for this meeting with such a short notice, especially those of you who are not from Stockholm.
- For those of you not knowing each other, he continued, I would recommend that you briefly introduce yourself and the purpose of your presence here - that is what you are doing - to the others.

Following the introduction from the host, the participants then introduced themselves to the other participants. There were representatives from the industry, the banks, the military, the police, the security police – SÄPO, and the

The Contract (The Mission)

politics (i.e. the government), more or less covering all areas of the Swedish society, apart from the unions, which in essence were regarded as "enemy territory", their behaviour and attitude after all being the very reason for the meeting.

- As you all are aware of we are here today trying to find a way to solve a delicate problem, that is how to solve the problem we are facing with our prime minister Olof Palme.

- Palme is increasingly not only becoming a domestic problem as he is also becoming a problem for our foreign policy in that he vehemently is interfering in any foreign matters, which he finds being important enough – or better said interests him – as a vehicle for improving his own personal ego - regardless what the subject may be, thereby more acting as a foreign minister than our prime minister, virtually making our foreign minister superfluous, which has the consequence that our foreign minister more or less has been degraded to the level of an errand boy.

- Also "Löntagarfonderna" is ultimately something, which will bring the Swedish industry to a grinding halt if we cannot find a way to get rid of them.

The host continued to explain what previously had been said and discussed between different parties before the meeting officially had begun, this in order to bring all participants up-to-date with the subject they were about to discuss.

After his recap of what had been said and discussed, each participant had the opportunity to explain his view to the problem.

One participant representing SÄPO was telling the others about Palme's obsession having to know practically everything, making their work very difficult to accomplish. He also told them about Palme's directives to stop SÄPO from having any further communication with CIA instead having to build up a corresponding relationship with KGB, something that he found utmost alarming. The question immediately arises, why? Are we here facing a socialist obsession or a blackmail situation from the Soviet Union?

Also the fact that Palme had or had had regular meetings with the KGB-agent Nikolaj Nejland only made his situation even worse.

The military representative commented that the issue they had had with Russian submarines at Karlskrona and Palme's lack of reaction regarding the incident also had raised the same questions regarding what Palme actually stands for politically.

One of the people representing the industry stressed that it had, as a result of "Medbestämmandelagen" coupled with "Löntagar- fonderna", gotten increasingly more difficult to do business, having to inform and agree with the union representatives all the time about what you are up to. Attempts to keep any business deals "hidden" from the public or from publicity, often as a wish from the customer site, has more or less become impossible. As a result of "Löntagarfonderna", the union has become cocky, probably already regarding the companies as theirs.

The government representative then commented on what he had found out by discussing the matter with trustworthy colleagues within the government. He said that although there seems to be a rising distrust, dissatisfaction and discussions over Palme's actions and how to act correspondingly, the probability that he will fall as a result of a vote of no confidence was very unlikely. Also to convince him to free up his position for someone else was at the moment extremely unlikely – he likes the power of his position too much. Also attempts to make him take a less provocative attitude when it came to foreign matters as well as towards the Swedish industry, thereby avoiding to jeopardise the Swedish industry and its exports seemed not to have had any real success.

- I believe many social democrats are afraid of their own

The Contract (The Mission)

courage, the government representative continued.

- What I wanted to say with these words is that I cannot see anything happen within the government in regard to getting rid of Palme in the foreseeable future. However this does not mean that unofficial support will not be provided, whenever and where ever possible, should any actions be instigated regarding Palme and what he may be undertaking outside the government. I cannot say what sort of support you can expect; just presume it. depends on what actions are due to be taken. Many people within the government are beginning to be afraid for the consequences from what Palme has started, including myself. From what I have come to hear, Ingvar Carlsson, Anna-Greta Leijon and Kjell-Olof Feldt are very unhappy the way Palme is carrying out his duties.

First all of the participants became silent from what they just have heard, but then they gave in and gave him a round applause for his speech.

Afterwards they discussed what has come about, without actually finding a solution to their problem. Different options were discussed, for example denounce him, but nothing was seen as something, which would lead to solving the problem fast.

One of the SÄPO guys – Hans Holmér - had an informal chat with the military guy Hans von Holbein - in a corner somewhat distant from the others, discussing the situation they were facing.

- I don't know how to have this problem be solved in the near future, without having to take drastic measures, the SÄPO guy – Holmér – said.
- What do you envisage with having to take drastic measures?
- As you cannot hurt or denounce him politically in order to have him be removed from his position, other, more

The Contract (The Mission)

decisive measures are the only ones left, viable as options; I mean means to get rid of him.

- How getting rid of him? Do you mean, well you know what I mean, without explicitly saying the word.
- Well, do you see another practical solution?
- But we live in a democracy, and the country is not run by a dictator, von Holbein replied.
- Are we not? Why are we then discussing the matter at all? Isn't it what it is all about, that he is governing Sweden as a dictator and not as an elected representative, in essence only concerned and obsessed with his own political goals and views, serving his own ego, regardless what the outcome may be for the country. The question automatically arises - is there anything more to it than just what he is stating in public? I believe there is. Unfortunately we don't have the time to prove there is. Therefore I believe we have to act. There are more than one country in the world where it is or was the only solution in order to "save" the country. We live in a democracy and we very much would like to have Sweden stay that way, the way we were used to call democracy before Palme came about and suddenly changed the rules.
- Are you aware of that Olof Palme has been classified as a security risk in Washington? The U.S. intelligence agencies DIA and CIA, in collaboration with senior British and U.S. NATO officers, is now working hard to weaken the Palme government. Palme was to be discredited and in the meantime neutral Sweden has been defined by the western defence alliance as an unsafe candidate and risk factor and that's what you get for being "neutral". I can imagine they might even be positive towards helping us in financing something leading to that Palme "disappears" from the political scene so to say. Palme is someone who long-term is devastating for Sweden as a sovereign country and therefore we may be forced having to take drastic

The Contract (The Mission)

measures.

- You are right but, I don't know. Such a drastic measure..
- What did you think then when we agreed to meet here. Was or is this that we are discussing just a theoretical game for you?
- No, but I assumed there were other options at hand
- Then please tell me which they are. Perhaps I can learn something here. From Sten we have come to hear that we cannot expect him to change his mind. At the present stage it is also very unlikely that he would loose a vote of no confidence within the government, as they do not seem to go for that option internally as a viable solution. And a vote of no confidence in the parliament raised by the conservative and liberal parties, will most certainly fail as a majority for such a solution is not at hand as the greens and the leftwing party will stick to Palme regardless of what he does and says. And to prove that he might be a traitor takes ages and a successful outcome is by far not guaranteed. Bear in mind that he also as prime minister has diplomatic immunity – he virtually is untouchable from outside the parliament. Only the social democrats can do something in that area and they are momentarily not prepared to take necessary actions, Holmér said.
- But how do you envisage us to accomplish such a task. You cannot just walk up to him with a gun and - Bang! He's got lifeguards and he is protected around the clock. Also any attempts which can be traced back to us would be even more disastrous for Sweden, von Holbein said.
- I know, but this is a different story, which has to be told in due course, Holmér replied.

  First action on the agenda must be to evaluate whether this is a price, which has to be paid to save Sweden from a political and economical disaster, and if we are prepared to instigate such a step.

The Contract (The Mission)

Second action then is the planning how to go about in exercising and carrying out the task. And the planning is not from us to be carried out. We will only more or less act as errand boys. The planning and later the execution of the task is something for a professional "assassination squad" to carry out, which still would have to be found, although I imagine it shouldn't be that difficult if the payment is high enough. There are enough "mercenaries" fighting in Africa either for some dubious guerrilla organisation, which are calling themselves "freedom" fighters, or working for some government, fighting some dubious guerrilla organisation. Now when Zimbabwe and Mozambique are likely to be lost to the guerrillas and South Africa is fighting the communists in Angola, trying to prevent them from progressing south, I believe there are enough Ex-military personnel available, I mean free to accept offers, and fighting as mercenaries in those areas. You might even find them in England, fighting the IRA in the name of the British Army in Northern Ireland but in essence they are working as freelancers. Unofficially of course, but even the British Army needs skilled and ruthless personnel to fight IRA the same way as IRA is fighting the British. You can also find a number of them defending and protecting diamond mines in Zaire for example. Africa is their gold mine, Holmér continued.

- And you mean they are capable of carrying out such a task. I mean do they have the corresponding experience?
- Oh, yes. Many of them are probably more experienced than any person you are likely to find in Sweden or all of Europe for that matter. Most of them are primarily trained to successfully carry out assassination and guerrilla tasks without being caught. I mean government-trained for successfully carrying out hit-and-run assignments, Holmér replied.
- And how are we to get in touch with any of them, may I ask? And what will it cost us? And what and how are we going to tell the others? You don't believe that any of them

The Contract (The Mission)

will get along with such a solution you are proposing.
- I know there would be a problem, having them to agree to such a solution. Therefore the solution cannot be bluntly presented as a solution. This would never work out. And neither can the solution be presented as THE solution. The solution must be wrapped in a lot of other stuff if we want to make the our solution come true. What we need is money, and a lot. I presume at least a million dollars will be necessary and it has to be made available from the military-industrial complex as well as from the banking sector, I believe.

  ... Or, if necessary, even other resources like "still our great Atlantic friend in Washington" - Caspar Weinberger - and people at Langley having a sincere interest in getting rid of Palme as well, I could imagine to support such a task, Holmér thought for himself.

- Our task will be to see to that the connection with the "mercenaries" comes about. The police will have to make sure that necessary cover up and divert actions and scenarios are put in place, for example see to that the inevitable crime investigation following the assassination is directed in the wrong direction, for example picking up and arresting the wrong guys, in essence aiming at delaying things, I mean producing a smoke screen scenario aiming at satisfying the public. The government will have to build up an official investigation with the purpose of finding the "murderer", in essence having the same purpose as what the police is doing, to satisfy the curiosity and demands from the public sector, especially the journalists might be a problem sometimes. We must not be caught up in a battle with the press - this must be avoided at any price. If the press starts to smell a rat, the shit will inevitably hit the fan, that is we all might then as well unison jump from the highest bridge in Stockholm, believe this is Västerbron (The Western Bridge), he said and smiled.

- I can see that you have paid some thoughts how to go about in coming to grips with our problem, von Holbein commented.

- Of course I have, the minute I got the phone call from one of the initiators, I immediately began to write down some possible scenarios as I am not prepared to all of a sudden have to switch partnership in favour of Soviet Union, just dropping old acquaintances, just because some elected political maniac tells you to do so. And as a result of what we have discussed here today, I can only see one viable solution, namely the one you and I just have discussed. We will have to have a chat with the host for this meeting, asking him to arrange for one million dollars to be made available on a foreign account. In this case I would prefer Gibraltar as I presume the connections will take place via Britain. For whatever reason, the "mercenaries" all seem to prefer Britain, as base for their work, which often includes Gibraltar as their money haven, with corresponding connections also having been build up there. Most probably has to do with the English language. Gibraltar is also close to Africa, Holmér explained.

- I understand. But let's further discuss the matter at a more appropriate time. I think we should join the others to hear their views on the problem. They might, without us being aware of it, share our views.

The discussion went on for another 2 hours, Holmér deliberately trying to steer the problem and its solution in the direction he previously had discussed with the military guy, von Holbein. He did not explicitly stress or mentioned the solution he favoured, but made the others aware of the difficulties in expecting to achieve anything viable by discussing the other options he had mentioned when discussing the matter with von Holbein. No one seemed to notice any connections between what they were discussing and what he was striving at. By taking the problem from that angle would make them eventually realise what options were due, which would make it easier to go ahead, mentally preparing all of them for the only viable solution

The Contract (The Mission)

without actually having proposed it, a sometimes used tactic in politics if you were after achieving something, without having to end up in endless and fruitless discussions over a particular solution. Afterwards your solution, in essence, has been their solution to the problem as well, without them really openly having realised it.

It was agreed that further information was to take place over the phone (or facsimile) or that further unscheduled meetings only were to take place over specific issues and that the host and Holmér were to coordinate, act on and plan for any further actions having to take place.

The guests left between 6 pm and 7 pm, in two groups, not to cause too much stir in case someone was to recognise one or some of them. Holmér stayed somewhat longer than the rest, wanting to discuss some "general" issues with the host more in private.

When all but the host and Holmér had left, they sat down over a cup of coffee in the dining room and Holmér then asked the host.

- What's your opinion of the meeting. How do you think it went?
- Apart from having reached a common understanding that there is a problem and realising that what we were not able to reach was a common solution and how to go about to solve it, we did not achieve a lot. I would have hoped for more decisive actions to have taken place, the host replied
- What action? What we actually did achieve is a lot. We have managed to scrap all solutions we discussed as non-viable solutions, regrettably not actually specifying a viable one, but in essence we are left to decide this one solution, or to be more specific, I believe to have a viable solution, however it will cost us a lot, however money is something which has to be your responsibility to organise, I believe, Holmér replied – to put it bluntly, at least one million dollars I reckon.

Anyway, I personally will see to that a viable solution is put

The Contract (The Mission)

in place. However I urge you not to force me to reveal what solution I am envisioning, in order to keep those involved at a minimum in order to avoid possible leaks. Just get the money organised and the rest will be sorted out through me. Please be advised that an "administration fee", amounting at 10% of the transfer sum, to be transferred for administrating any unforeseeable payments, has to be made available as well.

The host looked somewhat bothered, but did not say anything. He was suspecting what solution Holmér might have in mind, but refrained from asking him about the solution in order not to end up in a discussion over a solution, which he could not commit to anyway. Instead he just nodded a silent "yes" with his head telling Holmér that he agreed with the task split and would do what Holmér had suggested. He agreed with Holmér to arrange for the necessary amount to be made available through himself, his long-time friend and the two having represented the industry at the meeting.

Holmér left half an hour later, both having agreed to keep in contact on an as needed basis.

Holmér was to give give the host a number account in Gibraltar to where the money should be transferred and the money was to be transferred though different accounts in and via different countries, each separate transfer not exceeding $100,000. It was also crucial to have the banks transferring the actual money to the Gibraltar account all coming from countries not having any bank information agreement with Sweden. The money would be administrated by an accountant based in Gibraltar. After the money transfer had taken place no one in Sweden would have any knowledge of the account and consequently not any knowledge regarding the purpose of the account as well as any forthcoming payments, which might be due; it would all be handled by the accountant.

The host had a somewhat uneasy feeling regarding what he had instigated but tried to tell himself that it was the only

The Contract (The Mission)

possible solution to avoid jeopardising the future of Sweden where everything eventually would end in a financial and cultural disaster. Sweden, as an independent nation with a longstanding cultural history had never been closer to loose its unique identity and status as a sovereign country than now.

Hasn't Sweden born enough unique personalities like, Linné, Nobel and Celsius just to name a few and I am not prepared to trade in our uniqueness in favour of some spurious dogma, defined by foreigners, he thought for himself, becoming even more adapted towards solving the increasing threat they were facing as an independent nation.

Also, from what he had heard from what had been said during the meeting, it seems that the extreme right and the social democracy now share the same view regarding Palme's doings meaning both parties have a common interest in having the problem be solved ASAP, he thought. Therefore, an official investigation giving as a result plausible reasons and excuses for a possible assassination was probably welcomed from both sides and would therefore most probably not lead to any serious attempts in finding a possible assassin. Also serious attempts in trying to find the real reasons behind an assassination would most probably not come about, neither from the police nor from the politics.

Perhaps there were even discussions going on within the The Swedish Security Service - SÄPO - and the social democratic government being of the opinion that there was only one possible solution to the problem, although it was a very unsatisfying solution. However, any other alternative would prove to be far more serious for Sweden and the social democratic party, he further thought for himself.

What the host didn't know was that Holmér, having good connection with the Social Democrats, already had had some initial talks with a few officials about the rising problem they were facing with Palme, thereby also having reached some principal although presumptive agreements.

The Contract (The Mission)

After all guests had left, he then asked his butler to turn off the heating and close the house for the winter – it actually already had been closed, but the meeting had made him open up the summer house again. He then asked his butler to get the car – a BMW – 7 series - and they drove off for his house in Djursholm again, approximately an hour's drive.

The Contract (The Mission)

Stockholm, December 10th, 1985

Holmér was sitting alone in his office, trying to envisage how the so-called mercenaries were thinking when they were looking for new assignments. Most probably they were not people keen to advertise their profession too much as hiring mercenaries had become a very controversial issue in the recent past with the civil wars taking place not only in the African countries but also in Europe.

A feasible option how to find mercenaries might be to contact someone within the South-African Bureau of State Security – BOSS – where he had got some good connections from his time as head of SÄPO, despite Palme's never-ending criticism of the South-African apartheid regime. Regardless of what you may think of a certain regime – this is absolutely off limits to express your views in public if you work for the State Security, otherwise you would not be able to carry out any of your work at all.

Although BOSS now had been replaced by the National Intelligence Service (NIS) as a result of the Muldergate Scandal in 1980, in which government funds were used to buy a pro-government English newspaper, he still felt it might be useful in trying to get in contact with the former head of BOSS – Hendrik van den Bergh – to see if he might possess any useful knowledge regarding where to find useful "mercenary" leads.

Holmér phoned the head of NIS, Dr. Lukas Barnard, up from home and introduced himself as a former Head of the Swedish Security Police, saying he was an old friend of the former head of BOSS – van der Bergh – and would like to get in contact with

The Contract (The Mission)

him for old time sake. Barnard said that van der Bergh was no longer working and had taken up chicken farming instead (Holmér was silently smiling for himself), but then said that he would tell van der Bergh that Holmér had phoned and promised to give him Holmér's phone number. If he was prepared to talk to Holmér, he would surely phone him up, Mr Barnard continued, but more than passing on Holmér's phone number Mr Barnard was not prepared to do as he didn't know Holmér.

The Contract (The Mission)

Stockholm, December 14th, 1985

A few days later Holmér received a phone call from van der Bergh and after some general chat over "the good old days", Holmér asked him if he knew any organisation or government unit in South-Africa making use of "mercenaries" in order to accomplish their tasks.

Hendrik van den Bergh said he, following his resignation in 1980, was not up-to-date with what was going on within the South-African government anymore, but had heard that a new unit was in the making of being built up with the name CCB - Civil Cooperation Bureau, aimed to operate or was already operating under the authority of Defence Minister General Magnus Malan, whom he has come to hear took on an undefined number of "mercenaries" for fighting the communists at the border between Angola and Namibia He also knew that the organisation was very secret, hardly known as an operational unit even within the South-African Defence Forces - SADF - or South-African Police, neither outside nor inside South-Africa, which made it difficult to approach the organisation as some official unit within the South-African Defence Forces. The unit simply did not officially exist although unofficially it did already exist

Hendrik van den Bergh said he didn't know whom to approach within CCB or SADF regarding "mercenary" matters. However for someone possessing some military connections it might be possible to reach someone there having the corresponding knowledge.

Holmér thanked him for the information, which had been given to him, and wished Hendrik van den Bergh all the luck

The Contract (The Mission)

with his chicken farming and hung up.

He now had reached a point where he had to have some help from someone with military connections and decided trying to get in contact with von Holbein in getting to the right people within CCB in order to get at the right information.

Later the same evening he then phoned von Holbein up at his home, telling him that he had spoken to Hendrik van den Bergh and told him about the new CCB unit within the South-African Defence Forces and that he needed to talk to someone having sufficient knowledge where or how to find necessary information to enable them to contact some "mercenaries".

What he wanted was a list of skilled and professional mercenaries to be in the position to plan and carry out a most difficult task – he could not tell von Holbein what task he was envisaging – and also get away with it.

Von Holbein said, that he knew a person within the military complex, which might be able to help him and whom he had worked with in South-Africa in the past - **Carl-Fredrik Algernon**, however mostly unofficially, as Palme did not "favour" such connections at all. In essence, through Palme's ability to stick his finger in everything, the result was that he actually forbade people to pursue any contacts they might have with South-Africa. However, this fact did most of the time not prevent people from continuing pursuing the connections they had anyway – although unofficially - and therefore Algernon might be able to help Holmér getting at the necessary information Holmér was seeking.

Holmér said that due to the sensitivity level to do with the task to be accomplished, he very much would prefer to raise the question with people within the CCB himself, implying that he either wanted a name which he could contact or to have a person's phone number and phone him up to discuss the subject "in private".

Von Holbein said he would come back on the issue, if he could manage to come up with some task-relevant information.

The Contract (The Mission)

A couple of days later von Holbein phoned and told Holmér that **Algernon**, had given him a name and phone number of a colonel - Hannes Venter - working for the South-African Defence Forces, who was prepared to have a chat with Holmér and who might be able to help him with the information he was looking for.

The very next day he paid a phone call to Venter in South-Africa from home, explaining who he was and the purpose of his call - that he was looking for some utterly experienced "freelancers" for an exclusive assignment - and also mentioned that by giving him the desired information, Venter could also expect there would be some imminent advantages for South-Africa as a result of the information being given as well.

Venter did not say anything for a long time, as if he was considering what the advantages it might be, but then eventually said that he would consult with his superior how to go about with Holmér's request and would send him a facsimile if giving away the requested information was granted by his superior.

- I presume you have facsimile possibilities at hand, he said additionally.

Holmér said yes, as he had a combined telephone/facsimile device at home, both running on the same phone number, which he also told Venter. Holmér then thanked Venter for having taken the time to phone him and hung up.

The Contract (The Mission)

Stockholm, December 16ᵗʰ, 1985

A couple of days later a message arrived at Holmér's device, however the message neither did say from whom it was originated, nor was there a facsimile/sender number found with the message, something which was customary.

The message was only comprised of five Christian names followed by one word, specifying their major skills and the name of a newspaper and a word to look for, meaning how it might be possible to get in touch with them in case they were free to accept any new assignments.

Holmér took the facsimile off the device and studied it thoroughly. From what he could see there were at least three of them, who were of interest to him – one of them being a sniper specialist, another one skilled at planning and organising things and a third one a very good all-rounder. It also seemed to be possible to reach them through classified ads, which they regularly would put in Financial Times using the keyword "missionary". It was not very much to go for, but better than nothing, Holmér thought. The remaining two seemed to be more difficult to get in touch with and would therefore initially have to wait.

The next day, on his way home, Holmér went to Centralen, the main train station in Stockholm and bought the Financial Times. As it was a Tuesday, he could not find any classified advertisement resembling

the word "missionary". Consequently, he therefore threw the

The Contract (The Mission)

paper in the nearest bin and reminded himself to buy another copy of Financial Times the next day.

The next day proved to be more successful as there was one classified ad containing the word "missionary" saying **"missionary assignments welcomed - Answer under Chiffre....".**

Holmér felt his heartbeat rising when he saw the ad, realising that they now would have reached a point of no return if he was to reply to the ad he just had read. He then put the newspaper in his briefcase and went for tunnelbanan (the Stockholm tube) and took the train home.

At home he put together a reply to the ad, also requesting a reply via chiffre.

The reply he put together said

"Looking for 3 missionaries for assignment in a European country. Payment very good. Only skilled people. Reply with Christian name under Chiffre: ....".

He then facsimiled the reply to the chiffre specified in the ad to Financial Times and also requested them to set up a chiffre for him as well. He also asked the newspaper for payment information, requesting a reply with corresponding information to be wired to the same facsimile number. He also asked them if it was possible to have any replies be facsimiled to him, which they agreed to do.

The next day the payment for the setup was carried out through a secret Swiss account, he had had from the days as head of SÄPO - the Swedish Security Police - where covert operations and black payments often were paramount in order to get at the necessary information, although it was something which the politicians never got to know often stupid and naive as they were, mostly only interested in caring for their own ego, not really knowing or even interested in what resources were necessary to have at hand for actually running a country or there would not be any country left to govern long term, which - to them - probably didn't matter anyway – all idiots, Holmér thought.

The Contract (The Mission)

Durban, December 19th, 1985

The following week, a letter from Financial Times arrived to **Piet Van Cleef** in Durban, containing the reply from Holmér, which Holmér had sent off.

As the letter came from Financial Times, he assumed that the letter was a reply to his Classified Ad, which he put up once a week regarding his availability to take on an assignment, which also proved to be true. The letter contained an offer to execute his ability as a mercenary somewhere in Europe, which sort of surprised him. He then phoned Financial Times up, asking them to put in the other ad aimed for his friends Martin and Jose, for the following Tuesday, telling them that there might be a new assignment for all three.

He then put a reply together for Holmér saying that they were three people interested in the assignment also giving Holmér their Christian names and phoned Financial Times up a second time asking them to send his reply to the chiffre Holmér had specified, also requesting Holmér to have any replies for him be sent to the previous chiffre.

He then went for a beer and told his girlfriend that he just received a inquiry for an assignment in Europe. It didn't say where, but the only places he could think of were Northern Ireland or former Yugoslavia, where some unrest had emerged as a result of the death of the Yugoslavian dictator Tito, however he didn't know, he said.

His girlfriend, not too happy what he was doing anyway, got pretty upset maybe having to face that Piet might leave for

The Contract (The Mission)

Europe and not coming back for weeks, maybe even months. Piet replied that he still did not know what sort of assignment was up for grabs and that it might even be something not involving fighting but rather protecting or body-guarding someone or something. His girlfriend calmed down as she heard that fighting may not even be involved with the assignment. She even got somewhat exited when Piet told her that there might even be possibilities for her to visit him in Europe. After all Europe was a civilised part of the world, not like Africa and definitely not like Angola, he said and smiled.

Additionally, he already had catered for a "just-in-case" passport from a European country a couple of months ago as he thought there might be some work there due to mounting tensions in Yugoslavia and in Northern Ireland as travelling with a South-African passport in Europe might create unnecessary complications nowadays.

However, he eventually said they still had to find out what sort of assignment it was all about as he only had received an answer from someone as a result of his advertisement in Financial Times.

The Contract (The Mission)

Durban, December 22nd, 1985

December the 22nd was Holmér's last day at work before Christmas. As every year, he took time off between the 23rd of December and 6th of January the following year or thereabout as Sweden more or less came to a grinding halt during Christmas and New Year anyway. When he got home from work, Holmér had received a facsimile from Financial Times. The facsimile contained the Christian names of three people also saying that they were interested in Holmér's proposal.

Holmér then put together a reply and facsimiled it to Financial Times to the chiffre he knew, asking for a European address or a PO Box where additional information could be sent. Any subsequent correspondence from then on would primarily take place through an address, which still was to be revealed together with any additional information having to be sent in order for the mercenaries to be in the position to carry out what was to be accomplished.

The Contract (The Mission)

Durban, December 25th, 1985

On the 25th of December, Piet got a phone call from Jose, one of the three names found on the facsimile having been sent to Holmér on the 22nd interested in Holmér's proposal.

- Hi it's Jose, Merry Christmas. Saw you ad and phoned you as soon as I got your message. What's the "fuzz" all about?
- I've got a reply from my last Classified ad in Financial Times. From some guy who is looking for three guys for an assignment in Europe, with very good pay, he said. Incase we are interested he wants a reply with our Christian names. Somewhat strange, but I presume the guy has a list of people with names, which might be of interest to him - recommendations I presume. Can't think of any other reason why someone would like to have our Christian names otherwise.

Jose did not say anything for a couple of seconds, but then agreed it was the logical conclusion from the reply having been received.

- Would you then be interested in the assignment?, Piet asked
- Why not, could be just about everything. From guerrilla activities in Northern Ireland to protection duties for some politician on the Balkan – or mafia boss, he said and laughed. If you don't like it, you can always turn it down after you have heard what it is all about.
- That's the way I think as well, anyway I have replied to

The Contract (The Mission)

the ad on behalf of all of us saying that we all are interested. Let's wait and see what sort of offer the guy comes back with. I will come back to you on the subject as-soon-as-possible. Have you got a contact number where I can reach you? By the way, do you happen to know where I can find Martin?

As Jose was renting a furnished flat and a telephone connection often was provided with furnished flats in Lisbon, he only had to register the phone number in his name. Jose therefore gave him this phone number and said that, the 3rd guy - Martin, most probably was to be found somewhere in London but did not know where. Coming back from an assignment, he normally never stayed at the same place as the place he had been renting before the assignment. He also did not have a phone number from Martin where he could be reached.

Piet then said, that in case Jose got a phone call from Martin, he should tell him about the possible assignment and also tell him to pay Piet a phone call as soon as he could. As Jose was not much of an organiser, they also agreed to let Piet be the focal point for all correspondence with the client.

Piet then hung up and then tried to persuade his girlfriend come on other thoughts, at the same time eagerly waiting for a reply following his reply to the chiffre.

The Contract (The Mission)

Durban, December 28th, 1985

Three days later – **on the 28th of December** - Martin phoned Piet and said that he had seen Piet's ad and wondered what it was all about. Piet told him what he knew and asked Martin for a phone number where he could be reached, should there be an urgent need for communicating with the principal. Martin said he did not have a direct phone number, but what he normally did was using a "switchboard" - a small office run by a woman somewhere in London, who served many people or small companies as their secretary, simultaneously , and where people could phone and leave messages or having other minor tasks be expedited. Martin would then pick up any messages having arrived for him once a day and then call back. Piet found the solution being viable and also asked Martin if he would let Piet sort out any admin stuff which might arise and also be the focal point for organising and having correspondence with the client, something, which Martin happily could agree to as he was not much of a "desk" and admin man anyway.

The Contract (The Mission)

Durban, December 30th, 1985

On the 30th of December, Piet received Holmér's reply, read it and immediately phoned Martin's "switchboard" up, telling the woman in charge of the "switchboard" to give Martin the message to phone Piet up as soon as possible.

The Contract (The Mission)

London - January, the 2nd 1986

On **the 2nd of January** Martin phoned Piet up asking him what it was all about. Piet then asked Martin if he had a PO Box for acquiring the next batch of information. Martin said he did not have one as he had the "switchboard", but could set one up with short notice. Piet, preferring the PO Box option, asked Martin to set up one, however under another name, also saying that he would wait for a subsequent call from Martin giving him the PO Box information and hung up.

After he had hung up he asked himself what the fuck they were in for anyway and what sort of assignment they here were talking about as the initiator neither did want to reveal who he was nor did he want to reveal what sort of assignment they were talking about.

Seems to be something very special, which under any circumstances must not be revealed, he thought. Will be very interesting to read about what the assignment is all about.

The next day, Martin phoned Piet up and gave him the PO Box information. The following day Piet sent the information off to the chiffre he so far had been using for communicating with the client.

The Contract (The Mission)

London - January, the 5th 1986

On **the 5th of January** Holmér got Martin's facsimile with the requested PO Box information. He then put a letter together with the Gibraltar address (which in-fact also happened to be a PO Box) including a unique ID for the "project". The letter also comprised information what the assignment was all about. As follows:

Assignment	: Elimination
Where	: Europe
Payment	: $1,000,000 all inclusive (50% on acceptance)
When	: asap (End March at the latest)
Means	: Planning to be done by contractor.
Tools	: Is to be decided by contractor. Much is available on site.
Conditions	Once accepted, the contractor is on his own. Once accepted, communication through a pre-specified PO Box. Once accepted, no cancellation possible On acceptance, the target ID will be sent. On success, $500,000 immediately transferred Must not act under real name.
Generals	Acceptance is to be sent to the aforementioned

The Contract (The Mission)

PO Box and must not arrive later than January the 25th. Attach a phone number and time of day where further information and instructions can be given.
No reference to the assignment must be given in the reply.
Further information will only be revealed if the answer "missionary activities" is given to the question. And what is your occupation?".

He then put the letter in an envelope with the PO Box address he had been given. He then put the envelope in another letter and wrote the Gibraltar PO Box on the envelope. An additional letter to the accountant, specifying the unique ID, which was to be used, was also included. The letter to the "mercenaries" was then to be sent by the Gibraltar accountant. Holmér then took the letter and drove about 20 minutes and then threw it in a letterbox, just to be on the safe side.

London - January, the 10th 1986

On **the 10th of January**, the letter landed in the PO Box Martin had set up in London. He saw that the letter was from Gibraltar and opened it, read it and his face turned white and he said for himself - "fucking hell – A million dollars". It was just what he had been waiting for to be able to settle down in South Africa for good. Of course you had to do something for the money, but to eliminate someone and get away with it was not impossible, he thought, taken into account that they were three. Jeez, must be a pretty important guy to be worth a million bucks, he thought.

He then went into the post office and took a photocopy of the letter and put the original version in another envelope and wrote Piet's address in Durban on the envelope and put it in a letterbox again. He then went back to his furnished apartment took a bottle of beer from the fridge wondering what the next step would be.

The Contract (The Mission)

January, the 14th 1986

On **the 14th of January** the letter reached Piet in Durban, who read the letter and he consequently held his breath when he saw the sum – one million dollars. He then went out, took the car and drove to the nearest post office from where he then made a phone call to Jose in Lisbon.

- Hi, it is me. Listen, please don't use any names from now on when we are communicating with each other. We only address each one of us by using the first letter of our names, respectively. I have here the job spec for the three of us. The job is in Europe, is pretty urgent, but we are talking about a lot of money. To be more precise - one million dollars. Briefly, I believe it is about having to liquidate someone. I don't know whom they are talking about, and the reason for the liquidation, but I suspect we might be talking about a politician. Any planning how to go about in accomplishing the task is left with us. You don't have to decide right now, I know you have to think about whether you are prepared to do it or not. In-fact we all are. Should we accept the assignment, there is no turning back as they stress in the facsimile we have received and I believe them. Failure is not an option, neither is backing out. You cannot have a lot of people running around knowing what such an assignment is all about. The possibility anything might be leaking is too big, in-fact it sure will.
- Half of the sum will be made available up front. Momentarily I am not at home, but will contact you for your decision tomorrow again.

The Contract (The Mission)

- Een miljoen dollar, jis. Om verdeel te word tussen ons drie, neem ek aan, Jose replied in Afrikaans, quite excited.
- Yes, you are right, the million is to be split between the three of us.
- Have you spoken to M?
- Yes, I have. According to the last facsimile we have received from the client, it is to be between the three of us. It is all-inclusive, also meaning that we will be left on our own, how to go about in organising and accomplishing the task. Might get help in getting the necessary tools, they say.
- No, I have not spoken to M, but I am sure he will accept as he is constantly in need of money. However I will contact him as soon as possible. One thing, do you have any additional identification papers at hand?
- Yes, I am forced to have it otherwise I most probably couldn't enter Mozambique anymore as I am sure that the authorities there will keep records of my past. And that might render me some undesired problems, if they decide to carry out a check on me when entering the country with my original papers. Anyway I will think about what you've said. See you tomorrow then, Jose said and hung up.

Piet then called Martin's "switchboard" lady in London up and asked her to deliver a message to Martin saying that he should get in contact with Piet as-soon-as-possible. Piet then left the post office, climbed in the car and went home and waited for Martin to pay him the much awaited phone call.

One hour later Martin paid his "switchboard" lady a visit to pick up any messages and thereby got the message from Piet. He went down to the nearest post office and phoned Piet up.

- Hi, it's Martin, I just got your message. You asked me to phone you up. I presume it is about the "job offer" we just

The Contract (The Mission)

received.

- Yes, listen; don't say too much. I only want to know if you are prepared to accept the offer or not. If you do I have agreed with J to phone him up tomorrow for his decision. I will then let you know.
- I've thought about it and I am prepared to go forward with the task as it is. I understand it might not be an easy task but Angola was and is not particularly easy either.
- With what short notice can you pack and be ready to go?
- I might need a day or two to get things sorted out or settled.
- Any problem in getting an additional identification?
- No, I already have a couple of them at hand, all British of course. Entering South-Rhodesia or even South-Africa under my own name might be somewhat of a problem. Presume you have some additional IDs at hand as well.
- In fact I have, as travelling as well as acting with a South-African passport might sometimes have its advantages, but I cannot say how I got it.
- You don't have to, but I quite understand why and from whom you got it.
- Anyway, I will be waiting for J's decision. I will phone him up. And let's keep a low profile from now on, which means no names, only using the first letter when addressing someone. Call me the day after tomorrow after I have spoken to J and I will let you know how to proceed from here, Piet said and hung up.

Impatiently waiting for the next day to have Jose's decision, Piet could not really relax and went to the fridge to get a beer, although he knew that his girlfriend did not like when he had beer during the day, but he somehow had to come down. He went out on the terrace with the beer and sat down in their

The Contract (The Mission)

hammock, waiting for his girlfriend to return from work.

The Contract (The Mission)

January, the 15th 1986

On **the 15th of January** Martin phoned Jose up and got the message that he was prepared to join Piet and Martin in carrying out the assignment, although he was not too happy in not knowing the target before he had to accept the assignment, but as the client was talking about one million dollars, they had to make compromises, he thought. They also agreed to have Piet be the administrator for the money for all three of them until the task was accomplished..

The very same day Piet put a letter together. The letter said , s that they were accepting the assignment and also wrote down the bank account in Liechtenstein where the client was to put the money, something which he had set up as he started his mercenary activities using an alias id. Having an account in Liechtenstein was very convenient as you could use the account any time as if it was a normal salary account as well, enabling you to withdraw money using ordinary POS terminals. He then waited for Martin to phone him up the following day.

The Contract (The Mission)

January, the 16th 1986

The following day, on the 16th, he got the phone call from Martin and told him Jose's decision to go along with the assignment. He also asked Martin if it was all right to initially let him administrate the money, which Martin agreed to, although he requested to have $50,000 transferred to his account on the island of Guernsey once the first batch had arrived. He gave Piet his bank account credentials and Piet said that he would come up with additional information as soon as he got to know what the assignment was all about more in detail.

Subsequently, he took the car to the nearest post office, where he put a letter together saying that they accepted the assignment also giving the client the number of a phone box at the post office, where he would be every day between 01:00 pm – 01:30 pm as was specified in the letter. He then put the letter in an envelope, wrote the Gibraltar address on the envelope and finally he requested the letter be sent as urgent.

The Contract (The Mission)

January, the 20th 1986

Four days later, **on the 20th of January**, the letter reached its Gibraltar destination. The accountant then opened the letter, put it in his facsimile machine and sent it to Holmér's facsimile machine at home. He then filed the letter according to the instructions he had received from Holmér.

The same evening Holmér read the facsimile and then phoned the initiator of the project in Djursholm - a posh suburb in northern Stockholm.

- Hi it's me. I know I am phoning at a difficult time of the year, but I think we have to meet as soon as possible to discuss how to proceed further with our joint task.
- No problem, I fully understand the rush, the initiator replied and proposed Holmér to show up the following evening at 08:00 pm.

Holmér accepted the invitation and then hung up. He then put a facsimile together and sent it to the Gibraltar accountant using the agreed ID, explaining what was to happen with the money due to arrive in a few days time.

The Contract (The Mission)

January, the 21st 1986

At 08:00 pm the following evening Holmér arrived at the initiator's home as agreed and started to tell the initiator what had taken place regarding their common "project"., the last couple of weeks.

He then continued -

- The money transfer must take place as soon as possible and also a further $25,000 has to be transferred to another Gibraltar account using a specific "project" ID as reference, aimed to cover for the administration fees, something you will find in here, Holmes continued, and handed over another piece of paper, where said information was written down. The administration fee is 10% of the amount to be transferred. This means that another $50,000 are due for payment, when or if the next $500,000 are paid. I must stress that any additional payments depend on what sort of additional or let's call it unforeseen resources have to be allocated.

- The first batch amounting at $500,000 has to be transferred to this Gibraltar account, Holmér said and handed over a piece of paper where the account information was written down. It was an account, which the accountant exclusively had been set up for Holmér to manage similar situations.

The initiator agreed to make sure that the transfer got initiated as soon as possible. Holmér then left and the initiator subsequently phoned up his business partners and told them

The Contract (The Mission)

that things have been put into action and asked them to initially transfer $200,000 each to the Gibraltar account, which had been forwarded to him by Holmér - however not directly, as was agreed. He himself would transfer $100,000 plus another $50,000 to cover for the administration fees to the same Gibraltar bank. He also told them very clearly that any transfer must not take place from Sweden, but had to be handled through a foreign account, using a foreign bank, as had been discussed earlier, something which could be a minor problem.

Holmér's part of the initial payment which was carried out the following day was transferred from UK via Guernsey, the Bermudas and Cyprus, before the money finally reached its final destination - the Gibraltar accounts, a procedure which only took a couple of minutes. However, he did not have the slightest clue how the money transfer technically took place. This was a procedure, which had been set up a long time ago and could be applied for any money transfer between virtually any banks. He presumed that his business partners had the similar procedures set up on their behalf.

The Contract (The Mission)

January, the 22ⁿᵈ 1986

On the 22ⁿᵈ Holmér said to his colleagues that he had something to do and therefore could not join them during their normal lunch-break and went to the nearest post office to make the phone call to Piet. He was somewhat astonished having registered that it was a South-African number as the PO Box he had used for communication was in London, but never mind he thought, the guys must be of different nationality then, however it didn't matter to him.

At 01:10 pm a phone booth was free and he went to make the call to South-Africa.

- Hi, I have a question. "And what is your occupation?"., Holmér asked.
- "Missionary activities", Piet answered.
- Good, my name is of no importance to you as well as your name is of no importance to me. I am making this phone call to more in detail tell you what the assignment is all about and I sincerely hope that you are prepared for the information.
- No problem, Piet said in his Afrikaan dialect. Go ahead.
- The man we are talking about is Olof Palme, someone, who I believe is familiar to you.
- Piet didn't say anything for a couple of seconds, then Holmér heard him taking a deep breath saying "Jeez, now I understand why you are prepared to pay that much. May I

The Contract (The Mission)

ask you the reason why?"

- You may, but I can and will not give you a straight answer. However I will tell you this much: Palme has reached the level with his policy, where he is putting Sweden's status as a sovereign nation in danger and this is something which cannot and will not be tolerated by the main powers of Sweden.

- Does this mean that the assignment is officially sanctioned or at least officially sanctioned to a certain degree?

- This is something, which I will and cannot comment on. I can only say this much: It is of utmost importance for Sweden as a nation that the assignment becomes successful. Nothing less will be tolerated, as it otherwise would have unpredictable consequences for Sweden as a sovereign nation. If necessary, you can also expect help in certain areas. I also believe the outcome of this assignment could bring some advantages for your country as well.

- I understand why you cannot say more and fully understand the situation you're facing. And yes, my country would benefit from it as well.

- It is also very important that the task is accomplished before end of March as the object intends to visit a certain country, something that has to be avoided. anymore questions?

- If we have to, how do we contact you, once we are in Sweden?

- There will be no further planned contact than this. From now on you will be on your own. Should however any contact be necessary, you are to send us a letter to a PO Box in Sweden, giving me a phone number where and when I can reach you once you have arrived. Further requests for additional information or anything else will only be given through telephone - no communication is envisaged to be done in writing. Don't try to figure out whom the PO Box

The Contract (The Mission)

belongs to. The minute you try to do it an alarm goes off and you will be in real trouble. But as someone who has worked for CCB, I presume it is quite evident, what you can and cannot do. I also recommend you to rent a flat during your stay in Sweden to circumvent any hotel checks and corresponding phone records.

Piet all of a sudden got quiet, holding his breath for some seconds, wondering how the guy has come to know that he normally was working with CCB as its existence was supposed to be a well kept secret. He must have some real good connections. Must be a real important figure, he thought and Piet then finally said

- I understand, but how will you let me get hold of this information?

- I will send the information to the London PO Box today, meaning that you will have the information in two to three days. And I urge you to destroy the information after you have memorised it. There will also be a phone number, which you can call to get hold of any equipment you find necessary for your mission. When you phone, just say the number preceding the phone number and you should be able to get what you want. Please bear in mind though that the number is only valid for one call, meaning you cannot order things twice, so be specific the first time. There will also be a second page containing some addresses where you can find suitable furnished short-term apartments for rent.

- No problem. What about the money?

- The first batch has been initiated and should be in your bank account in Liechtenstein in a couple of days. anymore questions?

- Yes, one. Where does he live?

- At Västerlånggatan 31 in GAMLA STAN, that is Old Town. He wants to sell the image of himself as being "Close To the People" so he's staying in a "normal" flat for as long as he is

The Contract (The Mission)

Prime Minister of Sweden. Makes a good impression living where "normal" people live he says. Now see to that things get put in place and get going, Holmér said and hung up.

After they had hung up, Piet just couldn't believe that what he had just heard was true – an assignment to kill a prime minister. He just sat there in the phone booth with non-seeing eyes until a knock on the door made him wake up. He opened the door, said he was sorry, left the post office and went home. Coming home he directly went for a beer and went out on the terrace and sat down in the hammock to recap what he just recently had come to hear.

He now wondered if he had made the right decision when accepting the assignment, but as there was no turning back now and he had to live with his decision. He wondered what Palme had done to have forced the whole Swedish establishment to turn against him. Until now his views only seem to have been directed towards foreign powers. Although it had rendered him a lot of enemies outside Sweden, as well as influential people in his own country, still Sweden as a nation seems to have backed and supported him. But if he now even has made enemies within the Swedish establishment to an extent that they have decided to liquidate him, this was far more serious that anything else had been so far. The "Palme problem" seems to have reached a quite new dimension, he thought. The killing more or less officially sanctioned also most likely meant that any attempts to get rid of the bastard, would lead to that the inevitable hunt for the perpetrator is not likely to be that intensive and any ongoing investigations not that thorough, although it surely has to look as if this was the case. What a stupid guy. How stupid can someone be to bring a whole nation upon himself, just to prove that ones own weird views of things is the only viable option to go for. Isn't that what characterises a dictator in the end? Never mind, the whole roar about his person will make it morally easier to get rid of the bastard, he thought for himself.

When he got back home, Piet then paid a call to Martin's

The Contract (The Mission)

"switchboard", requesting Martin to phone him up as-soon-as-possible. Accordingly he also phoned Jose up to tell him about the latest "achievements". However Jose was not at home and he then had to leave a message in his answering machine, asking Jose to pay him a phone call as-soon-as-possible.

At around 7 pm Jose phoned, however Piet asked Jose to phone him up the following day instead, around noon, as Piet did not want to discuss their assignment when his girlfriend was around, as some crucial additional information had emerged, which could not just be presented and discussed in a couple of minutes, something which Jose fully understood.

When Holmér got home the same evening, he put together a facsimile to the accountant in Gibraltar, explaining what was to happen with the money due to arrive at the Gibraltar account and sent it off. He then destroyed the facsimile.

January, the 23rd 1986

The following day, on the 23rd, Jose phoned Piet up and Piet told him about the latest news, which had been brought forward by Holmér. Jose turned silent and then said:
- Fucking hell, they want us to knock off the head of a state.
- Yes, I know, but the whole thing seems to be sanctioned by the most influential people of Sweden, which, although it is alarming, it probably will make the task easier to accomplish than it otherwise would have been. I believe the police and security forces are involved as well, The guy I spoke with seems to have some decent power to get things done.
- If that is the case it more or less is a question of having to succeed, as was the case with John Kennedy, where more or less the same scenario was to be registered, from what I can recall as the investigation was a complete cock up or more or less a joke, deliberately leading the public in the wrong direction. A testable evidence and observations were quite simply ignored but in essence made everything look like it was a serious investigation going on. We have to watch out for not being the scapegoats ourselves in case anything gets haywire, because I can tell you one thing: If the killing is sanctioned from above as you presume, they will have to have a scapegoat in order to calm down the press and the public opinion, and they have to find him fast, which was the case with Kennedy and Harvey Lee Oswald. The sooner they find a scapegoat the better, as it will distract the press and the public opinion from the real

The Contract (The Mission)

perpetrator and reasons behind the killing. But as long as we are aware of what we are in for, it should not be that much of a problem.

- Good thoughts there, J. It cannot harm planning ahead for avoiding the shit hitting the fan.
- Anyway, I feel much better now that we know whom we are talking about. Also taking into account that he's a criminal in the eyes of the Swedish establishment as well, makes you feel real good. Any regrets having to liquidate the bastard are difficult to come up with, when you know what he, with his agitation, in essence is responsible for having destroyed countries like my own, countries, which have existed for centuries.
- We all know that it is easy to condemn and not having to give anything in return. At least it is good to know that the Swedes themselves seem to have realised what sort of person they have brought to power, running their country. He is probably about to destroy Sweden the same way as he helped destroying the African countries, Jose said bitterly.
- Agree, at least that is a relief. Anyway, good news. How are we to proceed from here?
- I am waiting for the first instalment to arrive in my account any day soon. M wanted $50,000 upfront to cover for his expenses, I can transfer the same amount to your bank as well, but then you have to give me the corresponding information.
- Why not, I have an account in Gibraltar, which I easily have access to. Just have to cross the border to Spain. and Gibraltar is only about 400 kms from Lisbon.
- Good, once the money arrives, I will see to that it gets done. In the meantime I will do some preliminary planning. We should take three different routes to get to Sweden. I would propose you take a flight to Frankfurt and then the train to Stockholm. M will take the ferry to Gothenburg and from

The Contract (The Mission)

there the train to Stockholm. I personally intend to fly to Frankfurt and then buy me a ticket to Stockholm from there. All three of us should travel using aliases.

- I sincerely hope this sort of arrangement is in accordance with your normal practicees - Piet continued - as we cannot afford to let the authorities get suspicious should they be checking arrival and departure records then having to register that there are people, which might have entered but never left Sweden or the other way around, It is paramount that we use passports from European countries, as we otherwise may be faced with having to undergo additional unnecessary checks .

Jose said it sounded ok, and then gave Piet his bank credentials for the Gibraltar bank. Piet then said that he would contact Jose as soon as possible, once all the money had arrived.

The Contract (The Mission)

January, the 24th 1986

The following day Martin phoned Piet up and Piet told him the same story as he previously had told Jose. Martin more or less shared the same views as those Jose had, also saying that he would have no regrets in getting rid of Palme, a person who had forced him to leave his beloved country and someone who vehemently was propagating for a takeover of South-Rhodesia by the communist Mugabe and his villains. He was also pleased to hear that even the Swedes themselves seemed to have had enough of Palme's way of doing politics.

Piet also made some a preliminary notes in – Afrikaans, Afrikaans being his native language - how to get and where to meet in Sweden.

- M neem die veerboot na Göteborg, Swede. Trein dan na Stockholm • J neem 'n vlug na Frankfurt, Wes-Duitsland en trein dan van Frankfurt na Stockholm

- P om die vliegtuig na Frankfurt te neem, dan 'n vlug van Frankfurt na Stockholm

- Ontmoet op 1 Februarie by Centralen (Central Station - Meeting Point). Tyd: middag

- P & M om woonstelle reg te stel - aanvanklik vir twee maande. - Geen hotel indien moontlik nie; te maklik om opgespoor te word.

(in english)

- M is taking the ferry to Gothenburg, Sweden. Then train to Stockholm

The Contract (The Mission)

- J is taking a flight to Frankfurt, West-Germany then train from Frankfurt to Stockholm
- P to take the plane to Frankfurt, then a flight from Frankfurt to Stockholm
- Meet at Centralen (Central Station - Meeting Point) on the 1st of February. Time: noon
- P & M to fix apartments - initially for two months. - No hotel if possible; too easy to get traced.

The same day, on the 24th, a part of the first instalment – what the initiator had initiated - was credited the two accounts and the accountant sent a facsimile off to Holmér reflecting the status.

The accountant then initiated the facsimile request from Holmér and had the $100,000 transferred to Piet's account in Liechtenstein. The next day the rest of the initial instalment - $400,000 - was credited the Gibraltar account and the same procedure was followed as was the case with the first $100,000.

The Contract (The Mission)

January, the 25th 1986

On the 25th, Piet phoned his bank in Liechtenstein getting the confirmation that the initial instalment in total had been transferred. He then sent a letter off to his bank requesting the bank to have them transfer $50,000 to Martin's account in Guernsey as well as transferring the same amount to Jose's bank in Gibraltar.

He then paid Jose a quick call, saying that the money had been transferred to his Gibraltar account and that he expected Jose to be in Stockholm for a meeting on the 1st of February at noon, place – Central Station. He also suggested Jose to take a no-return flight to Frankfurt and from there the train to Stockholm. Should they happen to recognise each other before said date, it was agreed not to make any attempts to meet, especially not in a hotel foyer.

He then phoned Martin's "switchboard" and left the woman on-duty a message to tell Martin to phone Piet up as-soon-as-possible.

He then went for a beer and sat down in the hammock on the terrace, waiting for his girlfriend to come home. In London, the weather more and more began to look like a typical London winter with fog and cold drizzling rain. Martin began to get somewhat restless and impatient having to wait for the "go ahead" command from Piet, who as usual was the organiser of the three of them. Martin himself was more a type prepared for action any time, although he understood that thorough planning had to forego a successful assignment, especially an assignment which he now was about to take on,

The Contract (The Mission)

where no errors were allowed. Nevertheless, just sitting around doing nothing was not his cup of tea and he felt like celebrating a bit. Coming from South-Rhodesia and having spent most of his life in Africa, he really did not have any real friends in UK. His real friends had all lived in South-Rhodesia but got scattered in all directions leaving the country as Mugabe came to power. He therefore just went down to the local pub every now and then for a beer and often met people, who were only after to have a chat as well. Around 8 pm, he therefore took a stroll down to the local pub, about 500 meters away. The pub was pretty full and the was only one empty chair at a table where already three people sat - one guy and two women, his girlfriend and her best friend, he reckoned. He asked if he could join them and they said – "no problem mate". Consequently he joined the table and spent a round as good will.

The evening went by with a lot of beer and drinks – can openers - and at 11 the guy and his girlfriend left and Martin then was left with the other woman. About midnight they left together and Martin asked if he could follow her home, something which she would appreciate she said. Arriving at her apartment, she asked him if he would fancy a coffee, something which he didn't object to, as it was evident what she was after, which also proved to be the case having entered the flat. No time for "Tango" there. Martin left the flat early the next morning with a pretty nice hangover, promising the woman to catch up with her when he came back from his assignment. Unfortunately he couldn't say when, he said, as he did not know when the assignment would come to an end.

The Contract (The Mission)

January, the 26th 1986

Martin phoned Piet up the next day, the 26th, around 3 pm and sounded as if he had a cold. Martin said that he had been out celebrating the night before and met a nice chick, who he went home with for some "wrestling" and did not come back to the apartment until early this morning, having a pretty bad hangover as a result of his "celebration". Went to sleep immediately.

Piet asked him if he had managed to keep his mouth shut. Martin said he had not revealed anything, apart from saying that he had got a well rewarding job as a freelancer and therefore felt like celebrating, but not mentioning what it was that kept his mouth shut, as he knew his tendency for bragging was all about. The lady was not curious either, seemed more occupied with more "important" stuff, he said and laughed.

Piet did not say anything, but sincerely hoped that Martin had kept his mouth shut, as he knew Martin's tendency for bragging about what he was doing and had done when he got drunk. Martin then said that they had got a letter containing two pages with addresses from Gibraltar.

Piet asked him to read the page with the PO Box information, which he also did and Piet wrote the address down, telling Martin to memorise the PO Box address and then destroy the page as it only was to be used for emergency matters. Piet also told him there should also be a phone number, preceded by a number written down somewhere, which he also had to have. The information, Piet said, was to a contact, which would

The Contract (The Mission)

enable them to get at the necessary equipment for the mission once they had arrived to Stockholm.

The other page, Piet said, contained a number of agencies which rented out furnished short-term flats and he asked Martin to take the information with him to Stockholm and get in contact with one of the agencies and rent a flat, two bedrooms, initially for two months for himself and Jose. Piet said they had to split as it otherwise might look suspicious and be noticed with three males staying in the same flat. Piet intended to rent a one bedroom apartment himself for two months. Piet then wrote down the addresses of the agencies, which Martin gave him.

Piet also suggested that Martin should take the ferry to Gothenburg in Sweden and from there take the train to Stockholm. He also told him how he and Jose envisaged to get there. He also told him only to buy one-way tickets as return tickets could be traced. He told Martin to be at Centralen at noon on the 1st of February, stating that there must be some sort of meeting point there, where they could meet. He also said to Martin that should they happen to recognise each other before said date, they were not to make any attempts to meet, especially not in a hotel foyer.

Finally Piet told Martin that the first instalment had arrived and that he had transferred the requested sum to Martin's Guernsey account something, which made Martin cheer up a bit despite his hangover.

Later the same evening, when Piet's girlfriend had come home from work, he told her he had got the lucrative assignment in Europe, meaning that he would be away for at least a month. He could not tell her what it was all about nor where the assignment was to take place, as it was one of the prerequisites from the client, but promised to phone her as often as he could.

Unfortunately, he had to leave the day after tomorrow, January the 28th he continued, as he must not show up later than February the 1st. His girlfriend was not too happy about it, but accepted his decision, hoping that the assignment would bring them some financial reward, at least.

The Contract (The Mission)

January, the 27th 1986

The next day, Piet booked a flight from Durban to Johannesburg and from there a connecting flight with South-African Airways to Frankfurt, Germany. The flight to Stockholm, he would have to book in Frankfurt.

In parallel, Jose had booked a flight from Lisbon to Frankfurt due for take off on January the 29th. Arriving in Frankfurt he would have to book the connecting train to Stockholm, roughly a 24 hour journey, due to arrive in Stockholm on the 31st.

He then went to visit his parents place to say good bye, not telling them what the assignment was really all about, only telling them that he had got a well paid assignment in a European country and that he, for contractual reasons, was not allowed to tell them where the assignment was to take place and what his task was, but told them not to worry. He hoped to be back in two months, he also said.

In the meantime Martin had also booked the ferry from London to Gothenburg for the 29th, due to arrive in Gothenburg on the 30th of January. He would buy a ticket for a connecting train to Stockholm once he had arrived in Gothenburg. As he did not fancy having to sleep together with people that he did not know, he had booked a single cabin on the ferry.

The Contract (The Mission)

Durban - January, the 28th 1986

Piet woke up early, as the had to take the shuttle flight to Johannesburg at 07:35 am, being in the position to take the connecting flight to Frankfurt at 11:20 am, scheduled to land in Frankfurt approximately 11 hours later. He said goodbye to his girlfriend and told her not to worry, but could not fully convince her that it just was an ordinary assignment, not involving any danger. He had ordered a taxi for 06:00 am to take him to Durban Airport and the taxi came a couple of minutes before 6. His girlfriend could not stop from shedding a few tears but despite her fears, she tried not too show it too much.

Piet landed at Frankfurt Airport somewhat delayed due to severe weather conditions around midnight and took a taxi to the Holiday Inn hotel, which was just around the corner where he took a room for one night. He also managed to get something to eat, before he went to bed around 02:00 am. He woke up around 09:00 am the next day, had a breakfast and checked out and returned to the airport where he bought a ticket for Stockholm, Arlanda Airport, due for takeoff in the afternoon. Piet arrived at Stockholm, Arlanda in the evening the 29th and took the shuttle bus to Stockholm city as, when using a taxi, they might be able to trace where he was heading. From the bus terminal he took a taxi to a nearby hotel and booked a room for three nights.

The following morning Piet phoned one of the rental agencies up asking the woman who had taken the call if they had a furnished one-bedroom apartment available to rent out for

The Contract (The Mission)

two months. They said that they had a vacant apartment very close to the MEDBORGARPLATSEN underground station – on the south side of Stockholm - from the 1st of February and Piet got the address and agreed to have a look at the apartment at 1 pm in the afternoon the next day.

At 1 pm he met the agent outside the house, Piet took a look at the apartment and agreed to take the apartment, initially for 2 months, as he did not know how long his assignment here in Stockholm was about to take, he said. He presented himself as someone coming from the Netherlands, which was plausible as his native language was Afrikaans, signed the contract which the agent had brought with him, showed the agent his passport and then filled in his name, address, nationality and passport number in a form, which of course was false. He also agreed to have the apartment lease be paid in advance and got a payment slip, which he also could use as down payment for the apartment if the job was to take longer than anticipated.

The Contract (The Mission)

Lisbon - January, the 28th 1986

In Lisbon Jose woke up on the 28th about the same time as always to make himself ready for the flight to Frankfurt, scheduled for 08:50 am with TAP, the Portuguese airline. He left his flat at 07:00 am and went down to catch a taxi to the airport - a 20 to 25 minute ride if everything went without interruptions - which shouldn't be a problem from the middle of the city where the flat was.

The airplane landed 10:25 am at Frankfurt Airport, one of the busiest airports in Europe, only superseded by the chaos airport number one – Heathrow in London.

After having passed through the customs, he then took a taxi from the airport to Frankfurt Hauptbahnhof – Frankfurt main train station – and bought a ticket for Copenhagen in Denmark as he did not want to give the authorities to be in the position to trace his journey, should there be any unforeseen problems. From Copenhagen, he then planned to take the Hover-craft over to Malmö in Sweden and from there buy a train ticket for Stockholm. Arriving in Copenhagen early the next morning, January the 30th, he went to the nearest taxi stand and asked the driver to take him to the place where the Hoover-crafts took off for Sweden. Two hours later he had passed the customs in Malmö, something, which did not present a problem, as checkups were virtually nonexistent and in essence not possible to carry out due to frequent commuting between Sweden and Denmark. Having reached the Hoover-craft terminal in Malmö, he then took a cab to Malmö Central Station, where he bought a ticket to

The Contract (The Mission)

Stockholm. The train left Malmö at 02:14 pm arriving in Stockholm around 8 hours later. He then took a taxi to a nearby hotel and booked a single room for 2 nights.

The Contract (The Mission)

London - January, the 28th 1986

In London Martin woke up on the 28th at 8 am, getting ready to take the connecting train to Immingham, from where the ferry parted for Gothenburg in the afternoon. He was scheduled to arrive in Gothenburg late the following day. At 11:05 am the train was sheduled to leave London, King's Cross, for Immingham, which meant he had time to pick up some money from his Guernsey account over an ATM terminal. As agreed he had made the booking, using an alias. He had made a couple of aliases in case he would get into trouble and had to vanish as a result of his "missionary" assignments, you could never tell. Having arrived to Immingham he took the shuttle bus from the train station to the ferry terminal, where he had to wait, as the ferry from Gothenburg still had not arrived. This left him with the only viable option - to go for a pint (or two) of bitter until the ferry arrived and he could get onboard and to his cabin. He went to the terminal bar and ordered a pint.

Beside him sat a woman in her early 30s, which he started to chat with. He presented himself as Nigel, living in London but originally coming from Bath and she said her name was Gunilla. She said she was from Stockholm, worked as a nurse for a big hospital and had been to London visiting an old friend of hers, which had moved to London about a year ago. Just to have something to talk about, Martin asked for the reason why her friend had moved and the woman answered that that her friend wanted to come away from the depressing job climate and high taxation in Sweden, where it was virtually

The Contract (The Mission)

impossible, due to the high taxation, to comfortably live on a salary, regardless what you were doing, unless you had the opportunity to make some black money on top. Sweden had become the country for non-workers and left-wing people, people not really interested in achieving anything anymore, she said. Skilled people got increasingly disinterested in pursuing any career goals and were leaving Sweden instead, something, which has started to become noticeable, and a problem for many companies when trying to find skilled people for certain demanding jobs. Martin tried to be ignorant about what politically was taking place in Sweden and continued innocently to ask her for further information about Sweden just to pretend being interested in her political views. From what he could hear from what she was saying, Palme seemed to find himself being some sort of a modern Robin Hood with what he was intending to do and Martin found it remarkable that there still were any people left in Sweden and he asked her why she did not leave as well.

The Contract (The Mission)

She then said

- It is not that easy as you might think. If you went for a job outside Sweden, you have to have a working permit regardless which country and what sort of job you were thinking of, and most companies were not prepared to go through the additional hassle with working permit for filling a position and in the end they went for a "local" instead.

Martin tried to be understanding and as the loudspeaker announced that they should board the ferry, he suggested that they should meet for dinner later and continue the chat, which she agreed to. They agreed to meet at 7 pm at the main restaurant. Martin said he would organise a table for two, and then they parted to go onboard and to their cabins respectively. Martin, somewhat of a womaniser, looked forward to what the evening might bring, but realised that he had to be very careful when talking about himself and his reason for visiting Sweden.

They met as agreed at the main restaurant at 7 pm and had a delicious three course dinner. During the Dinner he cautiously asked her about some private matters and it turned out that she had broken up with her boyfriend as a result of having more or less "caught him in the act" just before Christmas and this after having been seven years together, something which had hit her pretty hard. The trip to London was a direct consequence of this breaking up as she felt she had to breathe some new air and also chat with someone over her situation. And her friend was ultimately the right person for helping out in such occasions. After the dinner Martin suggested that they should go for something to drink, which she agreed to. Eventually the woman got curious what sort of person Martin was and he told her some fairytale about having grown up in England and having worked for the British army in Northern Ireland. He then felt being in the comfort zone when talking about military matters as any other profession might expose him. He also said that he now

The Contract (The Mission)

was working in the security and surveillance area and this was the reason for him going to Stockholm, where a client wanted to beef up his security and surveillance installations. As she asked him about the client, he said she must understand that he was not in the position to neither disclose the name of the client nor to discuss what sort of measures the client envisaged having to be undertaken. Martin found it very convenient to use the security and surveillance area as an excuse for not having to divulge too much of what his really was doing. People tended to accept his denial to talk about what he was undertaking without further comments.

Around midnight they agreed to break up and as the "alcohol level" then had reached a point where the "cautiousness" slowly began to disappear they started to get intimate and eventually they went to Martin's cabin where "further actions" took place.

As Martin woke up, he had a slight hangover and the woman was gone, however she had left a note on the desk, where she thanked him for a wonderful night and also her phone number, should he have time to meet up with her during his visit to Stockholm. Martin smiled and thought for himself that the trip to Stockholm promised not be that boring after all.

January, the 29th 1986

The ferry arrived to Gothenburg late in the evening the 29th and he took a cab to the Gothenburg central station, where he bought a ticket to Stockholm for the following morning. He then went out to the taxi stand and asked the driver to bring him to a comfortable hotel not too far away.

The next morning - on the 30th - after having had a comfortable breakfast, Martin called for a taxi, which took him to the Gothenburg central station, and waited for the train to take him to Stockholm. He arrived in Stockholm at Centralen - the Central Station - late in the afternoon on the 30th. He then took a taxi to a nearby hotel and booked a room for 2 nights.

January, the 31st 1986

The following morning Martin phoned one of the rental agencies up asking them if they had a furnished 2 bedroom apartment for two months to rent. They said that they had a vacant apartment not far away from MEDBORGARPLATSEN - the south side of Stockholm - very close to an underground station, from the 1st of February and Martin got the address and agreed to have a look at the apartment at 2 pm in the afternoon as the agent was meeting up with another client at 1 pm in the neighbourhood regarding a one room apartment. Martin smiled for himself when he heard it, realising that the client most probably was Piet. He then bought a map of Stockholm at the nearest newspaper store and also collected some brochures from the hotel, which they offered free of charge, including a map of the Stockholm underground system.

At 1:30 pm Martin took the tube 3 stations to MEDBORGARPLATSEN and walked for about 5 minutes before he reached the complex where the apartment was. It was situated in a fairly quiet area, close to a small park. At 2 pm, the agent arrived and they went to have a look at the apartment. The apartment would serve its purpose, Martin thought, nothing spectacular but had what you would expect to find in a furnished apartment including an already connected phone, which was available for incoming calls and was included with the lease. Any outgoing calls would be additionally charged for, the agent said. The agent also tried to have a chat with Martin, asking him about his profession and Martin told him the same fairy tale as he had told the

The Contract (The Mission)

woman on the ferry to Gothenburg, something, which evidently impressed the agent. Martin said he would take the apartment from the 1st of February and signed the contract, which the agent had brought with him, showed the agent the passport and filled in his name, address, nationality and passport number, which of course was false. He also agreed with the agent to have the apartment lease be paid in advance and got a payment slip, which he could use to pay for the flat.

The Contract (The Mission)

February, the 1ˢᵗ 1986

The following day all three checked out of their hotels, then taking a cab to Centralen and put their luggage in a locker respectively.

As it was agreed to meet up at 12 pm at the Central Station the Träffpunkt ("Meeting Point"), they then went to the nearest bar to have a beer and something to eat as well as discussing and planning for further actions.

Marin told the other two about the flat he had rented and it proved to be in the same block as the apartment Piet had just had rented, which was very convenient, should they have to meet.

They had to interrupt as a waitress came by taking their orders. The bar was not as crowded as normally would have been the case during this time of the day during the week as most Swedes preferred to have a meal in a restaurant during the day as they normally get tax free restaurant-vouchers from their employers which they then can use for meals in almost any restaurant.

Due to the noise level in the bar, it did not come to much planning and they decided to postpone the planning until they could have a meeting in one of the flats. Instead they joked about the frigging coldness, which none of them had experienced before and had a chat regarding what they had been through since they met last time. As they left the bar 2 hours later, the beer level having reached a decent height, they agreed to meet the following day around 12 pm in the flat

The Contract (The Mission)

Martin had rented. They picked up their luggage respectively and Jose then followed Martin at a distance as they left as he did not know where the flat was. They then took the tube from Centralen to MEDBORGARPLATSEN, which was three stops away.

Piet spent the evening doing some initial planning how to go about with the assignment.

The Contract (The Mission)

February, the 2nd 1986

Piet woke up around 8 am and got dressed and went down to a café, which he had seen the day before, for something to eat. He reminded himself to go shopping for some food and have the breakfast in the apartment in the future if he did not want to jeopardise being unrecognised. It was never good to regularly visit something as people tend to remember such people, when it came to the crunch.

The other two had also had their breakfast, however not in the cafe but at Mac Donalds, which was close to the underground station and therefore not too far away.

At 12 pm Piet walked over to the other flat, swearing over the unbelievable cold weather and reminded himself, that he had to go shopping for some winter clothes later the same day.

When they met, Piet asked Martin if he could make some coffee, in case the apartment was equipped with some instant coffee, which Martin said it was. There also were some biscuits, sugar and long-life milk, he said. Piet also said they should try to have breakfast in the flat, not to be recognised by visiting the same place every day, which the other two agreed was a good idea.

Piet then started to outline some preliminary plans.

- We have to write down his daily schedule and repeatable behaviour as follows:
- When does he leave home - I mean Palme - for work?
- How does he leave home? By foot, car or public transport?

The Contract (The Mission)

- Are there any bodyguards at large, how many and when do they come and leave ?
- What does he normally undertake over the weekend and are there any bodyguards at large then?
- He lives at Västerlånggatan number 31 in GAMLA STAN – Old Town not far way from the "GAMLA STAN" underground station, which is two stations from where we by-the-way call Tunnelbanan, one stop to T-CENTRALEN, which is very close to where he works. However, I presume he walks, presumably with bodyguards.
- How do we get hold of what he is up to?, Martin asked. We cannot just plan and correspondingly act out of the blue.
- Good question, I will have to contact the client and give him my phone number to the apartment, which will enable him to contact us for emergency matters. Also, as we from now on will have to stay outdoor a considerable amount of time for surveillance tasks, I find we will have to buy some winter clothes, like woollen cap, scarf, long-johns, socks, gloves and winter boots for that purpose as I believe we cannot possibly use our normal clothes, which we have brought with us, Piet said, something, which the other two could not more agree on.

None of them could actually understand how someone could live in such a climate and if it wasn't for the reward, which they would get if they were successful, they would most of all leave Stockholm as soon as possible. To them it was not a way of living, to them it was quite bluntly a matter of survival.

The Contract (The Mission)

- By the way, Piet said, I have brought you some women tabloids for you to read, where they write about and have pictures of Palme and his wife. Try to memorise what they look like and then throw the tabloids away.

Piet then asked the others what sort of equipment they would prefer or even need for the mission and they agreed on the relatively new Glock31, a semi-automatic .357 caliber gun characterised by extremely high muzzle velocity and superior precision even at medium range, even possessing the ability to penetrate a bulletproof jacket, a pistol harnessing the energy of one shot to reload the chamber for the next with ammunition for each of them, a stiletto knife for each of them, a sniper rifle either UTG or Mauser with telescope sight, ammunition for Martin being the expert in that area and three Walkie-talkies as well as a tool for unlocking locked doors. Martin said, professional and experienced as he was in carrying out sniper assassinations, that they probably would not get many opportunities and that he therefore would need bullets powerful enough to penetrate a bullet-proof vest should Palme be wearing one. They also reckoned they might need the tool for unlocking locked doors as they might have to carry out their mission from a building and therefore had to be able to enter the building fast and as they all had very limited experience with breaking up locks, they did not have the time to fiddle around with the lock then most certainly attracting suspicious and critical eyes from by-passers.

Piet asked the others to pay some additional thoughts what they might need in terms of equipment until tomorrow and then he would order the equipment through the clients connections, which he had been given.

Piet told the other two where to go for shopping and he also said that as far as he knew, from having read the tourist information brochures, the shops were open on Sundays as well.

The Contract (The Mission)

They then agreed to split up for going shopping and to meet the following day at the same place and same time again.

The Contract (The Mission)

February, the 3rd 1986

As Piet woke up the sleet - rain mixed with snow – an awful combination – had stopped and the weak sun had decided to come out and it seemed somewhat warmer than the day before. Piet made a quick breakfast, before he went for a warm shower and got dressed. He imagined being in Antarctica as he put on his long johns and a t-shirt with long sleeves.

He then went over to the others to continue with their preparations. However, none of them could come up with any additional equipment they would need to acquire for accomplishing their task, other than what they already had written down the day before.

After another cup of coffee, they went out to take a look at the building and surrounding where Palme lived. With their new clothes, they were certain that they now would pass as average Swedes with their woollen cap on over the ears.

They took the tube from MEDBORGARPLATSEN to GAMLA STAN – a less than 5 minutes ride. Old Town – the oldest part of Stockholm was comprised of small alley like streets only allowed for pedestrians and Västerlånggatan was no exception. Passing street number 31, they noticed a man in black standing in front of the door presumably from a company called Securitas, they reckoned, if you could trust what the name said on his jacket. Martin took a quick look at the houses along the street and came to the conclusion, there was no way in hell that you could make an attempt here where Palme lived, everything was far to narrow, the street

The Contract (The Mission)

probably not more than 5 meters wide and it would be virtually impossible to find an angle suitable for trying a shot from a nearby window. In order to be successful, Martin thought, you had to come very close to the victim and then the chances of getting away would consequently drastically vanish or better said be virtually nil. People would immediately notice where the shot came from and the time needed to escape would vaporise. One possibility might be opposite the street where Palme lived but he reckoned that this was something, which the security forces already would had taken into account. However, he abandoned this solution as being too dangerous as it would be too easy to find out from where the bullet came from, therefore the likelihood of getting caught was far too big. After a couple of minutes they turned right direction Stortorget – the Big Square - and went for a coffee at a nearby cafe. The cafe was just about half-full, making it relatively easy to find a table not too close to the other guests. As English was fairly common in Stockholm, Martin ordered three coffee, together with a "Wienerbröd", whilst the other two preferred to stay silent. When the waitress had left, Martin put forward his doubts against carrying out anything where Palme lived and the other two fully agreed with him. They agreed that they had to track his behaviour instead, thereby trying to find a more suitable spot or they might even have to be prepared for an ad hoc action if it turned out to be the only option.

However, this would literally mean they also had to be prepared to act with a very short notice.

After having finished the coffee, Piet and Jose returned to their apartments respectively, leaving Martin to have a better look around at the surroundings and also figure out when and how Palme returned home.

Having arrived at the MEDBORGARPLATSEN metro station Piet went to a public phone booth and phoned the number up, which he had gotten from Holmér regarding the ordering of additional "tools". The person at the other end of the line

The Contract (The Mission)

picked up the phone and answered with a simple "ja?".

Piet said

- Hi, I would like to buy something".
- Must be the wrong number, the other said. I'm not selling anything
- Hey, wait a sec., Don't hang up. I have a number here, Piet said, and told the guy the number Holmér had given him.
- Tomorrow at SLUSSEN, main entrance, 13:00, the other guy said. Put a DN from today in your left armpit. Bring the list.
- What is DN?, Piet said cautiously
- A newspaper, the other guy said and hung up.

Jeez, that was not much of a talker, Piet thought, immediately having recognised from the accent that the guy must have come from an eastern European country as he fairly often had come across such an accent from his time fighting the bloody communists in Angola. All of them extremely unfriendly and pissed off most of the time. Anyway, he could go fuck himself as long as the fuck delivered what they needed. He didn't care about his character.

He went back to the apartment to warm up and also to write down what they needed in terms of equipment on a separate piece of paper.

Martin came back from his "inspection" tour at around 9 pm, and Piet went over to the other apartment to inform the others what he had done and also to listen to what Martin had been undertaken.

Martin said that Palme had arrived home at around 08:00 pm followed by two security guys. The security guys having been standing outside the house then left and the other two took up their position outside the flat. He then had walked around for another half an hour but nothing relevant to their mission

The Contract (The Mission)

had happened. Martin reckoned that they would carry out their "changing of the guards" around 04:00am, 12:00 pm and 08:00 pm respectively every day.

They agreed to have Jose take the next "inspection" tour from around 06:30 and to follow Palme at a distance until he saw Palme entering the Swedish Parliament building. Piet would then come and take over around 02:00 pm depending on where the takeover was to take place. As incoming calls were included with the apartment lease, Jose could phone him on the apartment phone and tell him, as soon as he had found out, where Palme had his office.

Piet then said that he had phoned the number he had gotten for buying their equipment and said that he would meet the guy or someone from the same outfit at 13:00 pm tomorrow. He also said that the guy seemed to have come from a country in Eastern Europe also indicating that they often were pretty ruthless and consequently the guy probably was not someone, which you necessarily should fuck about with unless he was trying to play the "wise" guy.

Piet then left the other two and took a walk to the nearest McDonalds for a quick meal. He also bought a copy of today's DN at the MEDBORGARPLATSEN underground station newspaper kiosk before he went back to the apartment.

The Contract (The Mission)

February, the 4th 1986

Jose woke up at 04:30am, had a quick coffee and a cheese sandwich, before he took off for his "inspection tour". He took the tube around 05:40am arriving close to 06:00am at the place where Palme lived, however he did not put himself too close as it might have looked suspicious. Palme came out around 07:30 and took off direction Helgeansholmen and the Parliament building. The security guys accompanying Palme, one of them a couple of meters ahead of him, the other one a couple of meters behind, looking for anything suspicious. Jose followed them about 25 metres behind, trying to hide behind other people walking in the same direction. They turned right to Myntgatan and arrived at "Riksdagshuset" without anything spectacular having happened. Jose not really knowing what to do took a quick look at the surroundings and then took a stroll direction Drottninggatan, aiming at finding a cafe or something similar where he could get some breakfast and to warm up - which he also found, not too far away from the Parliament building.

Having had his breakfast, he first phoned Piet up and told him where to meet. He then went back over Norrbro to get a more broad view of the surroundings, but could not see any opportunity to accomplish their task where Palme carried out his duties. Everything was either too narrow or too far away and the surrounding buildings were all not accessible to the public. Besides, every street from where Palme lived to where he worked were marked as pedestrian zones, meaning that using a car was out of the question. The entrance of the parliament was from a pretty narrow street – Riksgatan - and

The Contract (The Mission)

surrounded by government buildings. So far the options weren't that encouraging, in fact there were not any viable options at all. Either the street was too narrow or there were only government building which you did not have access too. And you could not just approach the guy and "Bang" without most probably getting caught. The only positive thing was that the surveillance task was pretty easy as Riksgatan was a very crowded street and that made the likelihood of being regarded as a suspicious character when walking around the entrance were close to nil, Piet thought.

Piet woke up by the phone call from Jose, becoming the information from Jose where to meet. Having finished the phone call, he took a shower and then made some coffee together with two sandwiches with cheese. He thought about how to approach the guy he was about to meet, but could not make up how. Never mind, he thought, I will have to take it as it comes. Let us only hope that they can get hold of everything they had written down on the paper. He took the tube from MEDBORGARPLATSEN to the next stop - SLUSSEN - where he took the main exit. He looked around when he passed the exit barrier, but could not see any person resembling to what he had pictured for himself how the guy would look like. On the other hand had he arrived 10 minutes earlier than what was agreed. Suddenly a man approached him and asked him in english if he could take a look at the newspaper he had in his armpit.

Piet said - "Of course" and gave him the paper.

The guy took a quick look at the first page and then said - "You want to buy something?"

Piet said yes and the guy said - "Let us walk outside" and went for the exit doors.

Coming outside the guy said - "What do you want?" and from one of his pockets Piet took out and gave him the paper where he had written down what they wanted.

He looked at the notes and said -"Fancy stuff you want,

The Contract (The Mission)

expensive".

Piet said – "Doesn't matter. This is what we want and need".

The guy looked at the paper again and said "Will cost you at least five thousand dollars, my friend, and I will not rip you off as our common friend has told me not to".

Piet said that five thousand was all right with him and wondered for himself what sort of person their "common friend" was. Must be a pretty important bloke, he thought for himself.

The guy then said – The money is to be paid into a foreign bank account. I will give you the account information if you decide to accept my offer.

Piet said that he wanted to take the offer the guy had given him and he got the account information. The guy then asked him for a phone number, which he could use for contacting Piet when the equipment was ready to be picked up and Piet gave him the number to the leased apartment.

The guy then said – "The delivery of the equipment will not take place before you have transferred the money", and gave Piet an "order number", as an identification, which was to be attached to the payment.

Piet said he would initiate the payment immediately and the guy left. Piet went back to the underground station and took the tube to GAMLA STAN, from where he walked to the meeting point he had agreed with Jose to meet, something which took him in all about half an hour. Jose stood where they had agreed to meet and they went for a coffee to warm up. The cafe was pretty crowded at this time of the day as it almost was the end of the lunch break, but they managed to grab a table from a couple about yo leave the cafe. Having ordered a coffee and the "dish of the day", including either a glass of milk or light beer – they went for the beer – Jose did a recap of what he had found out and Piet saw the same difficulties as Jose when it came to finding a position, which

The Contract (The Mission)

would enable them to accomplish something during Palme's promenade to and from work.

They then agreed to have Martin take the morning shift the following day, so that he could get a picture as well of what was possible and what wasn't. After all he was the sniper professional and the one eventually having to carry out the assassination. They also agreed to meet at the same place Jose had met with Piet earlier that day.

Piet took over the surveillance and Jose then left for the apartment to have his well-deserved nap. He suggested Piet to take a look at the surroundings in case he found a different angle, which could thereby enable them to carry out the assassination after all, which Piet also did. He evaluated the options from all possible angles how to go about to carry out the assassination as well as taking the existing surroundings into account, However, he could not find any feasible way of getting away with it either from what he saw. He slowly began to realise that it would be a hell of a task to be in the position to successfully carry out what they had agreed to and to get away with it as well.

Palme came out at around 07:30 pm together with the two security guys and went home over Myntgatan and Västerlångatan before they arrived at number 31. Piet stayed "on duty" close to Palme's flat until around 10 pm despite a never-ending biting wind howling through the streets and a temperature below -10 degrees centigrades (14 F) and then left for the day and took the tube back to the apartment.

The Contract (The Mission)

February, the 5th 1986

The next day, it was Martin's turn to have his morning surveillance tour. He got there around 6:15, not really taking too much notice of what took place where Palme lived, when he suddenly came out in jogging equipment and turned left with the two security guards following a couple of meters behind.

Jeez, Martin thought for himself, in this weather the guy is taking a jogging tour at 6:30 in the morning.

Martin realised immediately that he could not follow him and could only wait for him to come back. Half an hour later Palme returned coming from the opposite direction. An hour later Palme came out turned right with his two body guards following a couple of meters behind., following the same pattern as they had followed yesterday. After having reached the Parliament, Palme entered the building and Martin passed and went for a breakfast at the cafe Jose had told him about. He then briefly inspected the surroundings and essentially came to the same conclusion as Piet, namely that there was virtually impossible to carry out something and at the same time securing a successful escape route between where Palme lived and where he worked.

At the same time Piet woke up, had his usual breakfast and got dressed. He subsequently wrote a letter to his bank in Liechtenstein, requesting the bank to transfer the amount of $5000 to the bank account he had been given and then signed it.

He then put the letter in an envelope, sealed it and went to the

The Contract (The Mission)

nearest Post Office, asked for express mail delivery, got the stamps and then put the letter in the letterbox. He also sent a letter off to the PO Box address he had been given by Holmér with the two phone numbers of the apartments respectively, stressing that Martin's and Jose's phone number was only to be used as second choice in case Piet could not to be reached.

He had also written a sentence saying that they needed to know as soon as possible when Palme was doing something and where he was going outside his normal daily pattern as his daily path was virtually impossible to use as a platform for carrying out anything useful.

Jose came to take over at 02:00 pm and Martin told him what he had been through. Jose then said that he agreed with the assessment Martin and Piet had done in that it was virtually impossible to accomplish anything between Palme's fat and the Parliament.

Martin then said :

- Palme changed his morning pattern today, went jogging for half an hour. Unfortunately I couldn't follow him so I did not see where he was heading. It would have been far too suspicious and dangerous as his two body guards were accompanying him as well. However this is something which we have to discuss as it might present a possibility to do something depending on how regular he is doing it.

Jose then said :

- At least something, which might be a possibility. Let us have a chat with Piet about it when I return tonight and maybe we can find a way of carrying out our assignment with this approach.
- Ok, lets do it, I will briefly tell Piet what I have found out and tell him to come over around 11 tonight to discuss the matter.

Martin then left for the day and Jose went looking for a place to have a cup of coffee and something to eat, something which

The Contract (The Mission)

was very easy to find in the city with heaps of cafes and restaurants serving their "meal of the day" including a non alcoholic beverage of some kind. A hour later he began to walk around the parliament building as if he was about to head off for something, more or less to keep the blood pounding to avoid freezing more than necessary.

Palme came out from the Parliament at around 7:00 pm as he did yesterday and took the same path home, followed by his two body guards. Jose followed them some 25 meters behind, arriving at the flat around 15 minutes later.

Jose passed the entrance as if he was heading somewhere not turning his head in direction number 31 as it might have been suspicious. Under no circumstances was any of them to be registered as more as just passers-by by the body guards as this most likely would mean the end of their assignment. They therefore had more than one woollen cap, which they swapped at regular intervals to avoid any recognition.

As he walked along Västerlånggatan he suddenly bumped into a woman walking in the other direction, whilst trying to protect his face from a fierce wind and the cold temperature being below -10 degrees centigrades. He suddenly stopped raised his head and saw that the woman in front of him was Listbeth Palme, Olof Palme's wife. He said a low "excuse me" – in Swedish, something which he had remembered from having ploughed through some travel guides and hurried to pass her. "Shit", he though, "hope that she will not recognise me, should we bump into each other again. I must watch out better, not letting the cold deviate me from better looking around when following someone and not make me loose my concentration regarding the purpose why I'm really here all-alone in this frigging cold".

He dared not to look back, afraid of that she might look back as well, and instead turned left into the next alley he come to see. He then waited a minute thereby also changed his wollen-cap for a different one before turning back in the direction he had come from, now having the wind coming from the back.

The Contract (The Mission)

Despite the "Collision" Jose kept up his "surveillance duty" until around 09:00 pm before returning to the apartment, where he found the other two.

- Jesus Christ, is it cold, Jose complained when he came back to the apartment, I couldn't stay longer as the wind together with the cold takes the breath out of you. Martin, can you please pour me something from that whisky you bought yesterday. I have to somehow warm up, before we can start talking.

Martin poured him a whisky and Jose also made himself a cup of tea, then he was just sitting there for 10 minutes without saying anything, desperately trying to "defrost". Eventually he felt better and they started to recap what had taken place during the day.

One issue was the sudden jogging activities by Palme. They agreed they could not do much but trying to track his whereabouts when he was jogging, before having got the walkie-talkies they had requested, which meant that firstly they had to find out whether there was a repeatable pattern or not. Therefore they all agreed to show up the following Wednesday morning in an attempt trying to trace what paths he might be taking, covering different areas. However, before Wednesday they had to find out, to best of effort, which paths were possible for Palme to choose, based on what Martin had come to register the previous morning. They agreed that this task should be accomplished by Jose the following day as Piet then was to take the morning and day shift and Martin the afternoon and evening shift.

Jose then mentioned his "confrontation" with Palme's wife, Lisbeth, saying that he believed she did not smell a rat or anything, but urged the other two to be on their guard when doing their "inspection tours", i.e. to be prepared for just about anything, e.g. sudden identification check-ups by the police or the security forces if you were staying in one place for too long, etc. He, therefore, suggested each of them to buy another coat or jacket for swapping purposes to minimise their

The Contract (The Mission)

presence wearing the same outfit. This to avoid their presence to be regarded as something following a possible suspicious pattern or someone wearing the same clothes. At any rate, their presence had to be diverted from being regarded as some sort of recurrent behaviour into a pure random pattern.

As Lisbeth Palme came home from a minor shopping tour at Järntorget, she said to her husband Olof that it was bloody cold and windy outside. She also mentioned that she had bumped into a stranger walking in the opposite direction. She said that although he excused himself she had the feeling that he did not "belong to" GAMLA STAN and from what she could hear the man was not Swedish although he used the Swedish word for "excuse me". He also hurried to continue his walk. She could not understand how someone could be outside walking in this horrible weather but maybe he was about to meet or visit someone, she said. She then left the subject and went to prepare an evening meal.

The Contract (The Mission)

February, the 6th[th] 1986

Piet had his usual breakfast, got dressed and took the tube at around 6 am to GAMLA STAN, arriving at Palme's flat around 06:15. Nothing spectacular did take place until Palme came out around 07:30 and went for the parliament to work, followed by his bodyguards. The sun had just started to rise over Stockholm and would be up around 7 hours before it said goodbye, something, which Piet found sort of depressing.

Piet followed Palme at a secure distance without any incidents and when Palme entered the Parliament building, Piet continued walking to the main shopping centre to buy an extra coat or jacket.

After Jose had woken up he got dressed and then went for a quick breakfast at the nearby McDonald Fast Food Restaurant. He then took the tube to GAMLA STAN to inspect possible jogging routes which Palme may take. Turning right instead of left at Västerlånggatan he eventually reached a small square – Järntorget - where Västerlånggatan and another street – Österlånggatan ended. He then took off to the left, along Österlånggatan. He walked that street until he could see the Royal Castle, a very impressive building, he thought. Having reached the castle, he then turned left along the castle and then after a couple of minutes he reached Västerlånggatan again. As he could not see any other feasible routes, he assumed that the route he had taken was the route Palme would take when he went jogging. He then walked the route again, this time more inspecting it from an assassination point of view and concluded that there were some possibilities, especially around Järntorget and the open areas around the Royal Castle, where they might be able to carry out their mission. A third option was at the end of Österlånggatan were a couple of trees were to be found and trees were always a welcomed hiding place. The only problem would be the bodyguards and how to escape them. On the other hand, he reckoned they would not be that alert after having been running for a couple of minutes. The primary task was to find the most suitable place and the secondary task was how and where to escape, which should not be that difficult with all the alleys found in GAMLA STAN. The obvious escape route would be to reach the underground station where trains come and leave almost on a minute basis during the rush hour. The question was, he thought – how to get there? - as the assassin would be on the other side of GAMLA STAN from where the underground station was located. He would have to walk through a couple of scenarios to know which solution to opt for if any.

Having gone through what seemed to be viable spots, he then walked the streets also having a street map of GAMLA STAN in his right hand, to get better acquainted with GAMLA STAN, realising that they must get to know every possible escape route worth considering and that they had to be taken inside out. No hesitation whatsoever what had to be undertaken after having completed their mission was to be allowed. Everything must run like clockwork, exactly the way they had learned to carry out their tasks in Africa. The weapon had to be thrown away at an agreed spot to be picked up by one of the other two and be made extinct. He would make a recap of his finding tonight when Martin had returned. Martin and Piet would then have to take the "tour" themselves and come forward with their estimates. Finally, a joint effort would then form the groundwork for further actions.

Having done and inspected what he thought momentarily was feasible and possible, he then walked to the main shopping district - not far away from GAMLA STAN - to buy an extra coat or jacket.

The Contract (The Mission)

Before Martin met with Piet, he also had bought an extra jacket which he gave Piet to take to the apartment when they swapped positions at around 2 pm. The temperature was still well below freezing and some light snow fell. Piet said that nothing worth reporting had taken place and asked Martin if he wanted to join him for something to eat, something which Martin happily accepted. They went in the direction of the shopping centre and found a pizzeria also having their usual daily special, something which, from what they could see, almost all restaurants and cafes had.

After having had their pizzas, Piet went to the nearest underground station – T-CENTRALEN – and took the tube back to the apartment and Martin went to take over the surveillance task.

Around 10 pm Piet got a phone call from Jose saying the Piet should come over for a quick chat to hear what Jose had found out during his " tour".

Jose told the other two from his findings and took out his street map of GAMLA STAN, saying that he saw three possible areas and told them why he found the three possibilities being adequate for carrying out their task. He also told them about possible escape routes and their pros and cons respectively. At the moment he did not want to recommend any particular spot before the other two had made their tour. After having delivered his findings a lot of questions came from the other two, questions which he answered best of effort. He also said that regardless of which spot was chosen, after the task had been accomplished a second guy must be responsible for taking care of the weapon and see to that it disappeared. Consequently, it was agreed to have Martin have his "tour" the following day.

Most probably it would be Martin being the one carrying out the actual kill, the other two supporting. Jose would take the morning and day surveillance tour and Piet would take afternoon and evening.

The Contract (The Mission)

February, the 7th 1986

The next day Martin woke up late, took a shower and went to a nearby cafe to have breakfast, the weather proved to be cold and miserable as usual. Martin then took the tube to GAMLA STAN and walked the way Jose had painted out for them. Reaching Järntorget he rounded the bend and to the left, he saw a small alley – Södra Benickebrinken continuing below. The alley also had a protection wall, preventing people from falling. He took a look at the surroundings and saw that there was another alley – Svartmansgatan - taking off from Södra Benickebrinken to the right then meeting Tyska Brinken, which then went all the way to the GAMLA STAN underground station. Martin found the place to be a splendid place for the kill as there was no way reaching someone at Södra Benickebrinken from Österlånggatan without having to reverse and then run uphill, which would take some time taking into account that someone had been assassinated. In between you would be long gone direction underground station, Martin believed. However, he would have to work through and try the scenario with his friends to be sure.

He then made an estimate how long it would take by running from the assumed spot for an assassination to the underground station and was satisfied with the result. He then returned from where he got started and continued his "tour" along Österlånggatan. He reached the trees, which Jose had mentioned, but after having investigated the surroundings for escape routes, he concluded that the "tree" option was not viable from an escape point of view.

He then continued until he reached the Royal Castle where he

The Contract (The Mission)

then turned right up the Slottsbacken looking for possible spots from where he could carry out their task. He saw at least two possibilities with feasible escape routes where you could escape through Svartmansgatan or Skomakargatan to Tyska Brinken respectively, but he found none of them being as good as the one at Järntorget, as you were more in the "open" being more exposed which meant it most likely would be very difficult to make the necessary preparations without being noticed by passers-by. However, he had to come here at a time of the day equal to the time of the day Palme went for his jogging tour to be in the position to estimate the number of people passing by. As it also was a joint operation, he firmly believed all three should come here at the same time to discuss possible options and their pros and cons. He would have a chat with them on how to further pursue the task this evening, proposing that all three should come for a " tour" together. He then went to a cafe for a coffee and to escape the frigging cold. He then returned to the apartment to make some notes regarding what he had found out.

Around 10 pm they all met again and Martin made a recap of his findings also going through some hypothetical scenarios, something, which the other two found to be very good and thorough. They agreed to go through the possible scenarios on-site on Monday as the coming weekend most likely did not reflect what would take place in the areas during a normal weekday.

Jose then asked Piet about the status of the tools they had ordered and he said that he had sent a request off to his bank on Wednesday. Taking into account that the letter probably would take 3 days to reach the bank, the bank would have it at the earliest on Monday. Having the transfer be carried out the following Tuesday, the guys would most likely not have the money on their account before Wednesday, which would mean that we could not expect any call before Thursday/Friday next week, Piet said. This would mean that we will not be able to pick up the equipment before next weekend, the 15th of February. They all agreed they were in

The Contract (The Mission)

for a tight schedule, taking into account that they also had to test and tune the equipment, something which could not be done where they stayed. It meant they had to rent a car and go someplace to test the equipment, which would cost them extra time, something which could not be accomplished before they had gotten the equipment, This would mean that they at least had to wait until the 16th before any testing and tuning could be made. This also realistically meant that the earliest date to carry out their "mission" would be on the 26th provided Palme went jogging on said day. They also agreed that it was no point in carrying out any surveillance tours during the weekend as long as they did not possess any equipment to work with.

They therefore agreed to postpone further activities until coming Monday and each of them was free to do whatever they fancied on their own during the weekend. Martin immediately saw the opportunity to meet up with the woman from the ferry as she had given him her phone number. The other two were not too happy about it and, knowing Martin, told him to be careful with what he said. Piet left the other two at around 1 am, asking Martin to buy some decent beer tomorrow, otherwise he wouldn't come over again, he said and laughed.

The Contract (The Mission)

Stockholm - February, the 8th 1986

The following Saturday morning Martin woke up, got dressed and made himself an instant coffee with milk, before he left the apartment. He first went to a nearby cafe for a breakfast and then went to the underground station went to a telephone booth and dialled the number he had been given by the woman. First he thought she was not at home, but on the 5th buzz she picked up

- Hallå
- Hi, do you remember me, the guy from the ferry from Engand?
- Oh, hi, good to hear from you, what are you doing?
- Busy working most of the time, but I am free during the weekend and I thought maybe we could meet for a dinner somewhere, only if you've got time, of course,
- Oh yes, that would be nice, where?
- I don't know that many places in Stockholm. I leave it to you to decide.

The woman then suggested a nice little restaurant in Vasastan, not far way from where she lived. She told Martin to take the tube to RÅDMANGATAN underground station, the rear entrance and she would pick him up from there. They agreed to meet there at 07:30 pm the same evening. Martin said he thought it would be nice to meet her again, something which she wholehearted agreed to as well.

Satisfied with the arrangement, he then went to one of the

The Contract (The Mission)

state owned liquor stores – Systembolaget – in the neighbourhood and bought a 6-pack of Tuborg export lager together with a bottle of French red Bordeaux to bring with him instead of flowers, something which cost you a fortune, he thought, and then went back to the apartment. Jose was still sleeping, so he turned the TV on. Although Sweden did not have English as their official language, all English movies and TV series were shown in original, only with Swedish subtitles. The same was the case with the cinemas, something which was a relief. Jose must have heard the TV, because he came out of his room, sleepy, asking Martin what time it was. Martin said it was almost 12 and Jose said, that he must hurry.

- I intend to satisfy my intellectual needs by visiting the VASA Museum, whilst you presumably are after satisfying your physical needs, Jose said and laughed. Any luck with the pickup ? he then asked.
- Sure, no problem. I am off for a dinner this evening. Meeting the chick at RÅDMANGATAN underground station at 07:30. We'll see what surprises the night will bring, Martin said and smiled.
- Does this mean that you are not coming back tonight?
- Judging from our come together on the ferry, most probably not. But you can never tell.
- Be careful with what you are saying though, I know you.
- Jose, I'm not that bad. Surely I will not jeopardise our mission, just for a one-night stand.
- Hope not, Jose said. Anyway, I must get ready for my intellectual tour. Believe they are closing the Museum at 6 pm
- What sort of museum is it? - Martin asked innocently, trying to be interested in what Jose was telling him.
- Supposedly it is a warship, build some 350 years ago, which

The Contract (The Mission)

sank on its maiden trip, just because the then king demanded to have the ship built too top-heavy with all its guns, leading to that she got unstable and overturned and sank in the harbour as it was pretty blustery that particular day, I've read.

- Jeez, must have been a stupid prick they had as king.
- Probably not stupid, but at that time there were no guerrillas and terrorists. It was all a question for nations of winning battles – to sea or on land and the one that had won the battle got what he demanded. It was not as difficult to win wars as it is nowadays. As the king always was present at a battle, it virtually meant that when a king surrendered, the whole war was more or less over, easy eh?
- Sounds interesting. Tell me about it and I might take a look at the ship myself.
- Sure will. Even you might need some intellectual refurbishment.
- Get stuffed, mate, Martin said and laughed. See to that you get ready for your "intellectual tour", and then bugger off. I must mentally prepare myself for tonight, Martin said and smiled.

Jose then got dressed, made himself a cup of coffee and a cheese sandwich waved a cheerio and then left for his "intellectual tour". He took the tube to T-CENTRALEN, walked out at the front exit where the main shopping district also was, took a 10-minute walk through the shopping district, thereby passing Kungsträdgården – King's Garden – and caught a tram at Stureplan which then took him to the Wasa Museum. Walking through the shopping district, he thought that Stockholm was not too bad after all. You only have to have the right clothes for the weather and you might perhaps start to enjoy the beauty of the city, he thought for himself.

In the other apartment Piet woke up, got dressed and had his usual breakfast. He then went to the nearest post office for a

The Contract (The Mission)

long distance call to his wife as South-Africa had the same time as Sweden.

Martin, opened a can of Tuborg Export, sat down on the couch, and turned the TV on, waiting for the evening to come.

At 07:00 he took the tube and alighted at RÅDMANGATAN and went out at the rear exit of the tube station. As he was 15 minutes early, "his date" still had not arrived.

Women are never early, he thought. You can be lucky if they are able to meet the time, which has been agreed.

Eventually she came, 10 minutes late, excusing herself for being late. They left the underground station and came up at Sveavägen, one of the main streets of Stockholm. He said "Hello, nice to meet you again", and gave her a swift kiss, which she replied to. They went to a small Italian restaurant quite nearby, where she had reserved a table for them as it otherwise would have been difficult to get a table otherwise on a Saturday evening. They had a splendid dinner with beer and wine, chatting about their last rendevous on the ferry. With the coffee Martin had a Grappa and she took a Drambuie with ice. Around 10:30 pm they left the restaurant and she asked Martin if he would care to come with her for something to drink, something which he had worked towards the whole evening, hoping that she would suggest that he should come with her home.

Hardly having entered the flat, she walked up to him, putting her arms around his neck, dragging his mouth towards hers. He didn't protest, following her hands willingly. No time for anything to drink. Eventually they landed on her bed, letting their feelings and desperation take over. Having finally become what they both were aiming for, they fell asleep.

The Contract (The Mission)

February, the 9th 1986

Martin woke up at around 08:00 the next morning, went to the loo and relieved himself, got dressed and went to the kitchen. She had already made some coffee and had put some slices from the swedish bread "limpa" and swedish crisp bread together with butter and cheese plus two boiled eggs on the table.

- Good morning, she said and went up to him, giving him a kiss.
- Good morning, Martin said. Oh nice, I can see that you have made some breakfast.
- Hope you like it, she said, it is nothing spectacular, just an ordinary breakfast.
- It's ok, I'm hungry, will eat anything, Martin said, and sat down at the table.
- She gave him a mug of coffee and asked him how he preferred the coffee and he said with sugar and milk.
- How long will you be in Sweden, she then asked
- Don't know, he said. Depends on how long it will take to set it up
- And where do you stay? she asked
- I'm having an apartment together with another bloke, who also is working on the project
- Where?
- Doesn't matter, but I don't want to tell you where as the flat belongs to the client.
- Why?
- It is a matter of principle. In the security and surveillance

business you tend to be cautious. Also, not just me is staying in the flat.
- Strange, cannot be such a big deal
- Maybe not, but let us leave it at that. Does it really matter where I stay?, and he began to get hostile
- Not really, please don't get upset about it. I just wanted to know, she said as she saw that Martin started to get angry.

In order to make up for her curiosity, she came over to him and started to kiss him intensely. As Martin could feel the desire coming pounding again, he stood up and took her by the hand and they went to the bedroom again, something which she eagerly accepted as she had not felt like this for a long time. After another 2 hours, Martin got up, went to the bathroom and had a shower, before he got dressed. As he was about to leave, she asked him

- When will I see you again?

- Don't know, he said. I have to work during the week and next weekend, we might be in for some rehearsals, but don't worry, I will phone you.

- And I can't phone you?

- Unfortunately not, as I have no telephone, and he saw that she started to panic. As soon as I know more I promise I will phone you.

- Ok, she said, somewhat disappointed, but realised that she had to accept it. I will wait for your call then.

Martin gave her a swift kiss, waived a goodbye and then left her. Jeez, he thought, why must a simple one night stand get complicated? Sometimes he could not understand women, immediately getting "love feelings", when the only thing you wanted was a decent fuck. He realised he had to be cautious with her as he could not allow himself to let things get complicated now. He had to concentrate on their mission and could not afford to screw things up for a woman.

The Contract (The Mission)

He went down to the RÅDMANSGATAN underground station and was back in his flat around 5 pm. Jose was already back from his "intellectual excursion", watching TV smiling when Martin turned up.

- Success?
- Sure, man. Exhausted
- Kept your mouth shut?
- Sure did, but the bird was curious, Wanted to know where we're staying and the phone number. Believe she has fallen in love with me, Martin said and laughed
- And did you give our phone number to her?
- No way, are you crazy?
- I just wondered. One can never tell what happens "in the heat of the night", Jose joked and laughed.
- A lot of things happened but definitely that did not. By the way, how was your "intellectual excursion"?
- Not too bad, quite good actually. Saw a lot from the city as well. The city is awesome, very nice. Pity that there is such a shitty climate here, though.
- Read that the summer should be quite good. I guess we just picked the worst season to come here.

They continued with the easy going chat until Martin said, that he could fancy a cup of coffee, and asked Jose if he cared for one as well, which he did. After the coffee Martin said that he was tired and went to his room to have a nap.

Piet had not done very much during the weekend apart from having phoned his wife from a nearby phone booth. As he did not want to divulge where he was, for security reasons he said, she got cross and didn't want to talk and hung up. Piet got pissed off and promised himself not to phone her up again until the mission was accomplished as phoning her up seemed

The Contract (The Mission)

just to cause more problems, something which he couldn't need right now. He realised they had to take actions asap as he couldn't wait for too long to make the next phone call. Around 6 pm, he walked over to the other two to discuss what to do tomorrow Monday the 10th of February.

When he came over to the other apartment, Martin was asleep and Jose made some jokes about it. Piet went to the fridge and took a Tuborg Export and sat down in front of the TV, sipping the beer. On the TV some American series was running with Swedish subtitles, which he found being very strange but also quite amusing in that you could not keep from reading the subtitles although you did not have a clue what they were saying.

An hour later Martin woke up and came out of his room - sleepy, saw the beer can, which Piet had standing on the table and went to the fridge and got a beer himself. When he returned Piet said "congrats", smiled and took a sip from his beer.

After a couple of minutes, they started to discuss what they had accomplished during the first week, which was not too bad they thought, the only problem being that they still have not managed to come up with a solid strategy how and when they were to carry out their mission. The best bet so far was when Palme went jogging, provided he did it regularly, which lead to that they agreed to meet up the following day at the MEDBORGARPLATSEN underground station at 6 am for GAMLA STAN to go there and make some estimates, try some scenarios and to figure out how many people were out on the streets at the time, which they anticipated Palme was due to go jogging.

They also agreed to drop any surveillance the next day as there was not much more they could accomplish without having the right equipment.

The Contract (The Mission)

February, the 10th 1986

They met at 6 am at the underground station and took the tube to GAMLA STAN where they arrived around 10 minutes later. They walked up to Västerlånggatan but then turned right, direction Järntorget, instead of left to Palme's place. The weather was somewhat better than the last couple of days, although it still was below zero degrees, but no sleet snow or rain drizzle. They reached the place, which Jose and Martin estimated being the best spot and Martin explained how he envisaged the kill to take place as there were not too many people being underway at this time of the day. On the other hand, the streets were not empty, meaning that acting fast would be paramount for the mission to be successful. From where Martin thought being in the position to carry out the mission – Södra Benicke-brinken – they played through how long it would take for one of the security guys to reach that place, taking into account that Palme had been shot and that it inevitably would delay the decision making process of the security guys. One guy would most likely stay with Palme, maybe both. They came to the conclusion that there was no way in hell that any of the security guys would catch up on Martin before he had reached the underground station, in case they decided to go after him.

One of the other two would have to stay in the first alley to the left from Svartmansgatan, prepared to take and getting rid of the gun, most probably by make it disappear in the surrounding waters. The third one would have to stay on guard outside Palme's flat and to give the go ahead signal once he comes out. However, as they still did not have the

The Contract (The Mission)

necessary equipment, they had to wait for the final test until they had everything.

Then they went for the other two options, but by further investigation, the second one was regarded being too dangerous from an escape point of view and the third one, although it was good in terms of possibilities to carry out the kill, most likely it was too crowded, and would put innocent people in danger and also possible escape routes were not too good either, leaving the security guys a lot of space for taking up the chase. In essence, the third option was possible as well, but would require more skills, speed and also some luck compared to the first option. All three then agreed that they should concentrate on and plan for the first option. Any additional planning would require the equipment they had ordered.

After having finished their "inspection tour", they all agreed to that it was time for some breakfast and to warm up and went to a cafe at Stortorget, not far away from the third option.

After the breakfast, they then returned to their apartments respectively and Jose got the task to carry out the surveillance in the afternoon and if Palme then did go home directly then Jose could return to the apartment as well. After a week's surveillance, Palme's every day schedule did not seem to be changing very much on a day to day basis, apart from the jogging on Wednesdays.

The Contract (The Mission)

February, the 11th 1986

On the 11th, Martin took the morning shift, but nothing of importance happened. Palme went to work as usual and did not leave the parliament building until Jose came and took over at 2 pm.

Piet stayed in the apartment, waiting for the call from the guy from where they were to get the equipment, they had ordered, which came at around 11 am.

- Hello
- It's regarding your order, your payment has been verified and the delivery can take place in a couple of days, a voice said with an East-European accent.
- Good. And when?
- You may want to try the equipment out. In that case, let us meet on Friday at 10 am at the FARSTA metro station. We will then go to a place where you can have the equipment be verified for its functionality.
- Yes, we would like to try the equipment. Ok, we will be there
- How many?
- Three, is that all right with you?
- Should be all right, however it might be somewhat crowded in the back of the car.
- Doesn't matter as long as we get the equipment.

The Contract (The Mission)

Then they hung up and Piet felt a certain excitement, as everything now slowly started to be put in place and the nature of their mission slowly became more and more realistic.

As Piet did not want to approach the other apartment during daytime, he put his coat on and walked to the nearest underground station, from where he then phoned the other apartment. Jose answered.

- Hi, it's me. I just wanted to say that I got a phone call saying that our equipment has arrived and we will pick it up on Friday. We will also have the opportunity to verify if it is working as envisaged.
- Good, why don't you come over this evening as we have to make some planning for tomorrow.
- Ok, will come at 9 then

Piet then went for something to eat in a nearby Pizzeria, before he returned to the apartment. He then started to make some scenarios what and how they were to test the equipment, especially the sniper rifle which had to be accurately tuned.

Palme left the parliament at 6:30 pm and walked directly home, which made Martin take the decision to return to the apartment as well.

At 9 pm Piet came over telling Martin about the phone call as well, and that they would take the tube to FARSTA metro station – a borough in the southern part of Stockholm. They also made some planning for the next day, meaning that all three would show up at MEDBORGARPLATSEN underground station at around 6 am the next morning.

Martin was to cover option number one where the presumed the kill was to take place, Jose was to take the second option – the trees, and Piet was to cover the third option – the top of Slottsbacken, nearby the Royal Castle. Although there were not too many options, they could only assume what way

The Contract (The Mission)

Palme was running, implying that they might not catch the way he was choosing – they could only anticipate that the track they intended to cover was the right path.

Piet would then go to Palme's flat, just in case something out of the ordinary would happen. The other two were then to return to the apartment and they agreed to meet there the following evening to discuss what they had experienced in the morning.

The Contract (The Mission)

February, the 12th 1986

The following morning – Wednesday the 12th – at the agreed time they all met at the MEDBORGARPLATSEN metro station and took the first train heading direction GAMLA STAN. Arriving at GAMLA STAN, they took different streets to arrive at their respective spots they were to cover. Now they could only wait for Palme to come to see if they were right in their assumptions. Around 6:35 am Martin saw Palme coming around the bend, followed by two bodyguards. He tried to memorise as thorough as possible the way Palme had taken as well as the distance to Palme from which he eventually would take the shot.

At the same time he briefly thought about their mission and came to the conclusion that he did not have any regrets, did not repent and did not have any hesitation regarding what they were about to do. Palme, as one of those people being primarily blamed for and responsible for that he had been forced to leave his native and beloved country South-Rhodesia, he thought. He imagined receiving a silent satisfaction in what he was about to do from the more than 100,000 whites, which had been ruined, forced to leave their native country and forced to leave everything they had built up behind. The kill was a retribution for everything Palme had done with his never-ending agitation towards all whites in southern Africa. Why could he not have left our problems to be solved by ourselves? Martin thought. He wished he could make Palme feel the sorrow and pain he felt as a result of what Palme had done to him and all the whites, but he knew it was not possible.

The Contract (The Mission)

On the other hand, the kill was not a personal vendetta against Palme, but an assignment from influential people in Palme's own country, which could only mean that getting rid of the guy was both legitimate and justified and also a political necessity – the end justifies the means, he thought. They were out on a mission, not about to assassinate someone.

Martin then went for a breakfast at a nearby cafe. 20 minutes later Jose came through the door. Jose sat down at the same table and ordered a breakfast as well, loosely chattered about what each had seen earlier, They then walked back to the metro station and then returned back to the apartment. Arriving at the apartment, they more in detail discussed what they had experienced, Jose saying that attempting to accomplish the kill from where he had been standing would be suicide as the escape route was virtually non-existing, in essence meaning there was none.

The same evening Piet came over and all three had a chat about the possible spots they had been examining and they came to the same conclusion as they had before – the only realistic option was the one where Martin had been standing, as the other two options proved to be too difficult, primarily from an escape point of view.

Martin was to take the morning shift and Jose the afternoon shift the next day, however, should they face the same pattern as every day, they would stop half way through the shift. They also agreed to drop any surveillance on Friday as they had to collect the equipment they had ordered.

The Contract (The Mission)

February, the 14th 1986

Friday the 14th came and they met at the MEDBORGARPLATSEN metro station at 9 am as agreed and took the tube to FARSTA, which took them around 1/2 hour to get there.

As they were somewhat early for the meeting, they had time for a quick coffee. Whilst having their coffees, a guy came up to them, the same guy which Piet had met at the SLUSSEN metro station a couple of days ago, when he ordered the equipment.

- Hi, did you have a good trip here, he asked
- No problem. These are my two friends, Piet answered, pointing at Martin and Jose, not mentioning any names.
- Hi, ok then, shall we go?

They left the metro station and went to a huge parking lot. The guy walked up to an approximately ten year old, not too well maintained Volvo, opened the door and asked all three to jump in the backseat. In the front seat another guy sat, not saying a word when they entered the car. The guy was probably there to act as some sort of cover up in case any problems were to arise.

They left the parking lot and went for the motorway and then direction Nynäshamn, a small town south of Stockholm, situated at the Baltic. A couple of minutes after they had passed Västerhaninge, they left the motorway and turned right and then left onto a gravel road and stopped after a couple of minutes, having reached a clearing in the forest. The guy asked all three to step out of the car and come with him and then went to the boot and opened a case obviously comprising their equipment.

- We will stay here for a couple of minutes to give you the chance to check the functionality of the equipment, the guy said. I've brought some empty beer cans, which you can use as targets.
- Thanks, Piet said and took one of the Glocks out of the duffel bag and loaded it and aimed at the beer cans, which the guy had placed some 20 metres away.

The Glock felt very light and was easy to use and after a couple of attempts he managed to hit the beer cans. He repeated the same procedure for the other two Glocks and was satisfied with their functionality as well. The guy told him to pick up all shell casings and bring them with him. Then it was Martin's turn to check the sniper rifle, which was a Mauser. The beer cans were then moved around 100 meters away from where they were standing. At first the bullet went to the left but having made some adjustments to the telescope sight the rifle worked to perfection. The walkie-talkies were tested accordingly and found to be working to their satisfaction, in fact they were very good, no toy stuff.

Very satisfied with the equipment they had gotten, they put the equipment back in the duffel bag, then thanked the guy for his efforts and drove back to FARSTA metro station. The other guy in the car still had not said a single word as they arrived. They then left to take the tube, all entering different cars, back to MEDBORGARPLATSEN metro station.

Back at the apartments they tried out the Lock Pick Gun for unlocking the door to one of the apartments, which proved not to take them more than 30 seconds before they were in – very impressive stuff, they thought.

The Contract (The Mission)

February, the 15th 1986

Come Saturday the 15th, nothing of importance happened, apart from the fact that Lisbeth Palme came out of her flat at around 10 am, presumably to do her weekend shopping, thereby noticing Jose who had the first shift standing some 100 meters away from Palme's flat. Their eyes briefly met, Lisbeth seemingly not recognising Jose and continued walking. Some seconds later she however seemed to remember having seen him somewhere before, could however not say when and where and therefore changed subject and started to concentrate on what she needed to buy for the weekend instead. Jose hurried to disappear into the next alley, not to allow Lisbeth Palme to catch up on him, in case she should remember the previous unintentional "meeting" they had some days ago. He returned to the apartment at around 12 pm, after having come to the conclusion that the Palme's' had the intention to spend the day at home.

Arriving at the apartment, he went over to Piet. He rang the bell and Piet opened the door.

- Hi, what's up?
- I just wanted to have a chat with you over a couple of things.
- Sure, please come in. I was not doing anything of importance anyway.
- I've thought about our situation and how we are progressing and I fear we might run into problems in executing our assignment

The Contract (The Mission)

- What do you mean?

- We have been tracking Palme's movements for now roughly a fortnight and we have not achieved anything useful but the fact that he seems to be jogging every Wednesday morning. However we don't know if that's really the case, we are only assuming that he is doing it.

- I tend to agree with you. Momentarily we don't have any other option as what you are mentioning, it seems.

- This brings me to the question: What do we do if he diverts from this assumed pattern? I see a huge problem here. Just assuming a jogging exercise is not enough. If Palme decides to change his jogging schedule we would have lost. Apart from the jogging exercise, we have nothing else to go for and correspondingly react to and in my opinion this is not enough. Time is running out as there is no way we are in the position to react to any upcoming deviations from Palme's general behaviour ad-hoc, simply because we cannot prepare for anything in advance. We cannot for god's sake run around with the equipment all day just in case anything was to pop up. It is all ludicrous to believe that would be an option.

- I also see the problem and I have decided to write a request to our contact here to phone me up and then tell him to deliver more in detail information regarding Palme's agenda to us in beforehand and this as soon as possible. Otherwise, I will tell him, it may not be able for us to successfully accomplish the task although the option to cancel the mission is not at hand. I will also give him a recap and tell him what we have experienced and found out so far and explain the reason for our request.

- So you mean, to put it bluntly, we have to know more in detail know of Palme's agenda in advance?

- Yes of course, otherwise we are fucked and this has to be said as soon as possible. We have now as you said followed

The Contract (The Mission)

him for two week and in essence have not achieved anything useful but the jogging.

- Good to hear. This will make me somewhat more comfortable as I really began to doubt that we were to succeed in accomplishing our task as agreed.

Piet then offered Jose a beer and they continued talking for another 1/2 hour before Jose returned to his apartment. They also agreed to cancel the daily surveillance as the probability that they would be recognised got higher and the benefit from the surveillance was not proportional to the danger they might face in being recognised, especially now that Jose had been noticed twice by Lisbeth Palme. This meant that getting to Palme's agenda in advance was of utmost importance and a necessity.

He then wrote a letter requesting their contact to phone him up asap.

"Some non-anticipated problems have arisen. Need to talk asap"

He then put the letter in an envelope, sealed it, wrote down the PO Box address he had been given and put a corresponding stamp on the envelope, which he had bought as he sent off the first letter, and left the apartment to put the envelope in the nearest letter box. It had started to snow outside and he could not wait to get inside again. After having put the envelope in the letter box, the realised that it was past 3 pm and decided to get something to eat and went to get a take-away pizza from a nearby pizzeria before returning to the apartment.

As Jose came back from his chat with Piet, Martin was doing some exercises in the living room and stopped when Jose came in.

- Jeez, what are you doing?
- I felt I have to do something, not to loose too much fitness.

The Contract (The Mission)

- You are probably right, I should probable start doing it as well, but this fucking weather keeps you from taking any initiative in that direction whatsoever.
- I know, but I cannot just sit here waiting for something to happen. It makes me nervous.
- Agree. I just spoke with Piet and told him about my concerns regarding what we are doing.
- What did you talk about?
- That I see immense problem in what we momentarily are trying to accomplish as we virtually have not been able to come up with any real plan how to go about with the task, apart from concentrating on the jogging tour Palme is taking, something which we don't even know if he is doing that on a regular basis. We are only assuming he does, but we are not sure. What do we do in case he stops jogging? Then we are fucked, man.
- Thinking about it, you are right, but what do you the suggest?
- Piet has decided to request Palme's agenda. – what he is up to – from our contact as we otherwise cannot plan. Just running around with the equipment, waiting for something to take place outside the normal schedule, is not realistic. We must know what Palme is up to in beforehand in order to be able to react and plan. We also agreed to drop the daily surveillance until we get additional information what Palme is up to as we momentarily are not getting anywhere and the probability that we will be recognised gets higher, the longer we are doing it. For example, Lisbeth Palme passed me again today and I believe she might have recognised me from our clash we had last week. And being recognised is a risk, which we absolutely cannot take. Don't you agree?
- Sure, so you mean just stay low until we get at that information?

The Contract (The Mission)

- Yes.

- And how long will it take until we get that information? And what about the options we have planned regarding his jogging exercise? Will we stick to that?

- As far as I am concerned, we will. It is just that we cannot just base the whole assignment on something, we are not even sure of.

- You are probably right. This means that we will stay low until Wednesday morning?

- Yes, If we are lucky we might be in the position to finish our assignment as planned then.

- Ok, I have no problems with that. Then I am free to contact the lady again for some physical exercises, Martin finally said and smiled.

- I believe you are, but be careful, please don't gossip around.

- Of course not, my mouth will be sealed like a turtle.

    Jose laughed and Martin went for a shower and then went out to make a phone call.

- Hi, it's me. I have some time free over the weekend. How about meeting, only if you have not planned anything else of course

- Hi, that would be nice. No. I have not planned anything for today, in fact I was hoping that you would call.

- Ok, then. Is it all right with you if I pop up around 7 then?

- Yes, that would be swell.

- See you then around 7, then we could go somewhere and have something to eat.

- That would be nice, look forward to see you again, bye.

- They hung up, and Martin returned to the flat, waiting for the time to leave.

The Contract (The Mission)

When he returned, Jose had returned to his room for a nap and Martin took a beer from the fridge and then turned the television on, just to make the time fly.

As Martin left around half past 6, Jose was awake and said he would go to a nearby cinema and watch a movie. As he had heard that all movies were being shown in their original language with Swedish subtitles, he thought it might be worth a try, he said.

Martin returned to the apartment in the afternoon the following day, pretty tired, saying that had had a good time but that the woman was pretty demanding and said that he had to take a nap to "recover", which he also did. Martin woke up 3 hours later and asked Jose if he wouldn't care to go down and buy two take-away pizzas as he wasn't in the mood for entering the cold again.

The Contract (The Mission)

February, the 18ᵗʰ 1986

Tuesday the 18ᵗʰ came with even colder weather. The temperature fell to well below -10 degrees centigrades, which did not encourage any of the three to take any actions which would mean they had to go outside. Around lunchtime the phone rang at Piet's place. Piet picked up the phone.

- Hello

- You wanted me to contact you. I hope it is important

- It is important. We have a problem in that we have to have some additional information regarding the object and his movement and this in beforehand. Apart from one possibility, his daily schedule does not allow for any actions to be taken. There are, to put it bluntly, no possibilities at hand.

- In what way?

- No escape routes, the streets are too narrow, no car access, only pedestrian areas, for example. We have to know what he is about to undertake outside his normal schedule and this asap.

- I'll see what I can do, will do my best.

- You'd better, otherwise we'll have to abandon the task. We will finish the task if the provisions are there, but we are not prepared to commit suicide, I hope you understand.

- I said I will do my best, I can't do more

- Sorry, I understand, but you must also understand that we

The Contract (The Mission)

have to have some realistic options to work on, not just the "wish me well" crap. Time flies and the planning and the subsequent execution takes time for it to be successful.

- Ok, as soon as I hear anything outside his normal schedule, I'll let you know. But you will not receive anything in writing. Everything you receive will be through the phone, Holmér said and hung up.

The Contract (The Mission)

February, the 19th 1986

The temperature had fallen even more, but nevertheless they had agreed to meet at 6 am at the MEDBORGARPLATSEN metro station. Martin had brought the equipment with him and he had made all the preparations and the checks for the kill the previous evening. They now could only hope that Palme would take his regular jogging trip, otherwise they either had to wait for another week or hope for some change in his schedule, which would enable them to execute the task elsewhere. It was agreed that Jose would watch for Palme coming out of his flat and tell the others, using the walkie-talkie, when he came out. The other two would then have sufficient time to have corresponding precautions be set up to enable the assassination to be carried out.

Having left the metro station GAMLA STAN around 6:20 am, they split and Jose took off in direction Palme's flat, whereas the other two took off for Järntorget and the spot they had chosen for the kill.

Martin took out his rifle and got prepared. As he had to work without gloves his hands started to get numb from the temperature and he occasionally had to put down the rifle on the ground and put his hands in the pockets of his trousers to warm them up.

Piet impatiently waited for a call from Jose, but having been standing at the assumed position for around 15 minutes, he called Jose on the walkie-talkie and Jose said that there was no sign of Palme. Piet then said to wait until 7 am, then give him a second call and if Palme still had not shown up he then

The Contract (The Mission)

would return to the metro station.

The clock had passed 7, when Piet got a call from Jose saying that no Palme was to be seen. Must be too cold to run, Piet thought about what Jose had said and said to Martin that Palme had not shown up as expected and they consequently had to cancel the attempt and told Martin to put the rifle in the duffel bag again, something which Martin welcomed as he thought he was about to perish from the cold. They then returned to the GAMLA STAN metro station, where Jose already was waiting. Without saying a word they took the next tube back to MEDBORGARPLATSEN and returned to their apartments respectively, where they agreed to meet at 12 pm to discuss and plan further activities. Martin immediately poured himself a two-finger whisky and emptied the glass in one go, just to get warm. He then went to bed again.

At 12 pm, Piet showed up, accepted a cup of coffee from Jose and sat down.

- That was not that much of a success, Piet said.

- The fuck it was, said Martin. Was probably too cold to have a run. And we will have that problem every week. Depending on the weather, he might decide to run or not to run. And there we are waiting and freezing our balls off for something which eventually never comes true, fucking shit it is I tell you. We must have something else to go for, and this asap otherwise we're fucked.

- I also have realised that, but we have to stick to the "jogging tour" option until we have something else to go for, something which is more certain and accurate. And we hope to get this from our contact as soon as possible.

- This means we can only hope, pray and wait for something

The Contract (The Mission)

else to turn up then?

- More or less yes. Momentarily I cannot see another option, being more attractive than this - just hoping and waiting. I know it sucks, but please give me something else to go for. I sincerely hope that our contact here will give us some leads regarding what Palme is up to in the near future.

- How about following him on the weekends? He might be up for something outside his normal schedule then.

- We can do this, but as long as we don't know his intentions, it is difficult to predict what he is up to, meaning that the opportunity is gone before we get there, as we can't run around with a duffel bag full of equipment whilst trying to predict his next move. It is fucking unrealistic, but weekends are by far not off limits if we can get some indication what he is up to in beforehand and this "what" is what we are hoping to get from our contact. Anyway, Jose is not an option as he already has been sort of recognised by Palme's wife. If you want to pursue our mission differently you're welcome, but this is my view.

- I know that we don't have many options to pursue it differently but to wait for them to give us some sort of lead, but for god's fucking sake, why didn't they think about that from the beginning, this is what pisses me off. Palme is not some nobody which you just can walk up to, fire your gun or put a knife in his chest and walk away. You more have to compare it with the Kennedy assassination - he's the head of a state, he is protected, he is kept under surveillance and he has trained body guards, people who will take up the hunt for the assassin the moment Palme gets hit. The kill on Kennedy could be planned and the place could be decided based on information given to the assassins in beforehand. Those people who should have been there to guard Kennedy were more or less extinct the day Kennedy got killed, something which by the way was noted but has been totally

The Contract (The Mission)

ignored as something fishy by the politics and the investigation, and this information – the lack of protection - was vital to the assassins when planning the kill. And such information is something, which we also must have, not just what he is about to undertake but also under which premises. The number one rule in our profession is – don't get caught.

Eventually they agreed to wait for some leads to come from Holmér which they could act on, hoping that it would give them a better and more predictable opportunity to act on and correspondingly to finalise their mission. At the same time they would also pursue the "jogging tour" option.

In order to let out some steam and realising that they momentarily could not achieve much by just sitting around, they agreed to have a dinner together at a noble Italian restaurant not far away from where they stayed, trying to forget about the mission they were on and instead talking about "old times" and a more livable climate.

At the same time Holmér sat at home, thinking about yesterday's phone call he had had with Piet and slowly started to get nervous and impatient. The money has been put aside for the task and he could not allow something to happen, which would force the contractors to cancel what had been agreed. The financiers would not understand any difficulties, which would result in that the contractors were unable to carry out the task. No, as business professionals they were only interested in getting a return on their "investment" and would not tolerate anything but a successful outcome of their investments. Anything else would be devastating for him and inevitably mean his destruction. To put it bluntly, they would destroy him, both financially, mentally as well as socially. Most probably they would want their money back as well something, which he knew he would not be able to live up to.

The Contract (The Mission)

Of course he could put a hit-man on the contractors, but it would just be a primitive way of revenge and would neither solve the core problem nor bring the $600.000 back, which they so far had been given when they accepted the task.

He now realised that the task was more difficult to accomplish than he had anticipated and understood that the contractors had to have more specific information regarding what Palme was up to, Something had to be undertaken, that was inevitable, the question was only – how and what. One possibility was to let any information regarding Palme's whereabouts pass through him, something which was already done to a lesser degree, but the information often came too late and was more of informative nature that something meant to decisively act upon. As a consequence he also needed some help in getting hold of the necessary information. His thoughts steered in the direction the guy who had organised the equipment for the contractors although he was not very keen in having to use his often very questionable resources, however it was the only viable option he could think of at the moment and he had to act fast.

He therefore took the phone and called the guy on his private number.

- Hi, it's me. I need your help. It's a matter of urgency.

- Understand. What can I do for you?

- I need you to intercept someone's flat for a limited period of time

- Presume this means you want audio surveillance on someone's phone.

- Yes, but also what he is talking about when he is at home. However, we are only interested to know what he is up to, nothing else. Only what he intends to undertake, I mean where he goes and when. And this asap.

The Contract (The Mission)

- And may I know whom we are talking about?
- Depends if you accept the assignment or not.
- What sort of payment are we talking about and when is it due to take place?
- $2000 per day plus expenses plus costs for necessary equipment and start is ideally tomorrow. And I want you not only to install the equipment but also to organise and monitor the interception. Can you do it?
- I might, but I need to add someone to help out, hope it is all right with you.
- Should be all right, but only one. No one else is to be involved in the assignment. Is he reliable and trustworthy?
- Sure, he's a relative and a part of the family and we don't betray each other. The family is holy, he said and laughed.
- I know - can you do it? This only was a hypothetical question, as he already knew what the answer would be anyway.
- It is possible, but I cannot start until next week, as I have to finish something before. I also have to organise the corresponding equipment.
- Ok, but not later. Remember, the assignment is crucial to other ongoing projects
- Anything to do with the three foreign guys who you sent to me regarding equipment some time ago?
- No comments, will you then do it, starting next week?
- It's ok, I'll do it. Who's the guy we are to intercept?
- Olof Palme

The Contract (The Mission)

Nothing happened for a couple of seconds and then the guy said

- Jesus Christ. And where is the surveillance thought to take place?

- In his home at Västerlånggatan in GAMLA STAN. Can you do it or are you chickening out?

- No, but ...

- You don't have to understand why, don't you bother your brain with things you don't understand. Just find out where he goes and when, that's it. Got it?

- Ok, Ok "boss".

- And there's another thing. The stuff you would install immediately has to be removed when you get the call to do it, no delays whatsoever are allowed. This is crucial. Someone will phone you, saying "All Clear" and you are then immediately to remove the stuff from the flat. See to that you get a number to a phone booth nearby, where you can be reached – Do you understand?

- No problem. I understand. Whom is to phone me up? he asked in a naïve attempt to get to know more.

- Don't bother whom is to phone you up. You're getting paid for doing a job, not trying to be clever. It doesn't work out. So just remove the shit when you get the call – understand?

- Sorry, I didn't mean to be nosy, it just slipped out of my mouth.

- Whatever. And once you have finished having removed the stuff, the assignment has never taken place. I think you are aware of the consequences in case you try to be clever.

The Contract (The Mission)

- Sure, no problem, you know I cannot stand the socialist crap anyway. Most of my life I have been oppressed by that disease.
- As soon as you hear anything of importance you must call either of the following numbers, Holmér said and gave him the numbers of the two apartments.

Just report what you have come to hear and give the guy the number of the phone booth, nothing else. Then wait for the " All Clear" phone call. By the way, you have to be on call between 5 pm and midnight.

- Understand, the guy said, paying some thoughts regarding the phone numbers himself.

However, he had to stay put and not complain as he could only be in Sweden courtesy of the police, i.e. Holmér, as he often was helping out in executing things, which often tended not to be quite legal as now was the case, and they could throw him out at any time and without notice. Due to his connections with the crime scene in the socialist countries, he had made the deal with the police long time ago as this was the only way to let him and his family stay in Sweden. He did not regret it, as he "legally" could continue to make use of his skills and connections and the police was quite happy having someone who they could turn to in situations, which from a legal point of view were of questionable nature. As long as they played by the rules of the book he did not have to fear being thrown out and he had promised his family not to be "clever' in trying to find out the reason for the police using his skills and connections. Although he had come to know quite a lot behind what they have asked him to execute in the past. He also knew that you couldn't beat the system. Regardless if you lived in a socialist or a capitalist state, in the long run the system, i. e. the state, always won. On the other hand why should he try to be "clever", in the end he lived a comfortable life and the police paid him well for what he was doing for them.

The Contract (The Mission)

Eventually they hung up and Holmér's contact started to make some initial thoughts what might be necessary and how to go about to be in the position to carry out the assignment. As he realised that things had to move fast, he could not mock about for ages trying to unlock any doors. To move fast he ideally needed an Electric Lock Pick Gun for that purpose. He then needed some intercept equipment for the telephone as well as for covering the flat itself. He then phoned his brother in law – Stanislav - up who had a car repair outfit as a cover for being in the position to devote himself to more doubtful legal activities and told him they had an assignment and that they had to start on Monday.

- Monday? It is not possible. I have to finish off some stuff for a customer first.

- Fuck the customer. Tell him to wait as you have a job on the moon or whatever. The assignment is important. It is an assignment from our "protector" himself and it is fucking important to him. Cannot be postponed. Or do you want to return to the socialist paradise? Anyway it is only work which have to be done in the evening. Should not be impossible to do this job on top of the other.

- Oops, ok. I understand. I'll get it organised somehow. Should not present that much of a problem.

- Before Monday, you have to organise some intercept equipment, for telephone as well as for room. Cater for at least 5 rooms. Must also be so good so that you can receive what is taken place long distance. We will also need an Electric Lock Pick Gun for entering the premises as well. Price does not matter. Everything will be reimbursed.

- It will be difficult. I will need some time for that.

- I don't care how much fucking time you need as long as you have the stuff ready by Monday. Oh I forgot, see to that you get hold of two uniforms from Televerket - the Swedish

The Contract (The Mission)

state owned telephone company – as it looks less suspicious having them walking around compared to someone in civilian clothes. Also try to get hold of some Banners from Televerket to put on your van. Oh, I also forgot - we also have to have a Televerket parking allowance as we must park in a pedestrian zone.

- Ok, Ok. I was just about to tell you it is not that easy to get at such equipment, as the equipment cannot be legally obtained as it is illegal to use such equipment.
  - Since when has it bothered you whether things are legal or illegal? Monday is D-Day my friend. This is the drawback, having to adhere to what our "protector" wants, for being permitted to stay in this country.
  - Can you tell me what it is all about?
  - Let's meet on the weekend and I'll tell you. Can't do it over the phone.
  - Sure, no problem. Sunday all right with you?
  - It's ok. I'll come over at around 3 pm then.

He then hung up and started to plan the assignment more in detail, splitting it up in two parts – the physical installation and the interception. As the flat obviously had to be empty, when they installed the intercepting stuff, they had to have the flat under observation as from coming Monday. Presumably Palme lived there alone with his wife and the option that the flat would be empty for at least one hour, was not too bad he reckoned, as she most probably had to fill up the fridge again after the weekend. He also paid some thoughts regarding when she, i.e. Lisbeth Palme, might be off for work or doing her daily shopping tour and guessed that she either would leave for work or preferred doing her shopping in the morning. This meant they might have to show up around 7:30 am, waiting for Lisbeth Palme to leave the flat either for work or for her daily shopping tour.

  - In the meantime, he would have to make some initial

The Contract (The Mission)

surveillance regarding the habits of Palme and primarily his wife, at least from 7 am, to find out when she wa leaving the flat.

Holmér on the other hand phoned Piet's apartment up, just to tell Piet everything had been set in motion.

- It's me. I will keep it short. When something viable turns up outside the normal pattern, you will receive a phone call giving you information, which you might be able to act on.

- Good to hear that something finally is about to happen.

- Once you have finished your mission, you are to phone a number up, which will be given to you with the information. Understand?

- Understand, Piet said.

- Good. Once you are finished with the job you must phone that number and say "All Clear" – just that, nothing else. It is crucial and of utmost importance for guaranteeing the success of the whole job that you do this. Getting the picture ? Do you understand?

- I understand, no sweat, Piet said, not really knowing what it was all about, but reckoned it was the go ahead for some clear or cover-up activities starting to take place. It did not really bother him what they were up to as long as they got the rest of the money.

Holmér then hung up and Piet went over to the other two to inform them regarding what Holmér had said as one of them might have to do the call as well.

The Contract (The Mission)

February, the 21st 1986

The weekend was on and Holmer's contact woke up on Sunday morning around 11 am having a hangover from all the vodka he had consumed the previous night. He always said he had to cut down on the vodka but it hardly ever happened. At least - he though, he had managed to stay sober during the week as you cannot afford to get pissed when you are working. Here in Sweden people expected results when you worked, expecting that you delivered what you had committed to do and not, as was the case in his native country – the socialist paradise - no one was really bothering with what you did as long as the goal that was planned and what had to be produced by the state-owned factories in their five-year plan was met, regardless if it was realistic or not, regardless if you were sober or not.

No one really cared if what was produced did meet the demands and desires from the public or not - the name of the game always was to produce what had been planned by the state, i.e. by the communist party, just to satisfy the party officials, i.e. just to prove that what had been planned was correct and therefore the party officials got promoted correspondingly for their "accurate" planning.

Any adjustments to their fucking plan were unthinkable (would discredit their knowledge which eventually might be the end of their career or something even worse). As the demands and desires by the people were never met or even considered, the only way out of the misery often was to get pissed just to forget that you never would be in the position to

The Contract (The Mission)

fulfil even the smallest desire you had, unless you started to think outside that what the state had planned, i.e. started to join and work in and for the black and of course officially illegal market to make your dreams come true.

However, any political system is bound to fail where personal initiatives and opportunities, aimed at giving people the possibility to fulfil their dreams and hopes, are demolished or oppressed, thus only leaving them with the options - either to obey or face punishment. People are not made that way, regardless where they live. They then turn to other possibilities for fulfilling their needs and desires and this is what ultimately happened in the communist countries. As a result the black market started to grow and the state run market started to diminish.

In the meantime everything had begun to go down the drain or to put it bluntly – the shit had started to hit the fan. The party had - unofficially of course – realised that the socialist experiment could or did not work and started to become more and more dependant on what was produced or could be obtained through the black market. The result was that the black market was tolerated – against a fee to be paid to certain party and police officials – and a system was build up based on the give and take principle. In the black market no law existed, nothing was controlled regarding how and from where you got at things as long as the fee was paid. Even state produced goods started to appear on the black market (of course at a much higher price). Eventually the only way in even getting at state produced goods was through the black market.

In order to survive, people now had to turn to what the black market had to offer them as the state owned shops were constantly empty although the plan what had to be produced always was met. State produced goods got delivered to the black market and the head of the factories were now rewarded for having met the goals of the plan at the same

The Contract (The Mission)

time getting their rewards from those running the black market (i.e. the mafia) for delivering what the market demanded. This system gave certain people enormous opportunities in finding ways to get hold of just about everything as long as the fee was paid to party officials, the customs, the police, you name it.

Although he had lived a good and privileged life in the "paradise", he realised that the system was bound to collapse sooner or later and decided to leave the country. With his superior and exquisite experience in playing the system for his own benefit, exactly knowing where to push "the buttons", he managed to buy himself out of the "paradise", together with his family, claiming asylum in Sweden, which could not be granted. However, having worked and gained experience in such a system made you extremely valuable even for a capitalist system, as you knew where to get at and how to find ways in getting at virtually anything, things which often proved to be illegal. Even in a capitalist system, by paying a reasonable fee to circumvent the hurdles set up by the state proved to work as well – money is king everywhere, regardless where you live, he thought and smiled for himself.

And often even a capitalist run country needed to do and get at things fast and informal, things which would not have been possible to get at without a lot of hassle, time and probably corresponding negative publicity if you would have pursued the matter the official way.

This was the primary reason why Holmér's contact (with his contacts and experience) was so valuable - even to the Swedish system - and was used in getting hold of things fast and to act in areas where you by law were prohibited from doing anything – they had the experience.

With this knowledge he and his family were granted to stay in Sweden as long as he helped the state to circumvent its own rules and laws having been set up to "protect" the country.

The Contract (The Mission)

He took a couple of Aspirins and then went for a shower. Having finished the shower he went to the kitchen, where his wife was about to make breakfast, as usual having a pretty sullen mode, when he returned after having had too much booze the night before.

He went for a cup of coffee and said to his wife that he had to pop over and visit his brother-in-law asking her if she wanted to join him, which she agreed to do as their children, having reached the teenage age, were now living their own life and were already gone.

They left for his brother-in-law's house around 3 pm arriving half an hour later, his wife driving as he did not want to be caught with driving a car and having too much alcohol.

Upon arrival his brother-in-law asked them if they wanted something to drink. Holmér's contact looked at his wife and eventually said that a beer would do. His wife said a coffee would be fine. His brother-in-law asked him to come with him to have a look at the equipment.

- Man, it was difficult to get at everything with the time frame you had given me

- I'm sure you'd manage to get everything anyway, despite your moaning and groaning.

- Yes I did, but I had to put down extra money to get it

- Doesn't matter. It will be reimbursed anyway. Have you tried the stuff?

- Yes I did some tests and I could receive what was said from about 200 metres, maybe more, I reckon.

- Let's hope it will do the trick then. I've made some investigations when to install the stuff and I reckon in the morning should be ok. The flat then seems to be empty, at

The Contract (The Mission)

least for some time.

- Hey, I don't know what you are talking about. How about telling me what the assignment is all about.

- Oops, sorry, I forgot I have not told you anything about what we are going to do. Anyway, we are to intercept what is taken place in Olof Palme's apartment.

- What! Are you really aware of what we are up against? You must be crazy! Olof Palme, that's the Prime Minister for God's fucking sake. What if we get caught, Jesus, you must be crazy accepting such a job.

- We have no choice. Either, we accept the job or we face deportation, You know the rules as well as I do. We are not allowed to be here just because we are nice guys. We just have to see to that we don't get caught - it is that simple. Both of us will have to do the job. It's faster. You worry about the telephones. I'll take the kitchen and the rooms. The only problem is Palme's wife. We have to wait until she leaves the flat.

- It still is a pretty crazy job, though, don't you think?

- I agree, something is going on, but it is not our problem, Maybe they are trying the get rid of him. Would suit me fine, that fucking socialist. He's about to destroy this country the same way as they have destroyed our native countries. Hope they succeed with what they are up to.

- But if we get caught, there is no way we can avoid deportation anyway.

- Then we don't get caught for fucking sake! What's wrong with you? You don't get anything is this world for free.

- Sorry, I did not mean to upset you, but going after Number One is not really a piece of cake, something which you just

The Contract (The Mission)

do for fun.

- Agree, but as I said, this is nothing we can avoid or reject, so the only alternative is see to that the job becomes a success. Agree?

- Agree, sorry.

- What we will do is to go there tomorrow morning and wait for Palme's wife to leave the flat. Then we enter the building as employees for Televerket – by the way did you get hold of the uniforms, the banners and the parking allowance?

- I did, but I had to put up quite a considerable sum of money. Fuck, everyone wants to have more money nowadays, with the tax brackets we have here.

- Surprised? I'm not. No one can exist on what is left after tax anymore, by the way, what about the Lock Pick Gun, Did you get it as well?

- Yes, I got one. An amazing piece. Opens doors in no time. Presume it is illegal to possess one otherwise locks in general would be superfluous.

- Don't know, but I suspect they are illegal as well. Never mind, let's use them for now and get rid of all the stuff once we have completed the job. Anyway, put on the uniform and the banners and bring the rest of the stuff with you and come to my place around 7 am tomorrow. We will then drive to GAMLA STAN, where Palme lives – he lives at Västerlånggatan 31 - and wait for Palme's wife to leave the flat. Btw, I was there looking for three days last week and everyday she seems to leave the flat around 8 in the morning. Let's hope that she will do it tomorrow as well.

- OK, no sweat. I'll be there. Let's go back to the ladies before they start wondering what we are up to or do you have anything else, which you want to discuss?

The Contract (The Mission)

- No, on top of my head I cannot come up with anything else. I think that was all. You're right, let's go back to our wives to avoid any physical concussions, Holmér's contact said and laughed.

- They returned to their wives, who had prepared for coffee and cakes. Around 6 pm Holmér's contact and his wife left his sister and returned home for supper.

On the their way home his wife asked him what was so important that he had to meet his brother-in-law today. He answered that they had got an important contract from their "protector", which couldn't wait and had to be carried out asap. This meant that he had to start on the contract tomorrow. His wife then asked him what it was all about but Holmér's contact said that unfortunately he was not in the position to tell her anything about the contract – the contract was simply highly classified stuff, he answered prevaricated.

The Contract (The Mission)

February, the 22ⁿᵈ 1986

Stanislav – the brother-in-law – showed up as agreed at 8 am the next morning at Holmér's contact place. The van had the Televerket banner on the sides and a parking permit was attached on the front window. He also had put the Televerket uniform under his jacket. He also had a uniform for his wife's brother with him, which his wife's brother also put on before they left for GAMLA STAN.

The traffic was pretty dense, but they managed to arrive to GAMLA STAN in roughly ½ hour, eventually arriving at Västerlånggatan five minutes later. No-one passing by objected to the fact that a Televerket van was parked in a pedestrian zone. They had put the van so that they could see when someone was leaving or entering the building. Around 8 am a woman, resembling Palme's wife left the building in direction City centre. Two minutes later Holmér's contact and his brother-in-law left the van carrying a bag resembling the equipment the Televerket employees were using when they were on-call.

As anticipated, the front door to number 31 proved to be locked. Stanislaw took out the Lock Pick Gun and 10 seconds later they managed to enter the building. They had left their own jackets in the van just to make it visible to everyone that they were on a job for Televerket in case someone were to see them. Eventually they reached Palme's flat, Stanislaw took the Lick Pick Gun and they were in the apartment 10 seconds later.

The Contract (The Mission)

Holmér's contact told Stanislaw to take care of the phones, whilst he would intercept the kitchen, the living and dining room. There also proved to be a sort of office space, which got bugged the same way. The whole procedure did not take them more than about 10 minutes to finish. Before leaving the flat they listened for another minute if someone was in the stairwell, before they swiftly left the building without having met anyone. All in all the procedure had not taken more than 15 minutes until they were back in the van again and left to be back at around 5 pm to monitor what the Palme family might have on their minds in the immediate future. Back at 5 pm, they parked at a different place to avoid creating any possible connections to Palme's flat. Nothing of importance was broadcasted and they returned home around 10 pm.

February, the 26th 1986

Piet woke up around 5 am, took a quick shower, got dressed and then made himself a cup of coffee together with a cheese sandwich. Although he found the Swedish bread being very weird and awkward in the beginning, in the meantime he had got used to the sweet "limpa" they had and had even come to like it.

The day before they had been together to plan for another attempt today, hoping they would have more luck this time, however with the temperatures they momentarily were experiencing every morning they only had limited hope of succeeding with what they were here to accomplish.

They met at the metro station at 6 am and took the first tube that arrived to GAMLA STAN setting up the same scenario as last week. There was a fierce wind howling through the narrow alleys of GAMLA STAN, resulting in an even more hostile temperature.

All three thought that there was no way in hell that Palme would go for his jogging tour in such a weather. This also proved to be true as Palme did not turn up as they had hoped and Jose had to convey the frustrating message to Martin and once again they had to abandon what they had intended to accomplish. All in all they were pretty pissed off with the job as it seemed to drag on forever. The only thing they could do was to wait, wait for Palme either to start jogging again or

The Contract (The Mission)

waiting for a phone call telling them that he was about to undertake something outside his normal schedule. They were not in the position to plan anything themselves, as they had envisaged - something, which all three found more than dissatisfying and frustrating.

They then returned to the metro station and took the tube back to the flats however Jose decided to wait though and see when Palme really took off for work, which proved to be around 7:30, definitely not intending to go for a jogging tour in the present very cold and blustery weather. He then walked to the GAMLA STAN metro station and took the tube back to the flat, being in a pretty desolate mode. He sincerely hoped that something would turn up, which would enable them to finish off their "mission" and return back to the warmth, although Lisbon, this time of the year, probably was not to compare to what he was used to from Africa, but still better than Stockholm, he thought for himself and started to drift away with his thoughts, dreaming of "better days".

The Contract (The Mission)

February, the 28th 1986

The weather had become somewhat more bearable than the last couple of days – it was not that cold anymore and the strong wind had more or less disappeared. All three woke up pretty late. Piet made his usual breakfast and Martin and Jose went to a nearby café to have their breakfast.

As they now were more or less dependant on leads coming from outside, at least one of them had to stay on-call in case they were to get a phone call hopefully giving them the necessary leads to finish off their "mission".

Around 6 pm Piet's phone rung. He took the receiver and said "Hello".

- I have a message for you regarding your assignment, interested?

- Yes, I am interested, Piet said and could hear that the guy spoke with an Eastern European accent.

- Your man of interest is leaving the flat to watch a movie. No guards.

- I understand.

- The cinema is Grand at Sveavägen. The movie in question is Mozart, the movie starts at 9 pm. When finished you then have to phone the number .. - and the guy then gave him the number of the phone booth, which Piet immediately had to phone once the "mission" had been carried out.

The Contract (The Mission)

- Good, anything more?

- No, this is all I've got for you, the guy said and hung up.

Piet put down the receiver and took a deep breath. Think this might be what we have been hoping for, he thought and went over to the other two.

Martin opened the door and Piet said, quite agitated

- Hi, I've got news for you

- Anything useful? Martin asked

- I believe there is. Palme is leaving the flat to watch a movie tonight   – without bodyguards.

- Really? When? Jose asked.

- The movie starts at 9 pm, I don't know when he leaves the flat. This means we have to be at his flat ASAP and then follow him from there. I would suggest that two of us wait at the metro station, whilst one goes to the flat, waiting for him to come out. If he walks to the metro station it is ok. If he doesn't, the one at the flat will have to call the other two over our walkie-talkies. Does it sound   feasible to you?

Having discussed how to go about, they finally agreed with the scenario Piet had proposed. They agreed that Piet would take the task to go to the flat whilst the other two would wait at the metro station. They then agreed to leave individually not waiting for each other. Piet then returned to his flat and got ready, additionally put the gun and walkie-Talkie in his pockets, and left the flat.

He arrived at Palme's flat around 7:30 pm, hoping that Palme would show up as expected. The bodyguards were gone, a scenario, which would have been totally unthinkable to have in South-Africa when it came to guarding and protecting their Prime Minister Botha. Also how Prime Minister Botha lived, would have been out of the question.

The Contract (The Mission)

At around 08:35 pm Piet saw Palme coming out with his wife walking direction metro station "GAMLA STAN". Piet took his Walkie-Talkie and gave the other two the message and started to walk towards the metro station about 10 meters behind the Palme couple.

Martin is standing at a staircase about 100 meters from the metro entrance when he picks up the message. Jose is close to the entrance when the message comes. Both of them then start to walk in direction entrance and when arriving at the entrance they wait for the Palme couple and Piet to show up although they have agreed not to approach Piet. When the train arrives, Martin and Jose enter the same car as the Palme couple. Jose is very careful not to turn his face in direction Palmes'. Piet jumps in the car at the very last moment just to give the impression that he does not belong to Martin and Jose.

At RÅDMANSGATAN Palme and his wife disembark the train followed by Martin and Jose. Piet follows somewhat further behind.

The Palmes' then enter the Grand cinema and Martin and Jose continue with their walk as if they just accidentally happened to have left the train at the same metro station as the Palmes'.

Piet however does stop at the street corner and tries to reach Martin and Jose, telling them to wait somewhere for further instructions.

Once the movie has begun – around 09:10 pm - Piet approaches the cinema to find out when the movie is due to end and gets the information that the movie is scheduled to end around 11 pm, something which he also tells Martin and Jose over the Walkie-Talkie.

Around an hour later, Piet asks Martin and Jose to be prepared and have a look around for places, which might be suitable for finishing off their "mission", something which they

The Contract (The Mission)

already had started to do, they said. Piet then says that he intends to go to the other side of the street opposite to the cinema to get a better view of the entrance and the people that emerged once the film had finished. He then would communicate with them through his Walkie-Talkie, telling them in which direction Palme is leaving. As all three of them are fluent in Afrikaans, he suggests them to communicate in Afrikaans in order not to reveal to by-passers what they are up to.

At around 11:10 pm the movie finishes and the people start to emerge from the cinema. Palme and his wife turn right and start to walk in direction Hötorget.

Piet takes turns on his Walkie-Talkie calling Martin telling him Palme is on his way. Martin acknowledges the call. Piet starts to walk in direction Hötorget but on the other side of Sveavägen, keeping an eye on Palme and his wife.

Palme and his wife pass Jose and Martin approximately 100 metres from the cinema, not really taking notice of their existence. Jose and Martin are following the Palme couple at a 50 metre distance, realising they cannot wait much longer if they intend to take action. Palme stops at a display window and Martin sees his chance, taking his Glock pistol out of his pocket, cocking the pistol at the same time increasing his steps. As he is about 5 meters from Palme he raises the gun firing two shots at the Palme couple and without looking runs to a nearby entry of the underground station HöTORGET, buys a ticket to MEDBORGARPLATSEN and disappears in the waiting crowd.

Jose sees Palme and his wife fall, walks by as if he wants to help and miraculously sees the two shells from the two shots Martin has made, picks them up, then cautiously leaving, taking the same direction as Martin at the same time throwing she shells in a nearby litter-box.

From the other side of the street Piet registers how Palme and his wife fall and how Martin and Jose disappears into the

The Contract (The Mission)

underground station, then continues to walk, crosses Kungsgatan direction Sergels Torg and T-CENTRALEN, where he finds a telephone booth and phones the number he has been given, saying the two words "All Clear" and hangs up, taking the tube to MEDBORGARPLATSEN.

Holmér's contact gets the message and tells his brother-in-law that the message has been delivered, meaning they have to remove the intercept equipment at Palme's flat immediately as the police most likely will show up in the next hour or so. About 20 minutes thereafter the equipment has been removed and any visual traces revealing that an interception has taken place is gone.

They then return to Stanislav's car repair outfit to get rid of the equipment they' have used and the Televerket banner on the van and then return to their homes respectively, waiting for Holmér to phone and give them further instructions – if any - how to go about with their assignment.

Piet arrived at MEDBORGARPLATSEN around midnight and, from there, he immediately phoned the other flat. Martin answered the phone saying

- Hello

- Hi, it's me. Any news?

- Watch your TV

- Ok, will do. See you then, Piet said and hung up and turned on his TV.

The television was reporting about the Palme assassination and although he could not understand any Swedish, from what was shown, he understood that Palme was dead. He took a deep breath, realising that the mission they had had was accomplished and that they now had to make sure that they left the country ASAP, but in a orderly manner, i.e. without raising any suspicions. He suspected they had to stay in the flats for at least a week – perhaps even a fortnight, before

The Contract (The Mission)

even thinking of making any moves and thoughts regarding leaving the country. Maybe the best bet was to have them leave at different times.

The District Police Commissioner Holmér, being on vacation in Borlänge , a small town about 250 kms northwest of Stockholm and officially not to be reached, got the information regarding what had taken place from one of his most trustworthy colleagues being one of the core team members – Holmér had given him instructions where he was to be reached – some time after midnight. Holmér had to take a deep breath when he heard the news and poured himself a stiff glass of Tullamore Dew – Irish whiskey.

Jesus Christ, he thought. What have they done? Have they done the right thing? What actions now have to be undertaken? He realised that he had to take some action in order to divert the investigation from what really had happened, however he realised he had to act as if he had got the news the official way. He therefore went to bed and tried to get some sleep, setting the alarm for 6 am the following morning.

The Contract (The Mission)

March, the 1st 1986

As a result of the assassination the following events immediately took place:

- At 12:25 am: The official on duty at the National Police Board (Criminal Division), Christer Sjöberg, was informed and he then contacted the Director General of the National Police Board, Holger Romander.

- At about 12:30 am: Sandström - Head of the Police Department - and Welander - Deputy District Police Commissioner - arrived at the police headquarters and Welander then took charge of the police efforts.

- At 12:45 am: Ingvar Carlsson – the Vice Prime Minister - arrived at the Cabinet Office by cab. After 1:00 am several members of the Cabinet arrived at Rosenbad (the seat of the Government). Many of them came by taxi.

- At 1:15 am: The officer on guard at the military headquarters received a call from the military attaché in Washington, who wanted the rumours regarding the Palme killing to be confirmed. The officer on guard did not know anything about any assassination.

- At 1:30 am: The Supreme Commander of the Swedish Armed Forces, Lennart Ljung, was informed at his home by the officer on guard at the military headquarters.

- Just before 2 am: Welander ordered a nationwide alert immediately be sent out. He then made his way to Sabbatsberg's Hospital, where Palme was brought.

The Contract (The Mission)

- At 3:07 am: The Cabinet held a meeting, which began at Rosenbad. Thirteen members were gathered from the start. Welander and Hjälmroth were there informing the Cabinet members about the police efforts.

- At 5:06 am: Ordered by Welander. a correction of the nation widealert was sent out.

- At 5:15 am: The Cabinet held a press conference beginning.

- As the alarm went off at 6 am on the morning, March the 1st, Holmér got up and turned the television on facing that the assassination of Palme was on all channels. Realising that he could not wait much longer to return to Stockholm if he wanted to be in charge of the investigation that inevitably was to come about as a result of the assassination. He took a quick shower, got dressed and went for an early breakfast then phoning his deputy Gösta Welander up, telling him that he would be on his way to Stockholm as-soon-as-possible, just to make it look like he just had heard about what had happened over the Television, in order to avoid any possible suspicions. He then checked out but before he went to the nearest phone booth and phoned the guy up having helped him out with intercepting Palme's place and told him that the assignment was accomplished and that the money he requested for 10 days work - $20000 plus equipment – another $5000 - was to be transferred from Holmér's Gibraltar account to his Swiss account as had been done numerous times. He then phoned the one having initiated everything up at his home at Djursholm.

- Hi, it is me, no names please. Suppose you know the reason for my call.

- Yes, I know.

- The task has been accomplished and I must ask you to pay the outstanding $500,000 as agreed as-soon-as-possible

The Contract (The Mission)

plus an additional 10% to cover for the administration fee - that is $50,000. We also had some unforeseeable costs – we had to use some local resources to finish off some crucial work - work, which we couldn't do without - meaning that another $50,000 plus $5,000 as administration fee, will have to be paid as well. The $500,000 plus the $50,000 are to go to the same account as the first $500,000. Regarding the administration fee, please follow the same procedure as was taken last time. I sincerely hope that there will not be anymore costs, which have to be redeemed.

- Should not be a problem.

- As I will be pretty occupied in the foreseeable future, I must ask you to refrain from any attempts trying to contact me. If needed, I will contact you.

- Understand, said the initiator, agreeing to what has to be undertaken, however finding it utterly discomforting having to be told off like this. On the other hand he fully realised that he didn't have much experience in these areas and therefore had to rely on outside help.

- Bye, Holmér said and hung up

Realising he had just might have earned $25,000, depending on the outcome of the investigations, he then took off for Stockholm arriving around 11:00 am, immediately taking charge of the search for the murderer.

With his business partners, the initiator organised the outstanding payment to be carried out the same way as was done with the initial payment.

The very same day a managerial group was put together within the police force and Ingvar Carlsson, the Vice Premier Minister, in reality just a puppet for Holmér and SÄPO and their doings, was appointed as the new Prime Minister of Sweden. Carlsson and Holmér had known each other since they had been working together in the beginning of the

The Contract (The Mission)

eighties and were on good terms, meaning that the bonds between the Government and the managerial group was reinforced. As a result of Holmér's close connection with the Government made it possible for Holmér to steer the investigation in the preferred direction or interpretation to be taken by the managerial group during their investigation.

Holmér realised that he soon had to come up with a convincing "story", aiming at steering the investigation in a direction to enable the three "missionaries" to leave the country without being caught in a border clampdown. A good idea might be to listen to so-called "witnesses", people looking for getting some kind of recognition, therefore prepared to come up with all sorts of crap, just to have that recognition, even if it was for a couple of minutes. Holmér therefore ordered the managerial group to follow up on any leads, coming from the "witnesses". Should it prove to be a lead, pointing at the "missionaries", it could either be rejected or put on low priority. Was often a useful method for cocking things up if need be.

The Contract (The Mission)

March, the 3rd 1986

On March the 3rd, the rest of the money as well as his "administration fee" got deposited in the respective accounts with the Gibraltar accountant. The accountant already had received the instructions from Holmér how to go about with the money in his account and immediately organised a transfer to Piet's account in Liechtenstein.

In the meantime Piet was paying Martin and Jose a visit to discuss what to do next. They agreed that they had to get rid of the equipment as-soon-as possible, preferably dumping it in the water somewhere, the problem only being that there had to find a place not covered with ice at this time if the year. From what they had seen from Stockholm, they thought the water close to Stockholm Harbour might be a possibility, although the possibility to get caught when trying to get rid of the equipment there was bigger.

Although they saw the problem they all agreed to look for a suitable place somewhere around SLUSSEN, where the waters - as far as they could recall - were free from ice. They also agreed to do it on an individual basis, i.e. each of them doing it on their own - one dump per day, starting tomorrow with Jose. As from now on each of them were to act on their own, no more meetings, no - nothing. They also agreed on letting Jose leave Sweden first, only staying in the flat for another week and then Martin staying for two weeks and then leave and finally Piet leaving Sweden after three weeks. Each of them was to leave Sweden the same way was they had entered the country. Any outstanding payments were to be settled by Piet once he had left the country, provided the cli-

The Contract (The Mission)

ent had transferred the money to his bank account in Liechtenstein.

Before leaving Sweden, Martin and Piet were to settle any outstanding issues regarding the flats – no hassle, just pay what the agent requested. Piet then said good-bye to Martin and Jose, hoping they would see each other again, sometime in the future, in another "mission", and left the flat.

The Contract (The Mission)

March, the 8th 1986

Holmér arranged to set up hearings with known criminals and various people who in one way or another had been pinpointed as suspected a result of the flood of tips having come from the "witnesses". As a result of this strategy a 33-year old man became of great interest to the investigation as different witnesses stated that they had seen him not far away from where Palme had been shot, only a few hours before Palme was shot, something, which perfectly suited Holmes, as it could not possibly have anything to do with what actually had happened.

The guy also very explicitly had aired his hatred towards Palme, which was even better. On the 8th he was questioned, but was later released,

The same day Jose said good-bye to Martin, left the flat and took the tube to T-CENTRALEN and took the train to Frankfurt, Germany, having bought a one-way ticket to Frankfurt the day before.

However, on the 12th – due to new circumstances – the 33-year old man was taken into custody something, which was decided by the Chief Prosecutor.

The Contract (The Mission)

March, the 14th 1986

Martin was becoming increasingly bored, now being alone in the flat and thought about visiting the chick, whom he already had met a couple of times, before leaving Sweden. On the 14th he therefore phoned her up and excused himself for not having phoned her up earlier – due to work related matters, he said - and suggested, they should meet for a farewell dinner as he had to leave Sweden in the next couple of days. He proposed to meet at the same restaurant they had visited the last time. She said it would be nice and they agreed to meet at the restaurant and that she would book a table for 7:30 pm the following day.

The weather had become somewhat more bearable from a temperature point of view and the temperature now had risen to around 0 degrees, which made him skip the long-johns and the woolen cap as he hated being covered in piles of clothes all the time. At around 7 pm Martin left the flat and took the tube to RÅDMANSGATAN and the restaurant.

They had a gorgeous dinner chatting just about everything - from the Swedish weather to the assassination of Olof Palme something, which he tried to block as much as possible without raising any suspicions.

After the dinner they went to her flat, made love and then finally fell asleep.

The Contract (The Mission)

March, the 16th 1986

The next morning - on the 16th - breakfast was waiting for Martin, when he woke up. The woman already having had her morning shower, having put on a morning gown sat down at the breakfast table as well

- Want some coffee?, she asked
- Yes please, Martin answered
- Presume you want it with milk and sugar as all Englishmen.
- Yes I do, Martin said and smiled

    She then poured some coffee in a mug, together with milk and sugar and handed Martin the mug.

- Did you sleep well?
- Sure did, thanks for yesterday by the way.
- Your welcome. When are you leaving?
- Don't know yet but I believe, Tuesday. Just want the go from the client that everything works to satisfaction.
- Can't you stay a couple of days longer
- Sorry, but there are lot of work to be done elsewhere. Everyone is after having a security system be installed nowadays. Security seems to be the name of the game nowadays.
- It did not help to save Olof Palme from being murdered.
- I heard, he didn't want any security people around that

The Contract (The Mission)

evening

- And all of a sudden, just because there is no security around, he gets murdered, I find it very strange, don't you? How could the murderer have known that?
- Don't know, maybe he was followed
- Then he must have been under surveillance, but why. He didn't to anyone any harm and he fought against injustice and inequality especially for the black people of Africa, being against those countries oppressing the blacks.

Martin could feel that his face got red and he was about to burst – what had the fucker done for him, just because he was born white, anything but to ruin his life and the life of his parents and siblings?

- I don't agree with you. It is very easy to criticise something if you are not a part of it, not really interested in the outcome of your criticism.
- But he did, he wanted to help the black and the poor
- And what about those who where not black and poor, people who had build up the country and build up their life based on their assumptions?
- But they are oppressing the blacks and just using them.
- That's bullshit, no one were oppressing and using anyone. Before Palme helped ruin everything, they all lived together without anyone paying attention to whether you were white or black.
- What do you mean? He did not ruin anything. He tried to help.
- To help whom? And what about all the white people who lived there for generations, having build up there life there, Martin said, feeling that he started to loose control.
- They can live there as well, but the blacks must have their

The Contract (The Mission)

fair share as well.

- And what about South-Rhodesia and Mugabe? He more or less forced all whites to leave the country.
- What do you mean with South-Rhodesia? Do you mean Zimbabwe?
- No, I mean South-Rhodesia. Zimbabwe was the name Mugabe gave the country.
- Why do you get so worked up. It has nothing to do with you.
- Yes, it has, Martin now felt he had lost control. I was born and grew up there and my parents, my siblings and I were forced to leave the country for a country I had never seen or ever had any relations to. I just happened to be British, because South-Rhodesia happened to be a part of the British Empire when I was born.

  And Palme helped to ruin what we had possessed and built up. We were not privileged at the expense of the black population or ever had hostile feelings towards them. We built everything up with our own hands. We did not take anything from anyone. We even helped the blacks in that we gave them work and food. Fuck, the racists were the blacks, not the white population and Palme helped them becoming racists.
- The way you talk, you talk like you hated Palme and even were prepared to murder him.
- Yes, maybe I was, suddenly realising that he had let himself be too emotional and had gone too far.

The woman turned all white, realising whom was sitting opposite her at the breakfast table and raised and went for the phone, but before she managed to dial the Swedish Emergency number 112, Martin was at her, grabbing her with his left arm from behind around her neck and his right arm around her head and made a swift clockwise turn of her head, at the same time mumbling a low "sorry", and a low crack could be heard and the woman went limp – he had broken her neck.

Stupid bitch, Martin said to himself, why did she have to discuss Palme again? Why couldn't she just have used another subject?

Martin then realised he had to do some sort of cover-up, sat down thinking for a while and then came up with the idea that he could make it look like she had slipped on the bathroom mat, whilst going for a bath, banging her neck at the bathtub brim. He therefore dragged here to the bathroom trying to set up the scene making it look natural. He then tried to remember where he might have put any fingerprints and cleaned the dishes and cutlery from their breakfast and put them where they belonged. He then waited until it got dark, before he filled the bathtub with water and left around 8 pm, hoping that his cover up was sufficient in making it look like an accident.

He suspected that it would take a couple of days before someone missed her, but sooner or later her colleagues at work would start to wonder why she didn't turn up and would most probably try to contact her. At the latest he had to be out of the country by Wednesday, he reckoned, therefore he had to buy a ticket for the train and ferry first thing on Monday.

He decided not to tell Piet what had taken place in order to avoid additional complications.

Also on the 16th, a witness from the Ivory Coast picked out the 33-year old man from an arranged line-up something, which – according to the police - "strengthened" the circumstantial evidences against the guy. However, as he had failed to identify the man in a separate photo identification a couple of days earlier, this resulted in that the man was set free by the Chief Prosecutor on the 19th of March.

Holmér got furious when he heard about the decision and this led to ending any relation between Holmér and the Chief Prosecutor, which might have existed. As a result of the incident,

The Contract (The Mission)

Holmér requested the Chief Prosecutor be replaced, however his request was rejected.

The managerial group held on to the 33-year old man as a suspect, which in the end led to severe disharmony between the group and the Chief Prosecutors as the group deliberately tried to hold back any attempts in proving the man's innocence.

Later, as the 33-year old man finally managed to produce a reliable alibi for the evening Palme was assassinated and he consequently was dismissed from any suspicions, Holmér realised that another "prime suspect" had to be found to divert the investigation from what really had happened and the choice fell on PKK – the Kurdish Labour Party, which in fact had been of interest to the investigation from the very beginning.

The Contract (The Mission)

March, the 17th 1986

On Monday the 17th, Martin went to a travel agency and bought a return trip to London with train to Gothenburg and then ferry from Gothenburg to Immingham for the following day. He then went to the rental agency to finalise the rent for the flat, telling them that he would leave the following day. The agent told him – as everything had been paid in advance - just to leave the keys in the flat and close the door. Asking him if the flat had been to his satisfaction, Martin told the agent that the flat had fully lived up to his expectations and that he would gladly rent the flat again, should he get another assignment in Sweden.

The following day Martin took the train from the Central Station in Stockholm and left for London, happy to leave Sweden, its people and its unbearable climate. He bought a ticket for the ferry from Gothenburg leaving for Immingham the same evening.

As Gunilla did not turn up at work on Monday no particular interest was paid to her absence as you could claim sick, without your pay being cut in Sweden, however as Wednesday came and they still had not heard anything from her, her boss asked one of her colleagues to try to phone her up. As no one answered the phone, she told their boss, who then asked the colleague to try a couple of more times to phone her up and - if possible - to pay Gunilla a visit after work if she was unsuccessful in reaching her through the phone. As the colleague was unsuccessful in reaching Gunilla, she then went to her flat and rang the bell, but no one opened the door. She then

The Contract (The Mission)

realised that something must be wrong and phoned the police, which said that they momentarily were short of resources but would come and take a look at the apartment the next day and asked Gunilla's colleague to be there at 09:00 am as well, should she not have been successful in contacting the woman after all. Having been unsuccessful in contacting Gunilla, she told her boss that she had been requested by the police to show up at Gunilla's flat at 09 am the next day as the police might need some information from her.

The Contract (The Mission)

March, the 18th 1986

At around 9 am the next day, together with a police officer, she showed up at the apartment, rang the bell but nothing happened. The police officer then opened the door with a Lock Pick Gun he had brought with him, entered the flat and saw the woman lying on the floor in the bathroom, presumably dead since a couple of days. From what could be seen, the police officer suspected – as the bath tub was full of water and the fact that she was wearing a morning gown - that the woman was after going for a bath and must have slipped on the bath mat thereby hitting her head on the brim. Also no signs that a fight was to have taken place could be seen. Eventually he decided to call the homicide squad to make them decide what might have happened and what to do next.

He also took the address and phone numbers – work and home – from the woman's colleague, just in case the police needed some additional information.

The Homicide squad came an hour later and could only confirm the death of the woman, assuming the woman must have lost her balance when slipping on the bath mat, thereby breaking her neck when her neck hit the brim. Consequently they then called for an ambulance, which took the body to the forensics for further examination.

The colleague, totally devastated from what she had witnessed - was then allowed to leave the premises. She then went down to RÅDMANSGATAN underground station and took the tube to FRIDHEMSPLAN and St. Görans Hospital, where she worked and reported to her boss what she had witnessed. Her boss told her that she could take the time off for the day if she wanted to, but she declined, although she still was pretty shattered from what she had experienced.

The Contract (The Mission)

March, the 24th 1986 - Stockholm

The following Monday, March the 24th, at the forensic department, medical examiner examined the body and found it strange that the fall had not produced any signs of blue marks or bruises anywhere, not even on the neck, which was normal when having an injury. The medical examiner therefore decided to carry out an autopsy on the body, just to be sure.

He then found out that the neck injury causing the death, could not possibly had come from slipping on the bath mat and hitting the neck on the brim, but rather resulting from some sort of physical impact having taken place. He further investigated the reason for the broken neck and came to the conclusion that the neck had been broken through a violent act, most likely from someone violently and unexpectedly having twisted the neck. Presumably it must have been a very strong person, knowing exactly how to go about carrying out such an act and also must have done it before as it was very professionally done. To the medical examiner it now was no longer an accident but a murder case.

The very same day, Piet went to a travel agency and bought a single ticket to Frankfurt for the following day and then went to the rental agency to finalise the rent of the flat. The agent said the same thing he had said when Martin checked out and also asked Piet the same questions. Piet also stressed that he had been very satisfied with the flat and most likely would rent it again, should he get another assignment in Sweden. He said that he intended to leave the flat as of the next day and

The Contract (The Mission)

the agent said that he only had to lock the door and throw the key in the gap normally used for getting the post.

The Contract (The Mission)

March, the 25th 1986

The next day – on Tuesday the 25th - Piet took a cab to Stockholm International Airport – Arlanda – and left for Frankfurt, Germany. Once having landed in Frankfurt he then bought a connecting flight to Johannesburg, South Africa in Frankfurt – using his real name - scheduled to leave the same evening, happy to return home to South Africa and Durban and the warmth.

In Johannesburg, whilst waiting for a connecting flight, Piet ran into one of his neighbours who also worked for the Civil Cooperation Bureau (CCB), South Africa's "Green Berets", however employed to orchestrate and coordinate any work to do with counterterrorism, i.e. work being carried out by Piet and his likes.

As Piet often was off carrying out assignment tasks, they did not meet too often, the neighbour therefore innocently asked Piet what he had been up to in the recent past.

Piet said he had been to Europe for some non-CCB work, immediately realising that it might not have been so overly clever to brag about with his last assignment.

The neighbour then asked where in Europe Piet has been and Piet reluctantly said Yugoslavia as things had started to go haywire there he said.

Piet's neighbour found it somewhat strange that Piet was going all the way to Europe to carry out work as momentarily there was more work to be carried out in South Africa than they could possibly handle anyway, however it was not his

The Contract (The Mission)

business what Piet had been up to and stopped asking further; however back in his head his curiosity begun to build up and he wrote down some notes to help reminding him what to look for when returning to work next time. Being an admin guy, having access to all the information having been written down on all mercenaries, he wanted to see if anything had been written down and saved in Piet's folder in regard to what Piet had been up to next time he returned to the office - of course only out of curiosity he smiled for himself.

Somewhat later Piet embarked the aircraft for the last leg home to Durban.

Having landed at Durban Airport and disembarked the airplane the neighbour asked Piet if he would fancy a trip home with him as his wife was picking him up but Piet politely turned the offer down, saying that his wife was picking him up as well, not particularly interested having to answer all sorts of weird questions regarding what he had been up to in Europe.

During the trip back home – he had taken a taxi from the airport – he realised he have to be very careful in what he was saying and to whom he was talking to, in avoiding the shit from hitting the fan.

His neighbour on the other hand could not quite understand why Piet was so reluctant in answering questions regarding what the assignment had been all about. After all he only had been body guarding some important Serbian guy, he had said. On the other hand; it shouldn't really concern him what people being hired as externals by CCB were doing as long as they were fulfilling their obligations towards CCB.

Anyway - I will be on holiday for 3 1/2 weeks and shouldn't be concerned with what other people are up to, he thought for himself. I might come back on the subject once I am back from my holiday.

March, the 26th 1986

In Stockholm the medical examiner put his report on Gunilla together and sent the report off to the appropriate homicide department the following day – Wednesday, the 26th.

The Contract (The Mission)

Stockholm, March, the 28ᵗʰ 1986

On Friday the 28ᵗʰ, a police officer within the homicide squad got to read the report from the forensic team and decided to phone the colleague of the deceased victim having found the body up. He managed to get hold of her, just before she was about to leave work, and they agreed to meet at a nearby café during her lunch-break the following Monday.

The Contract (The Mission)

March, the 31st 1986

On Monday the 31st, when he entered the café, he saw only one woman sitting alone and presumed she was the colleague he had agreed to meet, he approached her table and asked her if she was expecting an interview with a Police Officer. Having said yes, he then presented himself as the Police Officer and she asked him to sit down. Having sat down, he ordered a black coffee and started with some nonsense talk just to make the woman feel more at ease he then asked her

- Did you know your colleague Gunilla very well?
- Not that well, but we often went together and had lunch.
- Did she have a boyfriend?
- No I don't think she had, she had had one but they split and she got pretty upset from the split up. Did not want another serious relationship she said.
- Do you know the name of her then partner?
- I only know that his name was Lars but not his surname.
- Anyone else?
- Only that she went to London end of January to visit a friend. She also mentioned that she had met a good-looking Englishman on the ferry back from England, whom she also seemed to have met here in Stockholm.
- Which ferry line was it?
- I don't know, but I know she took the ferry from Gothen-

The Contract (The Mission)

burg

- Did she mention the name of her acquaintance?
- I think his name was Nigel, but she did not mention any surname.
- Was he living in Sweden?
- No I think he only was here for some sort of security installation.
- Did she say anything how long he would stay?
- No
- Did she say where he stayed during his visit here?
- No, she only said he was very secretive about where he stayed. Had to do with what he was doing, she said
- Do you know when she returned back from England?
- I am not sure but I think it either was on the 29th or on the 30th of January. But as I said I am not sure.
- It is ok, anything else you might remember?
- No, not on top of my head.
- Thanks a lot for the information, it might be helpful.
- You're welcome.
- They changed subject and talked for another 5 minutes and then she said she had to leave for work and said good-bye.

The police officer made some additional notes from the information she had given him. When he came back to his office, he looked up which ferry lines travelled to England and phoned them up one after the other explaining the reason for his call and asked to be connected to the booking department. After having been redirected to the booking department he then, after having said who he was, asked them if anyone with victim's name and someone with the Christian name Nigel

The Contract (The Mission)

had travelled with one of their ferries on the 29th or on the 30th from England to Gothenburg respectively. For the 30th one of the ferry lines found her name and 4 men with the Christian name Nigel having travelled to Gothenburg, 2 having bought a single ticket, two of them having booked a round trip for 5 days with hotel accommodation. He rejected those two as the "Nigel" he wanted as they have had their accommodation in Gothenburg. Regarding the other two, he realised it might be difficult to find out where they resided. He very much doubted they would have stayed in a hotel as they were talking about almost 7 weeks between arrival and the murder. He therefore assumed that they either used a private accommodation or had rented an apartment. He therefore intended to start with ploughing through the rental agencies asking them if they had had or had someone with the Christian name of "Nigel" having rented an apartment. As it already got pretty late, he decided to postpone the task until the next day.

April, the 1st 1986

The next day, Tuesday – April the 1st – the Police Officer took the yellow pages book and started to go through the rental agencies. The first 5 he phoned, said they have not and had not had a guy renting a flat with the name Nigel, but on the 6th one he hit bull's eye. The agent said there had been a Nigel Banks having checked in on the 1st of February for two months but had checked out on the 17th of March having paid for the whole two months. The name also was the same as one of the Nigels on the ferry. The police officer asked the agent if Mr Banks had made any phone calls from the flat but the answer was negative. Asking about incoming calls, the agent said that incoming calls were not being registered. The Police Officer asked the agent if he could have the phone number for the flat, as he might be able to trace any incoming calls through the local provider – Televerket.

The police Officer then phoned the ferry line up asking them if a Nigel Banks had booked a ticket for England either leaving on the 18th or 19th of March. The ferry line could confirm that a Mr Nigel Banks had bought a ticket from Gothenburg to Immingham for the 18th of March. The Police Officer started to get excited, as he could smell that something was ajar regarding Mr Banks. Presuming he had killed the woman – it could also be someone else -, the question was why? It did not seem very logical accidentally killing someone during your stay in a country also trying to make the kill look like an accident. Killing someone in a foreign country normally is a contract thing, however the Police Officer did not believe that the woman was killed through a contract assignment – she was most

The Contract (The Mission)

definitely not someone who you put a contract on her. So why was she killed and killed in a way, which only could have been done by a professional killer. At the moment he did not have an answer to that question.

He then called Televerket - the state owned telephone provider - up, telling the lady at the switchboard his name and in what matter he had phoned and she put her through to the department in question. They said, that it would take too long to have his request resolved over the phone, but promised to come back with an answer the very next day.

April, the 2nd 1986

The next day – April the 2nd - the Televerket employee phoned the Police Officer and said that there had been 2 incoming calls, both from a public phone booth at MEDBORGARPLATSEN, one on Tuesday the 11th of February at 07:12 pm and a second one on Saturday, March the 1st at 12:08 pm. The police officer said thanks for the information and hung up. He looked at the information he had received but could not come up with any conclusive presumptions. The only thing, which came to his attention, was that the second phone call came after midnight, but on the other hand he might have met a woman and she had paid him a visit and phoned to tell him to open the door.

Anyway, he thought, I must get some more information about Mr Banks, what he normally does, the company he works for and why and where he went to Sweden to work. He therefore sent a facsimile to the relevant police department in England explaining the reason for having contacted them, gave them the information he had assembled and kindly asked them to contact Mr Banks to get the information he wanted.

April, the 3rd 1986

The next morning – April the 3rd - the Police Officer had a facsimile waiting for him, saying that no Nigel Banks was to be found under the address they had been given. Perhaps the Police Office had given them the wrong address, they wondered.

The Police Officer then phoned the rental agency up again to have the address and the same address was given to him as the first time. Strange, he thought, why had the guy written down a faked address? He started to smell a rat here. He put together another facsimile to the English Police asking them if it was possible to find out if any Nigel Banks ever had ever lived on the address given and also had applied for a passport in the last two to three years. They replied that it might be possible, but would take some time as registering with the authorities was not compulsory in England as it was in most European countries and you could only trace it through a utility supplier, preferably for gas or electricity. You then could ask the authorities if someone with the name Nigel Banks had applied for a passport at said address.

April, the 4th 1986

The next day – April the 4th – a facsimile from the Londoner Police arrived saying that a certain Nigel Banks had lived at the address mentioned – at least had signed up with the electricity provider – 2 years ago, but only for a couple of weeks. He then seemed to have moved – new address unknown. They also had phoned the passport authorities and had it confirmed that a Nigel Banks had applied for a new passport during his stay at the address he had given. The birth certificate he had provided with his application said the he was born in Bath – a town around 150 km west of London – on the 23rd of March 1950.

The Stockholm Police Officer found it somewhat odd that Mr Banks had given an old address as his present when renting the apartment, although there might be a plausible explanation why he had done it. The reason might be that he might not have a permanent new address, which is not common, but possible. Another possibility might also be that he is staying at another person's residence and does not want to divulge his or her address.

As a consequence, he then looked up the phone number for the local Family Records Centre in Bath and asked the receptionist to be connected to them. Having been connected, he explained who he was and the reason for his call, asking them if there was a Mr Nigel Banks, born on the 23rd of March 1950, registered with them. They let him wait a couple of minutes and then the women came back saying that a Nigel Banks has been registered as born on said date. However, he had been killed in a car accident on the 12 of October 1979.

The Contract (The Mission)

The Police Officer held his breath, feeling as if he really had hit bull's eye - as if he had just come to hear something, which was not accurate and he could feel the tension rising. How could someone apply for a passport if he already had been dead for 5 years? Something was ajar. Why would someone need a false passport if not to hide his real identity. And why does someone need to hide his real identity if not to carry out some spurious work, not wanting to be traceable or his real identity would or might reveal something. He felt that he was on to something, but could not pinpoint what. He put the case aside, hoping that he was able come up with some other ideas at a later date. He then continued trying to find the victim's ex-boyfriend by ordering her phone to be redirected to the homicide squad to make it possible to have any incoming phone calls be intercepted and also traced.

April, the 6th 1986

Two days later – April the 6th - a late phone call came through, which they caught. The call was from one of Gunilla's girlfriends, having tried to reach Gunilla a couple of times without any luck.

When she heard what had happened she got all devastated and started to cry. She could not understand how and why someone should and could have killed her. After the Police Officer in charge had managed to calm her down, she was kindly asked to come down for an interview to the Homicide squad as-soon-as-possible, and they agreed to have her come by for an interview after the weekend – first thing on Monday morning.

The Contract (The Mission)

April, the 7th 1986

On Monday the 7th, Gunilla's girlfriend was met by the Police Officer in charge of the case, who asked her if she would like a coffee, which she agreed to. They then went to a nearby interview room to talk. Was in reality an interrogation room, the Police officer excused himself, but interrogation rooms was the only rooms they had for interviewing people. She didn't mind, she said. Having sat down the Police Office asked

- Did you know Gunilla well?
- Since we went to school, over 20 years in fact
- Is it ok to say that you were her best friend?
- Yes, I think you can say I was
- How often did you meet?
- As we both had partners and job – I also have a son – it was not that often, but we phoned each other pretty often, maybe once a fortnight.
- What was the name of her ex-boyfriend?
- Lars Björk
- Have you got his address?
- Yes, in fact I have, hang on for a sec, she said and rummaged around in her handbag, eventually found her address/phonebook and Lars's address and handed over the address and the phone number to the Police Officer.
- Did she ever mentioned having met an Englishman when

The Contract (The Mission)

she was on Holiday in England last January?

- Yes, in fact she did and I think she was pretty fond of him. From what she told me, he must have been pretty good-looking.
- What was his name?
- I think it was Nigel. Surname, I don't know.
- Do you know if they met here in Stockholm?
- Yes, at least once, I think. She told me they even had dinner together
- Where?
- There is a restaurant nearby, which she likes, sorry liked, very much, she said and gave the Police Office the name of the restaurant.
- Did you happen to meet this Englishman?
- No, unfortunately I did not.
- Would you mind identifying your girlfriend
- No, if I have to I can do it
- You must not do it if you have problems seeing dead people, but I would very much appreciate if you could.
- Should be ok

They then went down to the morgue in the basement, where the bodies were stored. And she identified the corpse as Gunilla's. The Police Officer thanked her for coming and hoped she wouldn't mind if he contacted her again, should there be anything of importance, which had to be sorted out, She didn't, she said, still being pretty upset from the identification procedure, and left.

Later the same day – Monday the 7th - the Police Officer phoned the ex-boyfriend up and told him what had happened and he immediately started to cry when he heard it. He felt

The Contract (The Mission)

very sorry for how they had separated, he said he always wanted to phone her up explaining why, but he never had had the courage to do it. As for the time his ex-girlfriend was murdered, he had an alibi, understanding that he might be a suspect, he said. However, he had returned from a ski holiday with his new girlfriend in Zell am See and Kaprun in Austria on the Sunday after the murder had taken place.

The Police Officer thanked him for the information and said that he might come back, should there be any outstanding issues, which had to be sorted out/resolved.

The Contract (The Mission)

April, the 8th 1986

The next day, on the 8th, the Police Officer took the tube to RÅDMANSGATAN to visit the restaurant, that the victim presumably was to have been visiting together with the Englishman. He entered the restaurant and ordered one of the cheap lunch offers with a Lyckholm's light-beer, which always was on offer by Swedish restaurants at lunchtime.

The restaurant was pretty crowded, so he had to wait talking to the owner until he had finished his meal. Eventually, he got some breathing space and went over to the police officer and asked him about the reason for his request wanting to speak to him. The police office reassured it had nothing to do with what he - the owner - was doing, but more to ask him if he could give the police some additional information regarding a case, which they momentarily were pursuing.

- Do you know this woman?, the Police Officer said, showing the owner a photo of the victim, which he had found in her apartment. Of course he could have taken a photo from the morgue, but he often found it easier to get information from someone if you showed them a photo of a person looking to be alive than a photo of a dead one.
- Oh, yes. This is Gunilla, she quite often comes here or better said came here. I have not seen her for quite some time now. Has anything happened to her?
- Unfortunately, yes. She was murdered a couple of weeks ago
- But this is dreadful, the owner of the restaurant gasped.

The Contract (The Mission)

Have you found the murderer?

- No, and this is the reason why I am here. I presume she has been seen with an Englishman dining in this restaurant some time ago, am I right?
- Yes, I think she was here twice with someone I had never seen before. From their conversation, I could hear they did not speak Swedish, believe it was English. I did not actually listen to what they were discussing, but I could hear the conversation was not in Swedish, as I said.
- Could you describe the man?
- Well. Good looking, charming – womaniser type of guy, looked physically very fit, hair colour - ashen blond, I would say. Looking from his complexion, he looked like someone being more of an out-door guy – not office guy.
- What do you mean by out-door guy?
- Well, someone being out in the sun most of the time, he definitely was not the pale type of guy, you regard as English.
- Sunburned, you mean?
- No, not sunburned, but maybe someone, having lived where a lot of sun is at hand.
- Size, weight, age, colour of the eyes?, the Police Officer `continued.
- Size is difficult as they were sitting – would say between 180 and 190 cm, judging from how he was sitting. Weight is the same - between 80 and 90 kg, I would say. Age - well, between 35 and 40, maybe. The eyes, I cannot say. But not brown, I believe.
- Any other particular characteristics?
- No – as I said, we had a lot to do and I just caught a glimpse of him every now and then.

The Police Officer thought about what he had heard, and could not come up with anymore questions and decided to finish the interview. He thanked the owner for having had the time for this interview and left the restaurant.

Later in the office, he sat down and wrote down some bullet points from the interview. What he found being of particular interest was how the owner had described the guy's complexion characteristics. Out-door guy. Much sun. Ashen blond. Where do you find someone with these features ? Definitely not in England or Northern Europe, he thought. Maybe South America, but they did not speak English. What about Australia or New Zealand? This would fit. Or maybe Southern Africa? This would also fit the description. Could also be the Caribbean, Cyprus, Malta or even Gibraltar although he did not believe that was the case. The guy could even be English always having worked in sunny areas. In fact it could be the whole British Empire. On the other hand, what sort of occupation must an Englishman have in order to enable him to work out-door in a sunny climate? He didn't know on top of his head. Anyway, he thought, the information might be something you could use for further investigation, he thought and put the case folder aside and went for a cup of coffee.

A couple of days later a member of the managerial group came to hear about the case and - as it had taken place not far from where Palme had been assassinated - told Holmér about the case. Holmér asked to have the report be sent to him, but after having read the report, Holmér rejected any speculations and conclusions, stating that he did not – based upon what he had come to read - think the case to have any relation to the assassination of Palme. As a result the case got more or less forgotten by the managerial group as almost all resources were used for other leads in solving the Palme case.

Holmér, on the other hand, immediately realised that the case could have something to do with the Palme case as the way the woman had died was typical for how mercenaries carried out their work – decisively fast and silently. He only wondered what possibly could have gone wrong if one of the guys had

The Contract (The Mission)

been forced to kill the woman. He might have to keep an eye on what happened with the investigation regarding the woman, he thought. This was the sort of unforeseen complications, he had hoped to avoid realising that if things were seen to be heading in the "wrong" direction, he might have to take some action.

Having arrived home, he subsequently decided to phone his "mafia"-contact up tonight to get some information on what the mercenaries looked like as the contact was the only one who had seen them, this just to get the confirmation in case one of the mercenaries had committed the murder and also in case something unforeseen had to be undertaken.

- Hi, it's me. Only a courtesy call. I have a couple of questions
- Ok, what do you want to know
- Remember the guys I sent you buying some additional tools?
- Sure I do
- What do they look like, you know I never saw them.
- Well, one of them was ashen-blond, Swedish looking, suntanned, good looking, spoke English like an Englishman. The other two more seemed to have English as their second language. One of them speaking with a Dutch accent, I believe – northern European complexion, suntanned, but not blond, the other one more with a south-European accent, south-European complexion, suntanned although it is difficult to say when they're from southern Europe – could have been a Spaniard or Italian.
- Thanks, this was my only question. If I need more information I'll come back to you – bye, Holmér said and hung up.

Holmér thought about what he had come to hear, and was now pretty sure – based on the information he had got from the homicide division – that one of the mercenaries, namely the "Englishman", had committed the murder for whatever reason

The Contract (The Mission)

– an unforeseen and perhaps hazardous complication. Something has gone astray and he sat down thinking about if anything might have to be undertaken, depending on what the police officer at the homicide division had found out, if anything.

At the other end, Holmér's contact also paid some thoughts regarding the phone call. He could not understand why Holmér wanted the information other what something unforeseen had taken place, something, which was not planned. Either one of the guys had been seen doing something outside the actual assassination or they want to know who the mercenaries actually were for whatever reason. Do they have to be silenced? He could not say, but he found the phone call from Holmér being somewhat disturbing, he though for himself. Never mind, he thought, after all it is not my business. Time will tell if he will be used for anything in connection with the phone call or not.

The Contract (The Mission)

April, the 16th 1986

The Police Officer was not particularly happy with the outcome of his investigation so far. He could not fully dismiss the thought that the murder, one way or the other, might be connected to the assassination of Palme, however he did not see how. Having the feeling of not getting anywhere, he therefore started to read the witness protocols and it became clear to him that by concentrating on the number of Walkie-Talkies having been observed to have been in use, more than one person must have been involved in the assassination. This observation could not have been done by accident as it was registered having been seen from more than one spot.

Also the assertion that either Dutch or Swiss-German had been spoken could not just be ignored.

As a result, he decided to return to the rental agency in order to find out if there may have been more than one flat having been rented out for the same period.

He therefore took the phone and started to call the number to the rental agency but hesitated and decided make the phone call the following day.

April, the 17th 1986

The next day, he phoned the rental agency up around 09:15am and yes - there had been more than one apartment having been rented out having had the same rental period - 2 months, however one day apart. The latter one had been rented by a Dutch citizen - Martijn Bomhoff - living in Utrecht in the Netherlands. Mr Bomhoff had checked out on the 25th of March, having paid for the full 2 months.

The Police Officer got quite excited and then asked the agent if there was more apartments, which had been rented out for the same period, but the rental agent said no, however Mr Banks had rented a 2 bedroom apartment and Mr Bomhoff only had rented a one bedroom apartment. He also asked the rental agent if any phone calls had been made during his stay, but the answer was negative - no phone calls had been made. He then asked for the phone number of Mr Bomhoff's apartment with the intention to see if there had been any incoming phone calls.

Subsequently he called Televerket - the Swedish state owned phone company - up and inquired about any incoming calls on the apartment phone.

Later the same day a Televerket employee phoned the Police Officer and said that there had been a couple of incoming calls, however only from public phone booths and asked the Police Officer if he also wanted to have their position, however the Police Officer said no as he did not know what to do with such information and thanked the guy for the effort and hung up.

He then phoned Televerket up again to get the phone number

The Contract (The Mission)

of Mr Bomhoff in Utrecht.

He then phoned Mr Bomhoff in Utrecht up, but no one answered. The Police Officer then decided to wait with further phone calls until the following day.

The next day he tried to contact Mr Bomhoff on the same number again but with the same result.

The Police Officer then assumed that Mr Bomhoff was away for a new job assignment and therefore could not be reached and decided to postpone further attempts until the following week as the weekend was approaching.

However, he could not quite put the subject aside as there has been witnesses stressing to have heard Dutch being spoken where Palme had been murdered.

He also could not fully understand why his theory was so vehemently rejected by Holmér and the managerial group. On the other hand he fully understood the pressure the group and its members were experiencing. Also; solving the Palme murder was not his case; his case was to solve the murder of the woman Gunilla. He therefore decided not to push his theories too hard as he then might be jeopardising his own investigation as such as well as being in danger of facing disciplinary reprimands, something which most definitely would not serve its purpose at all.

The Contract (The Mission)

April, the 21st 1986 - Stockholm

Monday came and the Police Officer responsible for solving the murder of Gunilla made another attempt in reaching Mr Bomhoff in Utrecht. After some signals had gone through, someone picked up the phone at the other end.

- Hello, am I speaking with Mr Bomhoff?
- Yes
- Do you speak English, the Police Officer asked.
- A little
- Very good. This is the Swedish Police - Homicide Squad - and I am phoning from Sweden in regards to a murder. I assume you were in Stockholm last February and March?
- No, I have never been to Stockholm, Mr Bomhoff answered.
- But we have information, that you rented a flat for 2 months there.
- Must be wrong. I was at home working all the time.

Strange, the Police Officer thought. Well let's take it from another angle.

- When did you last time go abroad, Mr Bomhoff?
- Last September. I went for one month to South-Africa. The Police Officer now got really excited and started to feel that something was considerably astray. Who had then used Mr Bomhoff credentials and passport for renting a flat for two months? He then continued

The Contract (The Mission)

- Have you changed or renewed your passport recently?
- Yes, I had to as I was robbed on a bus in Capetown. They stole my wallet with my passport and some money.
- And they did not find your passport?
- No, I had to apply for a provisional passport at the Dutch Embassy so that I could return home.
- Sorry for having phoned you, but unfortunately we have to follow up on every lead there is on the case I'm working on.
- No problem
- May I phone you again if the investigation so requires?
- You're welcome. And what about the flat?
- I have to find out whether the information is accurate or not. From what you are saying it seems like the information might have been wrong, the Police Officer said avoiding to further explain what it was all about.

The Police Officer then said goodbye and hung up.

Now it really got interesting the Police Officer thought. A Dutch passport stolen in South-Africa. As far as he knew the main language used by the white population in South-Africa was Afrikaans – a sort of ancient Dutch dialect. A Dutch passport might come in handy if you did not want to reveal your real nationality, especially if you were of South-African origin.

He also recalled from having read the witness protocols that one witness should have said that she had heard someone looking Swedish presumably should have spoken Dutch or Swiss-German. A second one - a taxi driver - should have seen 3 different people having used walkie-talkies – a very strange coincidence – and he did not believe in coincidences.

All of a sudden it struck him that the woman might not have heard someone speaking Dutch or Swiss-German but what she had heard was Afrikaans!

The Contract (The Mission)

But Swedish-looking? As far as he could recall, having spoken to the rental agent, Mr Bomhoff did not look Swedish. So who was it looking Swedish speaking Afrikaans, he thought?

He then suddenly recalled from the interview he had had with the restaurant owner regarding the "Gunilla" murder, the person having accompanied her – Mr Banks - seemed to have had a Swedish or Scandinavian look. But he spoke English with Gunilla. This assumption might lead up to the conclusion, that he was not of Swedish origin. Then the Police Officer realised that he originally also might have come from South-Africa, but had decided to move to England sometime along the way, something, which would explain why someone had seen a Swedish looking guy speaking Afrikaans using a Walkie-Talkie.

This assumption would connect Mr Banks to Mr Bomhoff, which also would enable him to pursue the "Gunilla" murder from a different angle, i.e. as something being connected to the "Palme" murder. Also the fact that both of them had rented their apartments in the same complex, made a connection between the two even more probable.

Also the fact that another witness said having observed a man with dark complexion would indicate the existence of a third person, being the one having stayed in the second bedroom in the flat having been rented by Mr Banks.

He then decided to find out if "Mr Bomhoff" actually had arrived between the 29th and 31st of January and left Sweden on the 24th or 25th of March as had been suggested by the rental agent.

He therefore phoned Information desk at Arlanda - Stockholm International Airport - up and asked them if they could help them in getting the information he wanted.

He asked the woman at the Information Desk to first concentrate on flights from Stockholm on the 24th or 25th of March for Frankfurt, London-Heathrow, Copenhagen-Kastrup and Amsterdam-Shiphol, as he suspected the person in question had had the intension to take a connecting flight to South-Africa from one of the European major airports.

She said it might take some time and asked him if she could phone him back. He gave her his phone number, thanked her for any effort and said goodbye.

3 Hours later the woman at the Information Desk phoned him up and – yes, there had been a Mr Bomhoff arriving in Sweden from Frankfurt on the 29th of January and leaving Sweden for Frankfurt at 11:10 on the 25th of March with Lufthansa.

He thanked her for her effort and said goodbye.

He was now sure that Mr Bomhoff was - one way or the other - connected to the Palme murder and decided to write down a report on what he had found out and then present it to Holmér and his group, keeping a low profile until he was ready to do so.

He was also pretty sure that a "Mr Bomhoff" hasn't taken a second flight anywhere from Frankfurt, presuming from then on that the person in question probably had decided to use his own credentials instead when returning to South-Africa.

He sat down at his desk trying to recap what he had accomplished in the last couple of days. He now was pretty confident that at least two people were connected with what had happened to Palme, most probably three as otherwise there would not have been any logic in renting one one-room apartment and one two-room apartment. He took some brainstorming and all of a sudden he realised that having only received phone calls from a public phone booth, they most likely were acting completely on their own not having any real connections to any permanent organisation and resources in Sweden. This conclusion was pointing at people being real professionals when it came to approaching and executing an assignment. As a result he phoned Televerket up again and asked the woman he had spoken with last time if it was possible to become a list of calls from the public phone booth, which had been executed between

The Contract (The Mission)

February, the 1ˢᵗ and March 31ˢᵗ

She promised to come back on the issue the next day.

The next day the woman came back with the information as promised. Excited what the information might reveal, the Police Officer immediately begun to evaluate the information he just had received. Apart from local calls within Sweden, there also were some calls abroad, to be more specific to a certain phone number in London, Great Britain.

The Police officer suspected that some regular calls were used by someone for checking the status of certain things whilst he/she was away on a mission. He wrote the number down, phoned his connection in London up and kindly asked them if they could find out who had the number in question. They promised to come back on the issue the very next day.

The Contract (The Mission)

April, the 21st 1986 - Pretoria

In South-Africa Piet's neighbour, whose name was Andreas Nydal, arrived at his desk in Pretoria, the seat of Minestry of Defence, and run by Minister of Defence, Dr. Magnus Malan, after his holiday. Andreas Nydal's ancestors had arrived to South Africa during the "Norwegian Exodus" in the 19th century where many Norwegians had left Norway looking for a better life, Durban being the primary destination for many Norwegian families during said time, something which he fully could understand having experienced the climate in Scandinavia a couple of times.

During his holiday he could not quite forget Piet and his assignment in Europe and had decided when he arrived in the office after his holiday, to have a look at what their mainframe computers at the office might reveal - if anything.

Having his first cup of tea of the day, he logged himself into a huge IBM mainframe computer. In searching for people working as freelancers he put "extern" and "availability" in as search pattern in the corresponding fields on the screen and got a list on the CICS terminal showing you all the people working for CCB as external resources – however only showing their Christian names plus first letter of their Surname as well as their skillset. In order to get the full Surnames – also giving you a more detailed view of a person's credentials, you had to have a corresponding clearance at a higher security level something which Piet's neighbour fortunately happened to possess. However, the information together with the querier's ID (i.e. password) credential and reason for the query were logged. What Nydal was not aware of was that each record being logged also got logged on a dedicated file specially put together for Minestry of Defence, Magnus Malan, only.

This meant that Malan received the information who had asked and what information he was interested in. Putting in the necessary query parameters, the computer now returned all freelancers and their availability. A number of freelancers now came up on the screen. He then scanned the content on the screen until he found de Cleefs - i.e. Piet's - record and the information he was looking for – date availability. With de Cleef the "date availability" field said 28th of April, meaning that he was available for a new assignment i.e. has given CCB a new date as from when CCB could give him a new assignment if there was any.

(CCB - Civil Cooperation Bureau - a government-sponsored death squad during the apartheid era in South-Africa that operated under the authority of Defence Minister General Magnus Malan. The Truth and Reconciliation Commission (TRC) pronounced the CCB guilty of numerous killings, and suspected more killings),

Another five people came up being marked as being available as from a specific date, but only two people being of interest proved to have a similar skillset as Piet including professional field operation experience. Anyway, he had found two additional people marked as being available as well as occupied around the same date as Piet. All three people supposedly being away on some dubious assignment in Europe, presumably - according to Piet - in Serbia. The only problem was that Andreas Nydal did not fully buy that story. He then called up the history display querying for their previous assignment and all three of them seemed to have finished their previous assignment around the same time - end of November, the year before.

If you are a person with professional field operation experience, you will most likely not go to former Yugoslavia to play babysitter for some local ex-Yugoslavian politician. And doing that crap for around 4 months – bullshit. There must be an-

The Contract (The Mission)

other reason, he thought, trying to remember what had taken place between November and March in Europe. All of a sudden he had the answer – the assassination of Palme, the Swedish Prime Minister! Could it really be that these three guys had carried out the assassination of Palme? You must be crazy thinking along these lines, he thought for himself but after a while the possibility more and more came up as a viable option. He felt a real blush of excitement also thinking of the reward he would receive for having delivered the information regarding those who had assassinated Olof Palme.

The problem was how to make said information be accessible to the Swedish Police, before some other wise-guy would get at the same information from a different source leaving him in the end standing there without a single cent from the reward, a reward which ought to be quite substantial, he reckoned.

Taking the risk of being identified and having to explain why you were interested in these three guys was minimal as everyone using the IBM mainframe had been cleared from any suspicions having to do with espionage – i.e. "the act of obtaining secret or confidential information without the permission of the holder of the information" - anyway, meaning that the possibility of being questioned, having to undergo an additional clearance check was pretty remote. He therefore decided to grab the possibility to earn the reward they must have set up by now.

He marked Piet on the display, pressed the return button on the keyboard and sent the query off. After a couple of seconds Piet's record information came up on the display. The unfortunate thing was, that Minister of Defence – Magnus Malan – now also knew what Andreas was interested in, something, whch was not particularly good for Andreas Nydal at all.

Nydal then pressed the "Print" button and the information was printed. He then repeated the same procedure for Martin and Jose and closed the CICS application and returned back to his desk.

The Contract (The Mission)

Having arrived at his desk, he went to the archive section and began to plow through newspapers, where the assassination had been reported as the main news, starting about a month ago and found out that the assassination was carried out on the 28th of February between 11 pm and 12 pm.

Based on the information having been provided to him, Malan intended to have a "chat" with Nydal in a not too distant future asking Nydal why he was interested in said information.

The Palme investigations had reported that two, maybe three people seemed to have been involved in taking Olof Palme down, one of them believed to have been speaking Swiss German or Dutch. However Andreas Nydal was pretty sure they were referring to Afrikaans - an old version of Dutch used by the major part of South Africa's white and coloured population.

Furthermore, the reports said that they seemed to have been communicating through Walkie-Talkies, something which sounded pretty viable as using english to communicate might have made people catch phrases of what they were up to.

Using Afrikaans instead of English for communicating with each other would not have been seen as a disadvantage, Nydal thought. Quite the contrary, he reckoned, as all of them from having worked for CCB were fluent in said language. You don't have to watch out what you are saying as Afrikaans is not that common, in fact only the countries in Southern Africa use the language.

Anyway, he was now pretty sure, that the three guys were the ones having carried out the assassination, the primary question now being – from whom had they got the task to liquidate Olof Palme as they most definitely would not have acted on their own, no way. On the other hand, it didn't really matter to him from whom they had gotten the task as long as some financial benefits came out as a result of what he so far has managed to find out. In essence he knew who they were and also knew the permanent residence where one of them lived and

The Contract (The Mission)

he did not intend to give away this information without a healthy financial compensation. Most probably he might also be in the position to reveal where they most likely were to be working in the immediate future, but that would have to wait until he had received the first instalment of the reward. The only problem left to solve was to find a secure way of letting the Swedish Police Authorities know who the three people were and where to find them.

And he sure could use some extra money, that was for sure. He had accepted the job he now had because it would give them more money, he thought. However, his stay in Pretoria showed to be somewhat boring, only going home every fourth-night. Not used to being away from home for such a long time, he started to visit the Pretoria casinos, hoping for some luck at the gambling tables. As almost always is the case with gambling, you end up having lost instead of having won - and a lot.

Eventually it lead to that he started to borrow money at an horrendous fee in attempting to make up for what he had lost, As was the case with most gamblers, their greed was bigger than their luck at the gambling tables. Eventually he was forced to borrow money on the black market (i.e. from the Mafia) to be able to cover the depts he already had, leading to constantly increasing depts. And then the shit will really hit the fan.

As a result he now only saw the reward as the vehicle for being in the position to return the money he owed the mafia by giving the Swedish police the names of the assassins. Not the difficulties how to get at them. The reward, he thought, might even cover all his outstanding depths, thereby giving him the possibility to start from scratch, which otherwise wouldn't be possible.

The Contract (The Mission)

April, the 24th 1986 - Stockholm

In the morning, the 24th of April, the Police Officer more or less had finished his summary on the "Gunilla" murder case as well as his suspicions regarding the two foreigners having rented the flats at MEDBORGARPLATSEN.

He decided to make a phone call to the Head of the managerial group – Mr Holmér - being responsible for the Palme murder and ask him for an appointment in order to tell him what he had found out with his investigation, which might be linked to the Palme murder as well.

He picked up the phone and dialled the number to the managerial group and asked for Mr Holmér.

A woman answered at the other end and asked him for the reason for his call and he said it was about possible leads in the Palme murder case. She then asked him to wait and directed the call to Holmér. Holmér who picked up the receiver.

- Hello, Holmér, whom am I speaking to?

The Police Officer said who he was, the reason for his call and asked Holmér if it was possible for them to have a meeting to give him the opportunity to explain in more detail why he meant his investigations might also be of interest to Holmér in solving the Palme murder.

Holmér, initially assuming that the guy was one of those that only wanted to brag about what he had found out. However, Holmes then slowly realised, that what the guy had concluded from his investigation, brought the level of the investigation

The Contract (The Mission)

on dangerous ground, and might be dangerously close to finding information, which eventually might lead to irrevocable questions why the investigation did not follow up on what the Police Officer had found out. The guy was smart, Holmér must admit and realised that he had to have a meeting with him to more in detail get first-hand information what his investigation so far had managed to find out. Of course, he might be able to divert some information as information only relating to the "Gunilla" murder case but most definitely not everything that the Police Officer's investigation had come to reveal. By ignoring everything the guy had managed to find out would then only make the man suspicious and the result would be that he might take the investigation a level higher in the police hierarchy, eventually leading to that he cannot prevent the investigation from taking its own uncontrollable path.

Holmér therefore decided to have the meeting with the Police Officer and agreed to have the meeting the following day, also asking him not to divulge his findings to anyone until they have met, this in order to prevent his findings from starting making its own gossip factory, something which would neither be beneficial for further investigations nor for the credibility of his investigation so far, Holmes said.

April, the 25th 1986 - Stockholm

The following day the Police Officer left his desk around 9:00 am to be in time for the meeting with Holmér. When leaving the office he bumped into one of his colleagues who asked him where he was heading. The Police Officer told his colleague the he was off to a meeting with Holmér – the Head of the managerial group, who wanted to meet him regarding some findings he had come to discover when pursuing the "Gunilla" murder case and which might also be of interest to Holmér in solving the Palme murder.

His colleague asked him what it was all about, but the Police Officer said he was not authorised to tell anyone before he had spoken to Holmér. His colleague said he understood his hesitation and did not pursue the subject further but instead asked the Police Officer to reveal his findings once he got the go from Holmér and the managerial group, which he agreed to.

The Contract (The Mission)

April, the 26th 1986 - Stockholm

The Police Officer showed up at Holmér's office at 10:00 am the following day.

Holmér asked him if he wanted a coffee before they started, something, which the Police Officer thankfully accepted and after some general smalltalk and smalltalk about the Palme murder in general, Holmér said

- Thank you for taking the time to come here to present your findings, I really appreciate it. From what you have told me over the phone so far your investigation sounds more interesting than I initially anticipated, compared to what I got to hear when we spoke to each other last time. I believe you also have put something in writing, which you have brought with you, but could you please verbally recap what you so far have managed to find out, things which might relate to or be relevant for the Palme investigation.

- Sure, but I should probaly take it from the beginning to make you better understand, why I have come to the conclusion that my investigation might have something to do with the assassination of Palme and then we can take it from there.

- Please do.

- Well, it all started with the forensic report, where the medical examiner, after having carried out the medical examination of Gunilla, the victim, came to the conclusion that her death could not possibly have been a result of an

The Contract (The Mission)

accident. The neck was broken from a twist, not from a fall. I then concluded that we had to do with a murder, not an accident. As a result I then decided to contact her colleague, who had found the body, for an interview. Her colleague told me that Gunilla – the victim – had recently been to England visiting a friend and that she, on her way back to Sweden, had come to know a good-looking Englishman, whom she later also did meet here in Stockholm. His name was Nigel, she said. I double-checked it and, yes, a man with the name Nigel – actually a few - was found having travelled with the same ferry line Gunilla had been travelling with.

- I then paid some thoughts regarding the information I so far had acquired and as it was almost 7 weeks between Gunilla's return and the murder, I thought the guy must either have used a private accommodation or rented an apartment as staying in a hotel for 7 weeks is not cheap. I was lucky finding a rental agency having rented out an apartment to a Mr Nigel Banks on the 1st of February for 2 months, in fact he checked out on the 17th of March, but paid for the full 2 months. I then phoned the ferry line up again asking them if a Nigel Banks had bought a ticket for England on the 18th or 19th of March. And Eureka, a Nigel Banks had in fact bought a ticket for the 18th of March to Immingham and I was beginning to smell a rat here. From my experience regarding the killing itself – based on how it had been carried out – must have been carried out by a professional, but I could not imagine that a contract had been put on Gunilla to have her killed. Are you with me so far?

- Yes, no problem Holmér replied. Please carry on.

- Well, I then sent a facsimile off to the relevant police department in England asking them for some information about Mr Banks based on the address he had given the rental agency, but on that address, there was no Mr Banks. I then sent another facsimile asking them if a Nigel

The Contract (The Mission)

Banks had ever lived on that address, which proved to be true. He also had applied for a new passport whilst he was staying at the address, stating he was born in Bath 1950.

- I then phoned the local Family Records Centre in Bath asking them for information about Mr Banks and they told me that there had been a Mr Banks with said credentials but he had been killed in a car accident 1979. A somewhat strange coincident don't you think?

- Yes indeed, Holmér replied and started to feel somewhat uncomfortable with the information he has gotten so far.

- We then decided to intercept the phone of the deceased and eventually a phone call came through from a girlfriend to Gunilla, whom I had an interview with a couple of days later. She said that Gunilla had been out eating with a Nigel a couple of times at one of her favourite restaurants and the restaurant could confirm that Gunilla had been there a couple of times with a good-looking man, looking very fit, presumably English as they could hear that they didn't speak Swedish, they said.

- It is very interesting what you have told me so far, but this still does not prove that the murder is connected to the Palme case in any way. Mr Banks could have been working for just about anyone, knowing what size the organised crime has reached nowadays, Holmér said.

- Wait, I am not finished yet. I then came to think about what some witnesses had registered when Palme was murdered and they had said that at least two, maybe three people had been communicating via Walkie-Talkies, both at GAMLA STAN underground station as well as in the area around RÅDMANSGATAN underground station. I then decided to ask the rental agency again if a second apartment had been rented out for the same period as the first apartment. And yes, a second apartment had been rented out to a Dutch national – a Mr Bomhoff from Utrecht – for 2 months as well. He had left the apartment

The Contract (The Mission)

on the 25th of March.

I then managed to contact Mr Bomhoff in Utrecht, but he said he had never been in Sweden. However, his passport had been stolen when he was visiting South-Africa last September. Quite a coincidence, don't you think? I then recalled that there was a witness having said she had heard someone having spoken Dutch or Swiss-German but if what she had heard was Afrikaans! This would better fit in the picture.

- It still does not prove any connection to the Palme case.

- No it doesn't, but circumstantial evidence is pretty serious and to my opinion telling us their own language, don't you think?

- I agree with you to a certain degree and it might be worthwhile follow up on what you have found out, but it still does not prove anything. Is there anyone else, apart from me, which you have informed regarding what you have accomplished?

- No, I have only had some minor discussions with the medical examiner regarding the way Gunilla was murdered and asked him what type of person might be capable of doing it and he said it most likely is someone being experienced in military, paramilitary or so-called "mercenary" activities, something which I think, would fit a broad description of the perpetrator, who had killed Gunilla.

- We then decided to intercept the phone of the deceased and eventually a phone call came through from a girlfriend to Gunilla, whom I had an interview with a couple of days ago.

- And experience with such activities you would expect someone to possess and, that to a very high degree, having gotten the task to kill someone like Palme and also involuntarily having killed Gunilla as I think the "Gunilla" murder was not planned. She was only a victim of circumstances unfortunately, the Police Officer finishing his "pledogy".

If you only knew how close you are with your investigation, Holmér thought for himself.

Holmér then finally replied

- Good. I will read your report more in detail at home. BTW, could you also tell me the name of the medical examiner in case we would like to or have to get in touch with him. One can never tell.

The Police Officer then gave Holmér the name of the medical examiner having examined Gunilla's body.

Holmér then asked if he could have the report the Police Officer had put together, something, which the Police Officer agreed to, however asking Holmér, if he could take a copy of the report he had brought with him. As he did not want any copies to float around before they had spoken to each other there was no copy of the report and what he had brought with him was his original. Holmér said it was no problem and told the Police Officer he would see to that the report got copied as soon as possible and would then return the original to him.

They then parted and Holmér promised to keep the Police Officer informed about any progress in the Palme case resulting from what the Police Officer has brought to light in his report.

After the Police Officer had left, Holmér took a deep breath and begun to sweat, grabbed the report and begun to read it. The more he read the report, the more he realised that he now most likely had to take some unplanned action in order to stop the shit from hitting the fan.

The report was far more detailed than what he had expected with references to witness protocols, a thorough analysis of his findings and also including an explanation why he found his findings to be linked to the Palme case and why they were of crucial value when it came to solving the assassination of Palme.

The Contract (The Mission)

The guy had begun to come dangerously close to "the truth", Holmér thought, and any further digging based on the report might lead to that further diversions might be impossible to instigate. Also distributing the report would inevitably lead to more people trying to be "smart-asses" and a cover up scenario would effectively be impossible. Holmér also realised that by distributing the report it also might jeopardise his credibility, probably leading to his replacement as head of the Palme investigation and by that time the shit would really have been hitting the fan.

By not killing the report as-soon-as-possible would most likely also lead to that the "mercenaries" themselves became a liability or even an incalculable risk factor, which additionally would have to be taken care of.

The Police Officer on the other hand was quite satisfied with what he had accomplished, hoping that his investigation would give his career a boost now that the head of the Palme investigation seemed to have accepted his findings as being beneficial for solving the Palme murder case as well. He said to himself, that he now must keep a low profile and he must be patient and not rush everything too fast as it might have the opposite effect. Just let his findings sink in, he thought for himself, and they will soon realise how important they are, for solving the Palme murder case.

The Contract (The Mission)

April, the 28th 1986 – Stockholm

The Police Officer went to work as usual. It was a wonderful day, the first day really reminding you of spring, he thought. The weather forecast said the temperature could reach 18 degrees Celsius.

Although the spring was there, minor sleets of snow still was to be found in shady areas. He lived in a 2-bedroom apartment in Bredäng - a suburb in the south of Stockholm. He had lived there for the last 2 years, since he got divorced from his wife, whom he had lived with for 12 years. However his job has taken its toll, often forced him to work overtime and often having irregular working hours. In the end his wife had started to look around for more interesting tasks than just waiting for him to come home and had met another guy more living up to her expectations. The Police Officer could understand why she had left him, but after having been with the police for more than 20 years, what he did was the only thing he could work with and he would have hoped for more understanding from his wife side, but unfortunately this had not been the case. Their only child – a daughter of 10 - now lived with his wife. He saw his daughter every 2 weeks, although it did not work out too well as his job in essence had prevented him from having the opportunity to foster a more deep relation with her. Maybe it also was a certain lack of interest from his side he must admit regarding what she did and undertook that made their relationship somewhat difficult.

He tried to concentrate on the work, which had to be done, but

The Contract (The Mission)

could not really do it to 100% as the meeting with the head of the Palme investigation team preoccupied his thoughts all day hoping for a phone call, saying that he had been right in his assumptions, to come, but nothing happened. Eventually he gave up and left for home.

His thoughts being preoccupied with the Palme case lead to that he did not notice the two men following him all the way home.

He made himself a supper, turned on the television to watch the news as there seemed to have been an explosion in a nuclear power plant in a place called Chernobyl, Ukraine two days ago and supposedly the radiation might even reach Sweden, they said, however he could not really concentrate on what the TV-news had to report.

He went to bed around 10:30 pm as he did more or less every day.

April, the 29th 1986 - Stockholm

On Tuesday the 29th, the Police Officer woke up at 6:30 am as he did everyday. He made himself a coffee and had two slices of bread – the Swedish Limpa - with cheese and a glass of orange juice before he took off for work. His mind was pre-occupied with what he had found out regarding the "Gunilla" case all the time and – as he saw it - its connection to the Palme case. He had not heard anything from Holmér since they had met last Friday, but told himself to be patient and not expecting Holmér and his team to immediately jump on the bandwagon.

He had a 5 minute walk to the Bredäng underground station from where he lived and he really enjoyed the walk now that it was getting warmer, although this morning it was a rather foggy and windy. He was so pre-occupied trying to cover his face from the wind that he did not notice the two men following him some 20 meters behind. As he finally reached the underground station, the platform was already pretty crowded with people waiting for "tunnelbanan" – the Tube - as about 90 % of the people in Stockholm used public transports to get to work. The Police Officer lined up as usual waiting for the train to come and as he saw it coming, he suddenly felt a heavy push from behind and he lost his balance and could not remain on the platform and instead fell down on the tracks and before he really was aware of what had happened the train was over him ending his life in a very gruesome way. People started to scream and some even fainted as they realised what had taken place before their eyes. The Police and medical assistance showed up some 10 minutes later, but

The Contract (The Mission)

there was nothing they could do but having to register that the Police Officer was dead. The two men having followed him had already left the area and returned to their car, which they had parked some 500 meters from the underground station. The Police Officer's death was later classified as having been an accident and no further investigation therefore took place. Unfortunately no cameras were installed on the platform in order to have a possibility to find out what actually had taken place.

The Contract (The Mission)

May, the 6th 1986 - Stockholm

On Tuesday the 6th, the Police Officer's funeral took place with a lot of police officials attending the ceremony including the colleague, whom the Police Officer had bumped in to just before taking off for the meeting with Holmér.

After the ceremony, the colleague thought – why not phone Holmér up and ask him if he could divulge what the Police Officer has found being of interest to Holmér and the Palme murder case and if he could be of any help to Holmér as he after all was working in the same department as the deceased Police Officer often sharing information.

Consequently he phoned Holmér , told him who he was and the reason for his call.

Holmér hesitated and took a deep breath realising that the shit no doubt would hit the fan unless some unforeseen measures, to bring everything that so far had been achieved under his control were taken. However, he tried to stay calm, not to create any suspicions, telling the caller that any leads being reported would be thoroughly investigated – also the lead having come from the Police officer - and no, what the Police Officer had reported could not be divulged until on-going investigations had been finished regarding said lead.

However, Holmér continued, a preliminary inspection seemed not to indicate that the Police Officers findings did relate to what so far had been found being related to the Palme murder case. Should there be a connection to the Palme murder case Holmér promised to call the caller. Holmér then thanked the caller also saying that he really appreciated his interest in

The Contract (The Mission)

what the managerial group was doing and hung up.

The colleague had to accept that he would not receive any information about the deceased the Police Officer's findings and decided instead to have a look at his desk in case he should have left any written notes – after all the Police Officer normally used to be very thorough in writing down what he had undertaken and having found out regarding cases, which he was pursuing.

The colleague went over to the desk, but could not find anything useful but a scribbled notice on the desktop wallpaper saying "Gunilla – Nigel – suntanned - english? - connections?" There seemed to have been some sort of private brainstorming, which he had carried out for himself, the colleague thought. However, the colleague found it pretty awkward not finding anything relevant to do with the "Gunilla" murder case on his desk as the Police Officer normally was very thorough in summarising what he has been doing.

He might have left something at home, the colleague thought for himself and left the desk to concentrate on his own work, at the same time telling himself not to forget to catch up on any further development regarding the "Gunilla" murder case.

A couple of days later he would be responsible for the case and consequently then would give him a better opportunity to go through all official protocols to do with the "Gunilla" murder in an orderly manner. This fact might then make him understand why the Police Officer had written down the name "Nigel" on the desktop wallpaper. However, from the official protocols he had read so far there was nothing indicating that there was a connection with the "Palme case" and he decided to put the case on a lower priority.

The Contract (The Mission)

May, the 8th 1986 - Stockholm

In the morning, the 8th of May, two Police Officers came to visit the medical examiner having done the autopsy of Gunilla. They showed him their badges and asked him if they could have a couple of questions be answered now that the Police Officer having been responsible for solving the "Gunilla" case had been so tragically killed in an accident 10 days ago. The medical examiner said it was ok and they went to a nearby meeting room. One of the Police Officers asked the medical examiner if he would care for a cup of coffee, which he thankfully accepted as they only had Canteen coffee machines in the building and you had to pay for each cup. A couple of minutes later, one of the Police Officers returned with the coffee. After another five minutes, after having asked some questions – in particular if the medical examiner had discussed his finding with anyone - the two Police Officers left the morgue and the medical examiner continued with his job. About 10 minutes later he felt a sudden pain in his chest and could hardly breathe and had to sit down. A colleague rushed to get him a glass of water but when she came back the medical examiner was already dead.

The Contract (The Mission)

May, the 9ᵗʰ 1986 - Stockholm

A couple of days later the colleague of the deceased Police Officer, now responsible for the "Gunilla" case, decided to at least have a chat with the medical examiner being responsible for the autopsy of Gunilla.

However, when he got to the forensic department he was confronted with the fact that the medical examiner suddenly had died just a couple of days before.

An examination has given as result that he had suffered a heart attack and his death had been written off as a natural death and no further examination had been carried out.

However the colleague found it somewhat strange that within a couple of days two people being connected with the "Gunilla murder case" suddenly had died and came to the conclusion that after all there might be more to the case than just a "normal" murder case and decided to dig further.

He asked some people at the forensic department if they had noticed anything not being normal regarding the medical examiner or if he had undertaken something being out of his normal schedule before he died.

One person said that the only thing he could come to think of was that the medical examiner had had an interview with two Police Officers in regard to the "Gunilla" murder case just before he died.

The colleague of the deceased Police Officer made a note of the incident but did not pay any further thoughts on what had been said.

The Contract (The Mission)

Coming back to his office he asked his supervisor about which Police Officers had been at the forensic department and having interviewed the medical examiner.

After having ploughed through the assignment and visitors lists, his supervisor said that he could not find anyone having gotten the task to have such an interview take place, which the colleague of the deceased Police Officer found more than strange.

He then continued by asking his supervisor some prophylactic questions like

- Was there more to the case than what one would imagine after all?
- Who were these two Police Officers?
- Why was there not any records of someone having visited the forensic department?
- If there was anything documenting that the meeting had taken place – where was it to be found?
- Did the medical examiner not suffer a natural death?

As a result of his supervisor being negative on all questions he tried to put through, he could not find any viable reason for having any further discussions with him, he decided to return to his desk to have his personal walk-through from there regarding what might have taken place in the Palme case.

After the colleague of the deceased Police Officer had left his supervisor, the supervisor paid a phone call to Holmér, telling him about the result of the meeting with the colleague.

Holmér then told the supervisor to stay low on what the colleague had said in order to avoid further diversion and "stealing" resources from the actual path they were following in the Palme case. He also told the supervisor to make sure that the colleague of the deceased Police Officer was not to spend too much time on what he seemed to have found out only making their work more difficult than necessary in

The Contract (The Mission)

handling journalists and TV reporters – to Holmér they all were a pain in the ass - when it came trying to solve the Palme murder case.

Holmér then suggested that an even better idea might be to give the colleague of the deceased Police Officer another case to work on, at the same time taking the "Gunilla murder case" off his list and put the case on the "cold case" (i.e. "pending" status) list, i.e. until new information turned up defending a "reopening" of the case – thereby giving the case an "active" status again. This scenario will also leave us with only one single point of contact with the general public, Holmér said, something, which he very much favoured.

The next morning the priority swap - with corresponding explanations why - took place and although the colleague initially got somewhat cross he eventually accepted the decision having been taken, to give the colleague a new case and remove him from the "Gunilla" case, something which effectively put further investigations and leads regarding the "Gunilla" Palme case to a grinding halt.

The Contract (The Mission)

May, the 12th 1986 - Pretoria

On Monday the 12th, Andreas Nydal woke up at around 7:00 am as usual in his small apartment, which he had rented not too far away from the CCB Office. The apartment was not much to write home about, but at least it was close the where he worked. He had tried to have it paid or at least subsidised by the Government, but no – the Government had its rules. He, therefore, had taken the decision not to go public with the address of the apartment, but to keep it to himself.

He had spent the weekend in Pretoria, but he wan't someone who particularly liked to be alone. So he had phoned his wife up a couple of times during the weekend, explaining to her, that a distant relative had recently died in Norway, and the relative having been pretty rich, from shipping cargo around the world, made his presence at the funeral almost obligatory if you wanted to have your rightful share from the testament. His wife was not too happy with having to spend yet another weekend alone, but accepted that he was going to Norway with gnashing teeth as they very well could need some extra money.

He took a quick shower, made himself a cup of coffee and had 2 toasts with English Marmalade before he was off to the office. It was a nice day, clear sky but somewhat chilly. The forecasts predicted the temperature to reach a maximum of 16 degrees Celsius.

Arriving at the office he had a cup of tea and a social chat in the breakfast room before he sat down at his desk, took the headphone and dialled the number to managerial unit,

The Contract (The Mission)

responsible for the Palme murder case in Sweden, which had been distributed to most major Police Organisations in the world, including South Africa.

He was connected to the phone switchboard in Stockholm, and the lady asked him for the purpose of his phone call. He told her it was about the Olof Palme case and asked her to connect him to the head of the managerial unit.

- Hello, whom am I speaking to, please?
- Is irrelevant at this stage, but I might possess information crucial to solving the Olof Palme case.

Very interesting, Holmér thought for himself, thinking he was talking to another weirdo. However, Holmér then saw that the caller's number was blocked, which was very uncommon to experience in areas where someone only wanted to report or reveal something, Holmér thought. This could indicate that the person was working for some government, most probably for the military or some non-official entity. It could after all indicate that the guy had some real information to give away and therefore it might be worthwhile to listen to what he had to say.

- That's what almost everyone is saying , trying to make an extra buck, Holmér replied. Unfortunately it does not work that way, Mr Nobody. You see, we are running the show – not you. If you have something definitive to come up with something which is easily verifiable, we can talk - otherwise not. And most definitely not on the number you just did call to get in contact with me. May I suggest you phone this number, Holmér said and gave him a scrambled high security phone number he had at home, which was not possible to trace, i.e. to find out where the phone number physically was installed. For security reasons, the number was also changed at regular intervals or if the number had been used for an incoming call.

- If you really have anything useful in solving the Olof Palme case, something which I doubt you have, may I

The Contract (The Mission)

suggest you call me tonight at 8:00 pm on the number I just have given to you, otherwise this call is the only and last time we speak to each other. If you don't call at said time on the said number, no other possibility will be open for you. Got the message? Holmér said.

The caller said that he would call at 08:00 pm and Holmér hung up.

The Contract (The Mission)

May, the 12th 1986 - Stockholm

After he had hung up, Holmér phoned Televerket up and requested a trace on the number he just had given Andreas Nydal, from 07:55 pm and onward, to find out from where the call was coming. Of course it might not be possible, depending on the security level the company or government entity had put on their phone system, but Holmér took the view that the phone call would probably not be officially sanctioned by the company or government entity and therefore only a pretty rudimentary security level would have been applied to the phone the guy intended to use. Holmér did not put much confidence in that what the guy was about to reveal. It was probably comprising the same crap as the rest of those weirdos eager in making an extra buck, without having to work for it, were delivering.

Holmér arrived at home around 07:30 pm, had a quick supper and went to his home office to wait for the call. He also made sure that the trace facility was turned on and working as expected. Almost exact at 08:00 pm the phone rang and Holmér picked up the headphone and said

- Hello, this is Holmér. What do you have to deal with?
- I might know the whereabouts of those who have killed your Prime Minister. However, I will only reveal what I know if there is a reward put up to compensate for the information I then intend to reveal.
- "Always the same story", Holmér thought. They are all only interested in getting a lump of money – not that they might have helped the Police to catch the murderer, which

The Contract (The Mission)

in essence was good for those people being ultimately responsible for having planned the mission and ultimately having seen to that the mission was executed.

- I am not aware of any reward having been publicly announced. You can expect a reward corresponding to the importance of having solved the case in case we catch the murderer based on your information. How much I cannot say at the present stage, Holmér said slowly getting pissed off having to talk with the guy.
- It has better be substantial or I will go to one of the most important newspapers or weekly magazines and I am sure they will pay for the information and will not hesitate to give the Swedish Police a bashing.

Holmér did not comment on what Nydal had just said, but memorised it as a serious attempt to threat the Swedish Police, something Holmér would not forget. Instead he said:

- What information have you got, which is so crucial in solving the murder of Olof Palme? You are free to go ahead please.

And Andreas Nydal told Holmér about the tree mercenaries and why his information was first-hand and unique and not something fabricated. As he mentioned that one of the mercenaries was from South-Rhodesia although the name of the country was not used as the official name of the country anymore, Holmér was now certain that the guy was talking about the same mercenaries as the ones having been contracted by Holmér to carry out the kill.

Corresponding authenticity of the information he had would be handed over to Holmér as soon as 50% of the reward money had been transferred to a bank of his choice, Nydal said.

Holmér listened intensively and realised that Nydal's information was real and not made up and that the guy would have to be silenced as soon as possible or the shit would hit the fan. He was also pretty sure that the information he was trying to sell came from the same database as the information he originally had received from Hannes Venter from the South-African Defence Forces (SADF). They agreed to have a meeting on neutral ground to finalise what they had agreed on. They agreed on having a meeting in Holiday Inn at Frankfurt Airport in about one week's time; The date and time was to be confirmed in the next two days by Andreas Nydal via facsimile as soon as he had the go from his superiors to take some time off to go to Frankfurt. Of course he gave his superior a different story, blathering about an old aunt who recently had died and his distant relatives wanting him to visit the funeral.

Holmér was now pretty certain that the guy he was talking to was from South-Africa, something which later was confirmed by Televerket after they had evaluated the trace output from the phone call Holmér just had with Nydal. They could also say the call came from Pretoria. However they were not able to pin down the exact number as they only could trace the number to the company switchboard. The line from the switchboard to the local phone unit was blocked and therefore not accessible from external resources.

He also did not have any intention to go to Frankfurt; that would have to be taken care of by local resources, so he would have to contact his "Russian friend" again to help him out with that problem.

About an hour later he phoned up his "Russian friend" from the scrambled phone at home and told him he needed some support but this time it would be abroad.

- Where and when, his Russian friend asked Holmér
- Most probably next week and place is Frankfurt
- And what sort of help do you envisage?
- Someone's trying to be too clever and needs to be taken care of, permanently, but not until he has given us the

The Contract (The Mission)

necessary information he possesses – it is information, crucial for the whole project we are doing, without revealing what the project was all about.

- Will cost you an arm and a leg as usual , bro, the Russian contact said.
- I know, but don't you try to be too clever either or you might in for a Surprise, Surprise situation which you suddenly cannot handle, Holmér replied somewhat irritated as he was not in the mood, trying to be funny.
- No problem, boz, I always do what you say
- Agree, but see it as a reminder not to be too clever
- Understand, boz

And they talked through what had to be undertaken and the contact agreed with Holmér to have everything organised and supervised from Stockholm.

The contact was to contact a Go-between in Frankfurt asking him to carry out the actual tasks in Frankfurt.

The Go-between man would listen to the name Abraham Rosenstein. wearing an orthodox jewish outlook. When Holmér asked him why such a weird outfit, the contact answered that due to what happened during WW2 there were still tensions between the Germans and the jews and by wearing an outfit only meant for orthodox jews, people tended to give in regarding what the jews were requesting instead of starting a lengthy and boring discussion about the request as such.

In the Soviet Union – apart from having had an official position within the KGB organisation - he had had an important and powerful role within the Black Market organisation, organising the ordering and distribution of foreign goods. Being fed up with the "Soviet bureaucracy" and a never-ending bribing system, he finally decided to leave the country continuing to do what he was good at in "Soviet

The Contract (The Mission)

Union"- finding demanding goods for the Russian Black Market and the demand was huge.

Working in a system, where something like a black market entity never was allowed to officially exist in the Soviet Union, as a KGB "comrade", it immensely helped him to circumvent many bureaucratic hurdles when "importing" goods to Russia, hurdles which you otherwise inevitably would have faced.

Money was and had never been a problem in Russia – the only problem was to find secure ways of having the goods reach their final destination through the "Soviet bureaucracy" at a reasonable cost, which is not easy when everyone wants a piece of the cake in a system where nothing works.

As a registered jew in Russia there was a possibility that the Authorities would let him leave the country, he thought, something which also proved to be true.

Unofficially he also worked for KGB (after all, he was unofficially paid by the KGB anyway) and had the task to report anything, which looked suspicious to him and not following the daily urban pattern.

Organising the sending of luxury goods to Russia for the Politburo and KGB staff members to Russia was an additional task he had. Also any face being familiar to him as a dissident or people working for foreign Governments was reported back to Moskva. Organising girls for Government Officials visiting Frankfurt was another task.

He would be accompanied by his friend Kasimir Lebedev. However, he would not be directly present in the hotel lobby, but would merely wait in the car in the hotel garage (and for further "unplanned" actions)

The information regarding Holmér's contact was to be forwarded to Andreas Nydal - not immediately but a couple of days later via facsimile with the sole purpose to increase Andreas Nydal's adrenalin level (i.e. to make him nervous) – nothing else.

The Contract (The Mission)

Holmér was happy with what he had been told and said that he would come back with more specific information as-soon-as possible and then hung up.

The Contract (The Mission)

May, the 14th 1986 – Stockholm

Two days later when Holmér arrived home, Holmér had a facsimile waiting for him. The facsimile contained travel information when Andreas Nydal was to be expected in Frankfurt, to be more specific, Nydal was scheduled to arrive coming Friday, late in the evening, proposing the meeting with Holmér to take place the next day – on Saturday, May the 17th 1986.

Nydal had agreed with his superior to take 2 days off for the funeral in Norway: Friday the 16th of May and Monday the 19th of May, returning to work the following Tuesday.

Holmér took a deep breath thinking that nothing must go wrong now, or he would have a hell of a lot to explain.

Holmér then immediately phoned his Russian friend up to discuss the matter. A meeting the coming Saturday should not be a problem. Holmér then proposed "the meeting" to take place at 10:00 on Saturday and to have the South-African be picked from the Hotel 15 minutes earlier.

Holmér also said that he had suggested that Nydal should use the Holiday Inn resort at the Airport as the Hotel for him to check-in to – the hotel being big and somewhat chaotic with heaps of people staying in the hotel only for a very limited period of time more or less just waiting for their next destination to be announced.

The contact said he thought there shouldn't be any problem with what Holmér just had proposed.

Holmér then told him that the name of the guy was Andreas

The Contract (The Mission)

Nydal, arriving from Johannesburg, South-Africa and that he seemed to have in-depth information about the incident that took place end of February and threatened to make this public – nothing more, nothing less.

- He also demands heaps of money and threatens to go to the newspapers if we cannot pay and this is something which we absolutely cannot tolerate, Holmér mumbled for himself.
- It is paramount that this task becomes a success, Holmér continued. Nothing less than a success is acceptable.

After having spoken to his russian contact, Holmér put a facsimile to Andreas Nydal together confirming the date and time for the meeting, also saying that he was apologising for not being able to be there personally to pick him up. However, he would arrange to have someone to pick him up on Saturday at 09:45am and bring him to a more suitable place to hold the meeting. Would he therefore be so kind and tell the reception that he was expecting someone and have the reception give the visitor his room number to enable the visitor to pick him up?

Hoping that this arrangement would work out , Holmér then sent the facsimile, which he had put together off to Mr Nydal in Durban in South-Africa.

May, the 17th 1986 - Frankfurt

Saturday the 17th Andreas Nydal woke up at around 07:00 am, excited over the day and what the day would bring. If he played it carefully, maybe he had $25,000 in cash in exchange for the information he got by just making some elementary queries on the employee record file they had stored in their IBM Mainframe computer.

He took a shower got dressed and went down to the breakfast room for some breakfast.

Time was 08:30 am

As always when he was travelling he had an English breakfast and some coffee and a glas of orange juice.

About 45 minutes later he went back to his room and phoned the reception up and told them he was expecting a visitor to come and ask for him and that he would be very much obliged if they could give him his room number and let him through.

Time was 09:30 am.

He opened the safe and took out the information to do with the three mercenaries and sat down and waited for the guy to come and pick him up for the meeting with Holmér.

At 09:50 pm a knock at the door told him that the guy to pick him up had arrived.

He stood up, went to the door and opened the door. On the other side stood an orthodox jew, Nydal reckoned.

- Hello, my name is Abraham Rosenstein and I am here to

The Contract (The Mission)

pick you up for the meeting with Holmér.

Andreas Nydal looked surprised at Rosenstein, who was smiling somewhat crafty, but did not say anything. He just continued by saying "Shall we?"

Andreas Nydal just nodded and went for his briefcase and jacket Rosenstein waiting at the door still smiling.

When going for the elevator Rosenstein said

- Let's take the elevator down to the garage residing in the basement as we don't need to go through the hotel foyer. Still somewhat baffled over Rosenstein and his outfit, Nydal just nodded, not saying anything.

In the basement they went for the car – a Mercedes S-Class - and before they really took off Nydal felt an arm around his neck almost strangling him and an awful awful burning taste in his mouth before he went limp.

Leaving Holiday Inn, They took the German Autobahn direction south until they reached the exit "Seligenstadt" - one of Germany's oldest towns that already had been of great importance in Carolingian times - where they took off direction river Main and stopped at a house close to the river, where they unloaded Nydal and entered the building. The building belonged a very well-respected person within the Frankfurt high-society but in reality it belonged to the "Russian Mafia" often being used as a resource for interrogating people not understanding what the "Russian Mafia" meant with the word "Agreement" and if someone broke an agreement and what the consequences would be if you tried to be too clever in the eyes of the "Russian Mafia". More than one person have had to realise breaking an agreement with the "Russian Mafia" could ultimately have severe consequences to your health and you might end your days "swimming" in the river Main stripped of anything, which even remotely might connect you with said organisation. The "Russian Mafia" definitely was no Costume Club ("Trachtenverein"}, where you were practicing "sing-a-

The Contract (The Mission)

long" tunes.

Having entered the building they stripped Andreas Nydal of everything but his underwear and tied him to a chair, waiting for him to wake up. Eventually Lebedev – having been in the backseat of the car all the time - got impatient and poured a bucket of cold water over Nydal. Eventually Andreas Nydal woke up coughing, looking somewhat dizzy, wondering what had happened to him and where he was.

- Abraham Rosenstein appeared, this time without anything, which would even remotely resemble him being an orthodox jew.
- Don't worry where you are. It is irrelevant. You are here because you have threatened to use your knowledge to blackmail the Swedish Police and to force them to transfer a substantial amount of money to you or otherwise you would go public with your knowledge, i.e. you then intended to sell your story to the highest bidder. Is my assumption correct?
- I'm sorry, but I have no intention whatsoever to sell what I know about the assassination of Olof Palme to anyone but the Swedish Police.
- Why did you say it then?
- Just to make the Swedish Police believe that more people were prepared to bid for the information I have, but that's not true. The Swedish Police is the only part being interested in what I have to offer..
- And you want us to believe that?
- But it is true.
- And what would happen with the information once you succeeded in selling the information to The Swedish Police? Getting greedy and trying to sell it again to another bidder?

Andreas Nydal now realised that his attempt to play the wise guy had backfired, creating a very dangerous situation to himself. It now seemed to jeopardise the whole plan getting money for giving away information.

- How stupid can one person be, thinking that he could screw a Police Force at the same time attempting to sell the information on the open market. It does not work that way my friend, Rosenstein said.
- I never seriously regarded selling the information on the open market as a viable option, Nydal responded.
- Did you know that trying or withholding information, leading to that you are hindering or delaying a criminal case from being solved is a criminal offence, which would give you years in jail? Rosenstein said and smiled.
- So now tell us how much you know, what information you possess and how you got to this information, Rosenstein continued after having set up and turned on a tape recorder.

And Nydal told them about how he met Piet at the Johannesburg airport, Piet being a neighbour, what Piet had told him and finally about his own investigation and his resulting conclusions. He gave the Russians the names of the other two mercenaries but also told them that he had no idea where they lived. He said he had not written anything down for public distribution at all. Nydal was asked to open his briefcase, but in there was nothing resembling a public declaration or article aimed at the newspaper or printing industry. Only having met them a few times at work, Nydal said, he could only guess what the citizenship of the other two was but assumed that one of them could have his roots in southern Africa perhaps former South-Rhodesia. Being back at square one, the two Russians must admit they could not find anything new compared to what they already had come to know from their Russian friends in Stockholm. However it was paramount that no-one within the Swedish Police cadre was to get hold of the information. Therefore Andreas Nydal

The Contract (The Mission)

unfortunately had to disappear although he had not committed any crime in normal sense but having collected some information.

The two Russians switched off the tape recorder and left the room to discuss what to do. Returning from their discussion, they told Nydal, that they were in a very **precarious** situation in that they did not know what to do with him. They believed he had delivered everything he knew or had done. On the other hand, there is no guarantee that he would not go about selling the information to some entity at a later stage, no matter what they here and now agreed on.

Nydal was now close to a nervous breakdown, having to realise that his days might be numbered because of his own stupidity to brag about what he had found out, although Nydal couldn't know that Holmér already knew most of what Nydal has told them and that they primarily were interested in him as any physical person, not what he might know about the task the mercenaries had carried out in Europe. The danger was the avalanche syndrome: if someone became aware of what Nydal had found out and he subsequently started talking and pointing at the mercenaries, it wouldn't take long until they were found and taken in for interrogation. Obviously the shit would then have hit the fan as from there on you would not be in the position anymore to steer what was happening. Therefore it was paramount that no traces of what had taken place could be left anywhere, regardless of source or importance.

- Do you want anything to drink? Rosenstein asked
- Yes please, Nydal replied
- Will a glass of water be ok? Rosenstein asked
- Suits me fine, Nydal replied

And Rosenstein went to the nearby room, which in fact was the kitchen, for a glass of mineral water. Rosenstein returned a minute later with the glass, now with a deadly poison and

The Contract (The Mission)

gave the glass to Nydal who emptied the glass in one go. Rosenstein then went to the kitchen waiting for the poison to start working. After 10 minutes he returned to Nydal who now was dead.

A couple of minutes later Lebedev also returned and both of them left the premises and went back to Holiday Inn to pick up Mr Nydal's luggage and would return to the premises the next day to get rid of the body.

Later the same day, they returned to the premises with a Ford Transit and unloaded an old oil barrel to be used for getting rid of Mr Nydal. They then took the barrel and went into the room where they had left the corpse of Mr Nydal, undressed him and put him – head down – in the barrel, which to some ¼ was filled with hydrochloric acid, to speed up the decomposition of Mr Nydal. They then sealed the barrel and put Mr Nydal's clothes in a plastic bag and left the premises. On their way home, they made a small detour and put Nydal's clothes in s container for second hand clothes at a Red Cross reception centre.

The Contract (The Mission)

May, the 18th 1986 – Frankfurt

Around 6 am the next day they returned to the premises with the Ford Transit and loaded the oil-barrel, which they the day before had brought with them, onto the Ford Transit – this time with Mr Nydal.

They emptied Nydal's suitcase, which did not contain much more than a passport, air ticket and three computer printouts comprising some information to do with the characteristics of the three mercenaries and the suitcase and luggage which later got burned at a rubbish dump not far away from Frankfurt.

Next task was the disposal of the barrel with their content

A convenient way was to let people disappear was to use a scrap-yard, where everything got disposed without anyone really bothering what they actually were disposing and a scrapyard run by the "Russian Mafia" was an even better option and there were actually some scrapyards in the Frankfurt vicinity run by them.

As a consequence the barrel got disposed by such a "service" and that meant the end of Mr Nydal.

Rosenstein reported back to Stockholm that the task had been accomplished in accordance with what had been agreed. The content of the "interrogation" tape was relayed to the Russians in Stockholm over a normal phone line.

Holmér got to know what had taken place later the same day, which was not anything more than what he had expected. Additionally they also sent him a facsimile containing the

The Contract (The Mission)

computer printouts. He looked down at the names of the mercenaries, which he just had received and came to the conclusion that the third mercenary must have his roots in Mozambique as he possessed a Portuguese name. The second guy – Martin Carlisle – he reckoned, must come from either South-Africa or South-Rhodesia – not Europe - due to his complexion - Out-door guy, Suntanned, Ashen blond, the computer printout had said.

The Contract (The Mission)

May, the 19th 1986 – Frankfurt

An employee, working at the The Holiday Inn at the Frankfurt Airport noticed the next day – Monday, the 19th – that Nydal hadn't showed up for breakfast nor had he checked out, but no attempts were taken towards trying to find him. Instead they just collected Nydal's personal belongings and registered his stay as not checked out – not paid. In case he returned, he would have to go to to the reception to get his belongings (and pay the outstanding bill). Then the room was cleaned and prepared for the next guest to arrive – no hassle, the show must go on.

The Contract (The Mission)

May, the 19th 1986 – Pretoria

Monday the 19th came and Mr Malan decided to have this "chat" with Mr Nydal to find out what he was up to with the information he had gathered. He therefore phoned his secretary up and asked her to put him through to Mr Nydal. (A Minister never connects himself to anyone – that is a job for the secretaries)

After ca 5 min she came back with a somewhat puzzled face telling Mr Malan, that she could not get hold of Mr Nydal. Mr Malan told her to make another attempt to reach Mr Nydal in a couple of minutes. Mr Malan then asked his secretary about Mr Nydal's whereabouts and therefore couldn't be reached, however that was not the case either.

He then told his secretary to try a couple of more times before giving up and postpone it until the next day.

However, there was a problem finding Mr Nydal in that he had not left any address or phoneno where he was to be reached during the week.

The Contract (The Mission)

May, the 20th 1986 – Frankfurt

The following Tuesday Nydal's wife tried to phone her husband up at work, but no one answered the phone.

As it was not that uncommon that he wasn't at his desk, she just hung up and decided to call her husband later.

She made another attempt to phone him in the afternoon, but no-one picked up the phone. She then phoned up the switchboard to ask them to make a global search for her husband , but the result was the same – no-one took the call. She then said to herself to wait until the next day for a new call and hung up.

The following day she made another call to her husband at his office phone, with the same result as the day before. She then called her husband's supervisor up and asked him if he had seen her husband at work, but the result was the same – no-one had seen her husband at or arriving at work. However he promised to call her up in case anything of importance popped up.

She now started to become somewhat concerned regarding her husband and wondered if something might have happened to him.

She then called South-African Airways (SAA) asking them if they were in the position to give her information when he had left Johannesburg last Friday. The only information they had was that a certain Mr Nydal had left Johannesburg for Frankfurt in the morning, but had not booked any connecting

The Contract (The Mission)

flights to Norway the same day. She then asked the information if he might have booked any flight to Norway the next day – Saturday, but the result was negative as well – no flight for Mr Nydal bound for Norway.

Now being sure that something had happened to her husband, she phoned a couple of big Hotels up and asked them if a certain Mr Nydal had booked a room with them last Friday.

With Holiday Inn there was a hit – Yes, a Mr Nydal had booked a room for 2 nights with them. The odd thing was that he never checked out although his luggage was gone. She now became very puzzled as she couldn't find any plausible reason for her husband having stayed in Frankfurt for 2 nights. She then phoned the Police up in Frankfurt and asked them the same questions, no, no person fitting the description she had given had been found dead or injured.

Not knowing what to do, she finally went to the local Police in Durban and reported her husband as missing hoping they would find anything useful regarding his whereabouts. The Police contacted Interpol asking for help in finding her husband. Interpol asked for a case resume, description and photos of the missing husband asking Mr Nydal's wife not to panic and go home and wait for feedback to arrive from Interpol in Germany.

The Police in Frankfurt went to Holiday Inn reception at the Airport and asked them if they had come to notice anything unusual during Mr Nydal's stay. They said no, but then one of the employees at the hotel told the Police that someone had been asking for Mr Nydal and then went up to Mr Nydal's room. However, he never came back, nor did Mr Nydal as far as he could recall. He assumed that the guest must have taken the lift to the garage. What had happened to Mr Nydal he did not know, he said. Mr Nydal had phoned the reception and vouched for the guest, he also said. The Police then asked to have a quick look at Mr Nydal's room, but could not find anything spectacular. The Police then asked the employee if they could describe the person having visited Mr Nydal. He said

The Contract (The Mission)

the only thing he remembered was that the guest was dressed like an orthodox jew. The police then said they knew the trick, in that the outfit was just there to distract people, making them concentrate on the outfit instead of the person. Most often they were not jews at all - was just a disguise.

As the crime scene seemed to be Germany and therefore under German jurisdiction, the South-African Police couldn't do anything to speed up the process. They promised to phone Mrs Nydal as soon as they heard anything deviating from what they momentary had come to know.

As it is not exactly easy to chase a non-existing corpse, Mrs Nydal could not do very much but either to wait for Andreas' corpse to show up or to register Andreas as missed, which probably would take longer until he officially was declared being dead.

The Contract (The Mission)

May, the 22th 1986 – Stockholm

Holmér went down to the nearest shopping mall and bought a couple of postcards plus some stamps, one card of which he sent off to Piet in South-Africa the next day.

On the postcard Holmér sent Piet his condolences and deepest sympathies regarding Piet's boss Mr Nydal, whom he had come to hear had disappeared somewhere in Frankfurt.

However, Holmér continued, despite the fact Frankfurt not being the safest town, you can normally move around in Frankfurt without having to fear for your life as long as you stick to some basic rules, rules which everyone has agreed to live by. Otherwise there is no guarantee that you might not experience unpleasantness as a result of your behaviour – it is the same everywhere. There are rules, which everyone should adhere to, if they want a safe haven, Holmér finished the postcard.

He did not sign the postcard. Instead he just threw the postcard in the nearest letterbox the next day, unsigned.

The Contract (The Mission)

May, the 26ᵗʰ 1986 – Stockholm

Holmér was preparing to leave for work, when he got a phone call from the Gibraltar accountant asking Holmér what to do with the $400,000, which just had arrived.

To begin with, Holmér did not have a clue what the money was all about and asked the accountant if there was any message with the transfer and the accountant said there was only a short message saying

"Good Job/RWR", in the input folder of the account

At first Holmér did not quite understand from where or from whom the money could have come, but then slowly he began to understand why the money had arrived at the Gibraltar account and from whom and he smiled, happy that no one could see him. He told the accountant that everything was all right and that he should just park the money somewhere until further notice, thanked him for the call and hung up.

However, he could not understand how someone apart from a few distinguished friends could have known about the existence of the account. But then he realised that there were things and people having gotten organised and connected in the background neither having had his approval nor the unique knowledge he thought he possessed. He now also began to understand why the money for their "mission" was made available so fast and non-bureaucratic. Without his knowledge someone had given his go-ahead for the mission they just had brought to a successful end – someone whose words had far more weight and penetrating power than your own words, Holmes thought for himself.

The Contract (The Mission)

The same day Piet received the postcard from Holmér in Sweden.

The Contract (The Mission)

June 2nd 1986 – Durban, South Africa

He got all aghast when he read the postcard, as he not really having had the time to get informed about everything that had taken place in the recent past.

What the .... has Nydal done and why was he in Frankfurt? Piet wondered and decided to have a chat with Nydal's wife. He phoned her up and she answered with a voice having been weeping a lot.

She couldn't say a lot apart from the fact that he had told her that he was going to a funeral in Norway – a distant relative had died, he had said. But he never mentioned that anything could be connected to Frankfurt in any way. It was only about Oslo all the time, she said.

Piet then called Mr Nydal's supervisor up and asked him if he happened to know anything about Nydal's disappearance, but he could not say anything of importance either, only that Nydal had not showed up for work, which Piet also had assumed.

As a consequence, Piet phoned Nigel's "switchboard" up and told her to contact Nigel asap to tell him to phone Piet up. The next day Piet got a phone call from Nigel and Piet told him about the postcard and the conversation he had had with Nydal's wife and his supervisor.

- Something must have happened, Piet said, most probably a leak of some kind and that our client therefore is trying to seal the leak before the shit's hit the fan. In essence he is trying to help us, Piet continued.

The Contract (The Mission)

- What do you think of Nydal's disappearance?
- I think he has tried to be too clever and as a consequence they have decided to silence him – you will never find him. Please bear in mind that he was our superior and therefore had access to information we don't have.
- What do you think we should do, then? Nigel asked.
- Keep our mouths shut and don't brag about with what you know or what you have done and keep your fingers crossed that nothing will happen. They will always find us, whenever they want and regardless of where we are. Therefore I want you to have a chat with Jose and please tell him what I have told you. Please make him realise that this is our only chance we have to survive or we will be made extinct sooner than you think would be possible.

The Contract (The Mission)

1987 – Pretoria, South Africa

The rental agency now had waited for more than 6 months that Andreas Nydal should turn up and pay his outstanding debts, but no – nothing happened – it may be that he had got a new assignment somewhere and therefore cannot meet his obligations towards the rental agency, but even so, it does not free you from what you might have signed up with the rental agency - these debts have to be paid.

As Mr Nydal had written down "Ministry of Defence" as his employer when he signed the lease, the estate agent decided trying to find Mr Nydal by asking each government unit if a certain Mr Nydal happened to work on said premises.

Maybe I strike gold and find him, you'll never know, the estate agent thought for himself.

Consequently, he went up to each reception and asked the usher on duty if they possibly had a Mr Nydal in their department. It took some time, but then he struck gold and there actually was a Mr Nydal in one department, however he had not shown up for months

and the department said that he had not been given any new tasks elsewhere either. The real estate agent then took the decision to call the police and write off the rent for the apartment as a loss. A couple of days later, the Police showed up, opened the door to the apartment, but could only register that the apartment had not been used for a long time. Apart from some basic furnitures, the only thing they found was a binder with casino brochures and notes, primarily phone numbers,

The Contract (The Mission)

which Mr Nydal seemed to have assembled. When trying some of the numbers they connected you to some loansharks where you could borrow money at an horrendous interest rate or fee, something, which Mr Nydal seemed to have taken advantage of, from what you could figure out from the notes he had scribbled down. The Police phoned the casino up but no luck there either – they couldn't provide the Police with an address different from the one where they momentarily were either and took the decision, that there was not much more they could do, but to wait. The agent wondered if any of the scribbled numbers might have any address information. But the Police said that it was unlikely they had anything useful worth chasing and they advised the agent to stay away from and loansharks as they may come up with the "brilliant" idea to claim the debts from him instead.

The Contract (The Mission)

1988 – Durban, South Africa

A car drove up and parked at the curb where the deceased Andreas Nydal has lived when he was alive. The house was still inhabited by Mrs. Nydal, though she had the intention to sell the house and move elsewhere, most likely abroad – maybe to her sister in Australia, now when the probability for having an upheaval of the present social system in South Africa seemed to be rising with an unknown and unpredictable outcome as a result.

A man stepped out of the car followed by yet another man, the first one looking like a bodyguard from the way he was moving and acting. They went to Mrs Nydal's house and pressed the door bell.

After a couple of seconds the door opened and Mrs. Nydal showed up.

- Mrs Nydal, I presume.

- Yes, she replied

- May we have a short talk with you, the second man asked and showed her an emblem comprising the Coat of Arms of South Africa.

Mrs Nydal, knowing the importance of what just had been shown to her just nodded and they went inside. She was pretty sure that she had seen the second man before, however she could not recall when, but she assumed he must be of very high importance as he was travelling with a bodyguard. However she was sure she would remember who he was later-on.

The Contract (The Mission)

She invited the two men to have a seat in the living room then asking them if they would care for anything to drink. As it was a very hot day – they happily accepted the offer.

Having sipped on their drinks, the more important man then said -

- You may wonder why we're here, but it is all about your husband and we have reason to believe that he was involved in dubious business practices, eventually resulting in his disappearance and most probably leading to his death.

- We now know that he illegally – without corresponding allowance - has penetrated information residing in our computers in Pretoria and also extracted such information from the computers most probably aiming at selling corresponding information to the highest bidder, which you, most likely, would find in Germany. We assume that something must have gone wrong when the transaction was about to take place and therefore we believe he was paying for the unsuccessful transaction with his life.

  Should you possess any information having a direct connection to the type of work your husband was exercising, we strongly recommend you not to reveal or to discuss the nature of his work with anyone as it should not be of any concern to you or to anyone else what the work was all about or to put it bluntly is being none of your business or it might render you some unpleasent experience in areas being extremely unfamiliar to you – getting the point?

And she did, she said, and promised to keep hear lips sealed.

The more important man then continued:

- I can only say this much: the information your husband tried to sell is classified and would have rendered him many years in Jail if he would have been caught.

The Contract (The Mission)

- We also have reason to believe that he was addicted to gambling and most probably tried to find ways to clear his gambling debts, which according to the Johannesburg Casino seemed to have been pretty substantial. Having problems, not being in the position to clear your debts you may have with the underworld could be disastrous, I'm sorry to say. Either you pay your debts on the day having been agreed with money or with your life.

Mrs Nydal didn't know what to say, just trying to comprehend what she now has been told and could not really understand what sort of life her husband has been living outside their marriage. He probably having tried to stop what he was doing but eventually it was all too late. In the end his gambling debts were too severe to enable him to have them cleared the normal way and therefore the only way was to seek "help" from the underworld and the illegality.

She then had some second thoughts about what they now had told her and the reason for their coming here and wondered if everything really was the way she had been told or if there was more under the carpet than what she had been told.

The more important of the two men then continued by saying -

- We therefore firmly believe that your best option is to disappear from South African soil whilst you can as you can be sure of that the underworld - or let's say the mafia - want their money back no matter how many people will have to pay with their lives in their attempts to get them. Do you know anyone abroad, who you can move to or at least visit for a longer period of time?

- I have a sister in Australia, who moved there a couple of years ago with her husband and their 2 children.

- Good, the second man said, Have a chat with them to find out if you can go there. Then he continued -

The Contract (The Mission)

- The Mafia probably may not have come to the conclusion yet that your husband might be dead, but the moment they get to know it, they will start looking for relatives and we are pretty sure of, that sooner or later they will have found out where you live and then you are the next in line for being "questioned" and you have better knowing where "their" money is.

- I feel sorry for you having to experience the turn everything has taken here and it won't be better, I can tell you. The tension is rising in South Africa and a transition of the political power to the black majority seems to be inevitable.

And then she recognised who the second man was. It was the Minister of Defence – Magnus Malan - and in that very moment she was proud of having lived in South Africa all her life and proud that the Minister of Defence has taken the time to visit her personally in her home to clarify her situation. She said -

- How come everything has taken a turn for the worse? Why are things getting out of control? The situation for the blacks has improved a lot, I've been told, besides, Rome was not built in one day either, they say. Why cannot people show a bit understanding, patience and gratitude? They will eventually get their share. People should more appreciate what we are doing for them instead of moaning all the time. If they think they can run the country themselves without our support and experience then checkmate.

Malan replied -

- I personally think that we would surely be competent enough to master the situation and the task to rebuild South-Africa. It is more the influence and interference from abroad, which is new to us, that has worsen the situation and where there are problems having to be mastered. Influence and interference from countries like Cuba, China and the Soviet Union and people like the Swedish Prime Minis-

The Contract (The Mission)

ter running around yelling "freedom for the Blacks" all day and when he has finished with his gospel, he leaves the scene, and it is up to us to sweep up the crumbs of what is left of our intentions.

But as far as I have heard, he has got what he deserved. she said

- You may be right, but it does not help us that much in that such people once they have opened the eyes of the blacks, the damage is there and you cannot revert the damage they have caused – it is there, ignoring the economic constraints and level of expertise you always have to put on every project you start – once the beanstalk has started to grow, you cannot stop it - it grows and grows and grows ... it is like Jack and the beanstalk, the Minister of Defence finally said.

Mr Malan then thanked Mrs Nydal for the refreshment and the two men left the house and drove away. During their journey back Magnus Malan said -

- See to that some listening devices are installed in her house, so that we can intercept her to see if she is up to something as a result of her husband's death or if she knows about things, which she shouldn't know about, and tries to make a fast buck - just to be on the safe side. If you face any problems you know what to do.

The other guy said he understood and that he would organise to have the listening stuff be installed ASAP.

The eavesdropping equipment got installed in Mrs Nydal's house first thing on Monday the following week, whilst Mrs Nydal was out shopping.

Eventually, a couple of weeks later Mrs Nydal could not keep the recent development to herself and decided to phone her sister in Australia, just to have someone to talk to, someone to

The Contract (The Mission)

guide her how to go about in mastering all problems that seemed to pile up on the horizon. Se also wanted to find out what possibilities there were in moving to her sister, now that her husband seemed to have left this world

As Mr Nydal has been a good talker, his wife had come to get a pretty good view of what Mr Nydal was doing workwise and that made his disappearance even more exiting but also confusing and questionable from an outsider's point of wiew. Mrs Nydal sister was a good listener, however told Mrs Nydal that they only had a small semi-detached house, barely big enough for the family as such, however they were looking for something bigger and as soon as they had found something bigger and affordable, they would let her know, and she would be very welcomed to come and stay with them, her sister said. Mrs Nydal hung up, somewhat disappointed what she had come to hear from her sister. When it came to the crunch, in essence, she now really did not know what she should do or how to act, and she decided to invite her best friend for a cup of coffee and some biscuits to discuss her problems with her.

Eventually her neighbour recommended Mrs Nydal to wait and see what happened with her sister and a bigger house, hoping they were successful in finding what they were looking for, as South-Africa did not seem to be a realistic option any more with an ever increasing crime rate, political uncertainty as well as economic uncertainty.

The installation of the eavesdropping equipment eventually couldn't prove that Mrs Nydal should had revealed something, which would have rendered her a stay in a federal prison and a year later the equipment was dismantled.

In 1990 Mrs Nydal's sister finally had succeeded in finding a bigger house, and Mrs Nydal then accepted an invitation from her sister to come and live with her and her family and then moved to Australia.

The Contract (The Mission)

September 1990 - Stockholm

As Holmér returned from work one day, he registered that someone had sent him a facsimile. The facsimile did not have any "sender" information, something which he could recall having received years ago, or to be more specific, from a certain Hannes Venter working for the South African Defence Force (SADF). Holmér was on the verge of getting a nervous breakdown when he read the facsimile. What the facsimile said was that due to the present turmoil in South Africa the CCB had been disbanded and many former CCB agents now had decided to step forward giving the TRC (Truth and Reconciliation Commission) information about crimes and also seeking amnesty for crimes committed during the Apartheid era.

The facsimile also contained information concerning the Olof Palme assassination saying that "a certain South African national" had decided to step forward and give TRC information to do with the Olof Palme assassination as well. Although the name of the person in question was not mentioned, Holmér knew immediately whom the facsimile was referring to and once again the shit was about to hit the fan unless he took some action. He therefore phoned his "Russian Friend" up, told him about his problem and asked him if he knew someone in South Africa who could fix his problem ASAP. The Russian said "no sweat" and promised to come back the next day.

The Russian phoned back the next day and said the problem could be taken care of for a 10 Grand admin fee as he put it, which was ok for Holmér. Holmér told the Russian to go and fix the problem ASAP and hung up.

The Contract (The Mission)

October 1990 - Durban, South-Africa

Having worked for CCB as a freelancer in a "Death Squad" unit, a covert operation within the South African Defence Force (SADF) whose operations were under the authority of Defence Minister General Magnus Malan, it had become increasingly more difficult in finding another job nowadays, taking the present turmoil in South-Africa into account as well.

At first glance CCB appeared to be a unique and unorthodox security operations unit, providing the South African Defence Force with good covert capabilities. Its members wore civilian clothing and officially it operated only within the South-African borders, but later-on the operation was accused of torture, human experiments, political assassinations and the training and funding of militant groups throughout the world.

Resulting from information given to the TRC by former CCB agents seeking amnesty for crimes committed during the apartheid era, it became clear that there were many other covert operations similar to the CCB.

As a result of the TRC hearings the CCB was disbanded in August 1990. Despite all information put forward, no prosecutions were the result of the CCB operation.

Being in the process of changing the political power of South-Africa over to the black majority (ANC) as well as Piet being a South-African national, therefore not being in the position to escape from his role in the Palme murder case, eventually had made him take the decision to put forward what he knew about the assassination of Olof Palme before the TRC,

The Contract (The Mission)

including the role he had played himself, in a naive attempt to seek amnesty for himself.

Despite the political turmoil momentarily sweeping over South-Africa, Piet van de Cleef finally had succeeded in finding an American company, momentarily not present in South-Africa, which was prepared to give him a job interview for a build-up position as a Security and Surveillance Manager. Once the transition to black supremacy has started the demand for security and surveillance would be immense, they said and Piet tended to agree with them.

As the company did not have an office in South Africa yet, they agreed to hold an initial interview at the Durban airport a couple of days before Piet was to put his testimony before the TRC hearing committee regarding his doings working for CCB during the Apartheid era.

Before having agreed to testify he had a chat with a certain **Peter Castelton** - a South African Police Lieutenant, whom he knew from previous "cleansing" tasks having worked for the CCB and decided to reveal his involvement in the Olof Palme assassination. He thereby hoped that Mr Castleton could give him some good advise, being more experienced in similar matters, i.e. how to act before the TRC hearing committee. Mr Castleton promised not to reveal anything when testifying before the committee himself and Piet thanked him for having taken the time to listen to his concerns.

Piet sincerely hoped that Mr **Peter Castelton** - the South African Police Lieutenant – would keep his promise not to reveal anything regarding Piet's involvement regarding the Palme assassination when he had his testamonial before the TRC hearing committee as he had promised. But you could never tell – people often changed their minds.

However, as *the entire CCB operation was run via front companies*, employing operatives who formally resigned from the

The Contract (The Mission)

SADF and SAP (South African Police), implied that Piet, Mr Castleton and Mr Nydal, were effectively working for the same governmental unit – the Minestry of Defence, whose operations were under the authority of Defence Minister General Magnus Malan.

On this particular day Piet got dressed and had a regular breakfast. His girlfriend had already left for work. He closed the door to their house and went for the garage. As he was about to start the car he felt a sudden pain in the neck and then everything went black. From the backseat a person got out of the car, closed the garage and left – nobody had come to notice what actually had taken place.

As Piet's girlfriend later returned back from work, at first she did not register that something was not as it should. However, upon entering their house she found Piet not being at home. She found that being somewhat awkward that Piet had not yet returned from his job interview. She then went to the garage and there she found Piet dead in his car. She immediately phoned the Police but the only thing they could do was to proclaim Piet as dead, hanging over the steering wheel, presumably through a heart attack. None noticed the small read spot in the neck. The only thing, which the girlfriend could tell the Police was that Piet had planned to be off for a job interview with an American company. However, nobody had heard about the company and the Police assumed the girlfriend must have misheard the name of the company as the company could not be found as a registered company under said name in US either.

Regarding the two mercenaries having worked on the Palme assassination together with "a certain South African national", the problem was different in that they were not South African nationals and therefore could not be brought forward to testimony before the TRC without an adequate, and most importantly, legal reason. Although they had helped out in

The Contract (The Mission)

eliminating SWAPO members and supporters on South African soil, it would be difficult to prove their involvement unless someone decided to talk. On the other hand would it be stupid to stay in South Africa until someone started to talk, more or less just waiting to be caught, effectively leaving them with only one viable option left – to leave South Africa ASAP.

Regrettably this was the only option they had left, although they had planned for a quite different exodus. but you cannot change history.

The Contract (The Mission)

A few months later the war in former Yugoslavia broke out and would go on for more than ten years, ultimately leading to the breakup of the Yugoslav federation in 1992 This created immense possibilities for mercenaries to make "a fast buck" with the different armies – regular as well as irregular of questionable quality and origin – you would find there.

José Eduardo Tavares Silva and Martin Carlisle were amongst the mercenaries who joined the Croatian forces under the command of General Franjo Tuđman, in their struggle to win back those parts of Croatia, which had been "claimed" by the Serbs as a Serbian territory in their attempts to recreate a Greater Serbia.

In May 1991, they participated in the Krajina War – a "Blitzkrieg" - to reconquer the Republic of Krajina (from the Serbs) – comprising two successful military operations in less than a week.

The Contract (The Mission)

Granskningskommissionen (GK)
"The Investigation Commission"

"Granskningskommissionen", abbreviated "GK" (Part of the Government's Murder Investigation Commission) having had the task to investigate the work of the Police in regard to the murder of Olof Palme came to the conclusion that "those parts of the murder investigation that concerned the political situation in Sweden lacked a documented basic analysis. It was suggested that the police and the Swedish Security Service (Säpo) had been aware of the extremist organisations and persons around them and that they had investigated them in a competent manner". However the Commission also added, with regard to those exersizing a more extreme form of opposition:

"In one respect, this is not valid. The kind of political opposition to Olof Palme that existed during his tenure, and that in its extremes was expressed in malignant and repulsive forms is as far as we can see not examined and analysed anywhere in any murder investigation documents."

The many coarse attacks on Prime Minister Olof Palme, intensified after his re-election in 1982, were intended to discredit him and make him appear suspicious. However, GK came to the conclusion that such a hatred was too vague as a motive to be considered as an independent murder hypothesis, and argued that the lack of a basic analysis about this topic was the reason why important aspects never were investigated.

As an example of events that should have been analysed in such a context, GK mentioned the territorial violations of sub-

The Contract (The Mission)

marines by the Soviet Union, and the debate around this where Palme was accused of an inadequate response, and from the most extreme critics also for treason, as well as the forthcoming journey to Moscow in April 1986 to meet with President Gorbachev (which by the most extreme critics also was seen as evidence of treason).

The GK found that it was unacceptable to ignore these issues simply because they "were not related to [the scene of the murder at] Sveavägen", and that it could not see it as anything but "... a mistake that the manners in which the Palme-hate was expressed, as well as its more powerful forms, were not made the subject of a basic analysis."

The GK also states that the most extreme and vociferous attacks of this kind were not placed in their proper context.

The Contract (The Mission)

EPILOGUE

On 15 January 1987 a 61-year-old Rear Admiral (retired) Carl Fredrik Algernon fell in front of an incoming underground train in Stockholm. Suicide was the first word, that one came to think of. Or was it an accident?

Or was it ..? Algernon was a member of the military intelligence services for ten years and, after resigning, became inspector of war material, responsible for authorising arms exports.

Under Palme, the Swedish defence budget had been cut in half in just ten years. He did approve sensitive arms exports, to India for example. On the other hand he was vehemently propagating for disarmament. After Palme, Algernon was another person to die a violent death, the key figure in an investigation into illegal arms exports to the Middle East by Bofors (Swedish arms manufacturer).

There are indications that both Palme and Algernon had secret information relating to this connection. However, from an official point of view there has so far not been any speculations about a possible link between the two deaths.

The career thus far of Mr Palme's successor, Ingvar Carlsson, had focused largely on domestic affairs. Mr Carlsson's first challenge was to sort out the country's crucial bargaining over wages. Luckily Carlsson had several things going for him. The Social Democratic Party structure is very secure. The latest national election with Palme was held in 1984, and the next election being more than two years away together with a drop

The Contract (The Mission)

in oil prices helped to speed up the Swedish economic recovery. However, Mr Carlsson, who btw had been studying economic developments in other countries the past three years, wanted to keep Sweden competitive whilst sustaining Sweden's generous social welfare programs.

Palme's death, and his replacement by the more reserved deputy prime minister, Ingvar Carlsson, probably having realised that Palme had gone too far in stressing his own ego instead of concentrating to more act as Sweden's voice in the world, led to an immediate diminution of the Swedish voice in international affairs.

It also triggered some tumultuous—and very un-Swedish—fighting between Left and Right. And, by coincidence, the Swedish economy soon began an obvious downward slide towards disaster, meaning Prime Minister Ingvar Carlsson now had to rebuild the confidence in what Sweden really was able to offer before Sweden as a nation went aground due to Palme's mismanagement.

As a result of the gigantic economic mistakes by Palme in the 1970s - and the 1980s, leading to that Sweden almost capsized economically, Prime Minister Carlsson was forced to take forceful corrective actions. In a radical departure from Social Democratic practice, he sought to halt the country's runaway inflation by introducing an across-the-board freeze on prices, interest rates, and dividends, as well as a two-year ban on strikes.

At the same time, he also, with the help of one of the leading non-social parties, the Liberals, implemented a tax reform that reduced marginal taxation from a maximum of 90% to 50%. For the average family of four, the tax bite dropped to around 40 percent. However, despite such efforts, the economic situation even worsened, eventually leading to Sweden's worst recession since the 1930s. Not until 1994 did the situation begin to turn around for the better.

A question that often has been asked is:

The Contract (The Mission)

What would have happened to Sweden if Palme had not been murdered. What would have happened to Sweden's neutrality and NATO vs. Warsaw Pact. Had Sweden then followed the same path with Palme as was the case without Palme or had Sweden become a haunt for socialist "freedom" as an experimental workshop a la Cuba? How would Palme have reacted to Sweden's accession to the EC?

There also seems to have been a frightening incompetence and naivete regarding the Swedish official government's attitudes to the probably "friendly" communist regime in Moscow, given many incidents that had occurred as a result of Soviet Union provocations.

(For example, that a Soviet submarine ran aground in Swedish waters, after Sweden's highly trained navy could not detect it)

Peter Castelton – the South African Police Lieutenant - was mashed by his car in his garage, whilst he was repairing the car, just before he was about to testify about the Palme murder for the Truth and Reconciliation Commission in South-Africa.

The Contract (The Mission)

GAMLA STAN

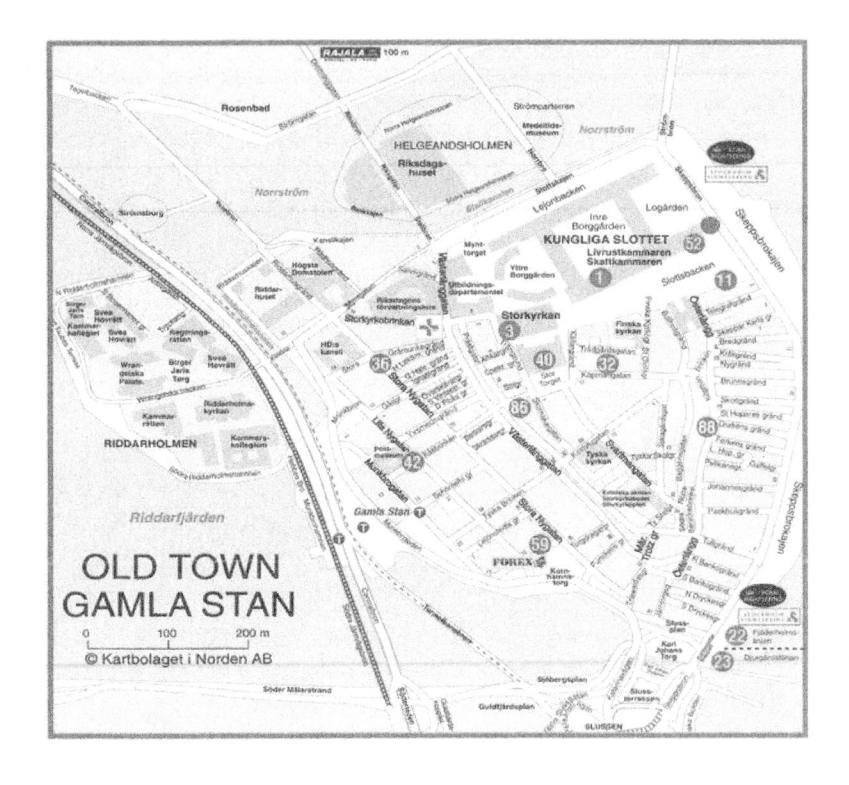

THE END

The Contract (The Mission)

The Contract (The Mission)

Numerous attempts have been started to find the cause and those responsible for the assassination of Olof Palme, one explanation more ludicrous than the other, full in line with the Swedish "Tomtebolyckan" (A happiness to be compared to that the Trolls live in. A Troll existing in Scandinavian folklore, dwelling in isolated rocks, mountains, or caves, living together in small family units). Naivety when it comes to describing a particular course of events - what is not likely to have happened cannot not have occurred, what is probable must have occurred - theories based on evidence lacking a practical reality basis like the Kurd problem, South Africa, Iran/Contra, Chile, CIA, EAP, a lonely drunkard, etc. - one theory more absurd and illogical than the other.

It is hard to have confidence in the Swedish Police and their investigation methods and ability to solve a problem when you hear and read the results of all investigations having been undertaken, resulting in the conclusion that the investigations so far can only be regarded as amateurish and naive in attempting to sweep the real events under the rug.

A conspiracy having its roots within Sweden's borders is something no Swede really and honestly has regarded as a possible option or really worthwhile discussing in Sweden. It is easier to put the blame on something or someone abroad than dwelling in looking for something, which does not lead to anything (cannot exist) anyway.

Consequently they start to search the guilty ones abroad. After all, there are enough potential and credible clients found there to carry a similar deed. Instead of concentrating on qualified causal research, based on Swedish history and culture, they shoot in all directions, the main task being finding someone or something, that fits the pre-requisites for a guilty sod.

Lately, however, a few credible scenarios have been publicized, that have lifted the investigations to a more serious level, from Swedes who have managed to "liberate" themselves from the obsession that all evil must come from abroad. Unfortunately these scenarios have (deliberately?) not been adapted by any official investigation or audit committee as creditable enough.

In the end it might lead to something, which also could be embarrassing, official investigations then only to regard as amateurish and naive attempts to sweep the real events under the rug.

This leads me to the conclusion that this case must be about a – for Sweden - much larger and more serious conspiracy than all the – sometimes naïve conspiracy theories that so far have been published.

The question : **Why did it happen?** must be answered

and this question is the path I have tried to follow and understand: How and why could someone have done this to the Honorable Swedes? It could very well be that for some people murder may be legitimate - others not. It may also not be the right solution to a particular problem, but it may help us understand in general why things have gone astray.

The Contract (The Mission)

A crime fiction/true story (factual fiction) book, based on a true story, recorded witness testimonies, logical reasoniing leading to a probable cause scenario over the assassination of Olof Palme, the Swedish Prime Minister. Had he more enemies than anticipated. Who were they? Is there more to the official version than what they say ..?